The
Coloring
Crook

Krista Davis is the author of

The Pen & Ink Mysteries

Color Me Murder
The Coloring Crook

The Domestic Diva Mysteries

The Diva Cooks Up a Storm
The Diva Sweetens the Pie

The Coloring Crook

KRISTA DAVIS

KENSINGTON BOOKS
www.kensingtonbooks.com

KENSINGTON BOOKS are published by

Kensington Publishing Corp.
119 West 40th Street
New York, NY 10018

All Kensington titles, imprints, and distributed lines are available at special quantity discounts for bulk purchases for sales promotion, premiums, fund-raising, and educational or institutional use.

Special book excerpts or customized printings can also be created to fit specific needs. For details, write or phone the office of the Kensington Sales Manager: Kensington Publishing Corp., 119 West 40th Street, New York, NY 10018. Attn. Sales Department. Phone: 1-800-221-2647.

ISBN-13: 978-1-4967-1643-9 (ebook)
ISBN-10: 1-4967-1643-4 (ebook)
Kensington Electronic Edition: December 2018

ISBN-13: 978-1-4967-1642-2
ISBN-10: 1-4967-1642-6
First Kensington Trade Paperback Printing: December 2018

10 9 8 7 6 5 4 3 2 1

Printed in the United States of America

Dedicated to
Susan Smith Erba
with love

ACKNOWLEDGMENTS

The coloring book called *The Florist* actually exists. In the 1700s, fashionable ladies and gentlemen passed the time coloring botanical pictures. The drawings were remarkably accurate, and it appears the intent was to color them according to the real colors of the plants in nature. As a writer, I enjoyed reading the introduction to the book as well as the charming quote at the beginning of this book. I think English is far easier today! There are a few copies of *The Florist* still in existence, mostly in the hands of museums. If you would like to see what it looks like, you can find copies of the pages online at Peter H. Raven Library/Missouri Botanical Garden: http://botanicus.org/title/b11968564.

The tiny van Gogh sunflower is, to the best of my knowledge, fictitious. Although van Gogh did paint a series of sunflowers, this tiny one is a figment of my imagination, as is the rest of the story and the characters.

As always, there are many people to thank. My lovely editor, Wendy McCurdy, is always a pleasure to work with. I owe her thanks for allowing me to write this fun series. I'm so grateful that my agent, Jessica Faust, is always only a phone call away. She keeps me targeted and is an endless source of encouragement.

I would be remiss if I didn't thank TiJuana Odum. Without her, this book would never have been written.

Special thanks to Amanda Leonardi, who helped me come up with the name of the coloring club, Hues, Brews, and Clues!

And I am always grateful for the friendship of Susan Smith, Amy Wheeler, Betsy Strickland, Daryl Wood Gerber, and Janet Bolin. There's nothing quite like friends to get you through the tough times.

I could wish you now and then, to exercise your Pensill in washing and colouring, which at your leasure you may in one fortnight easily learne to doe: for the practise of the hand, doth speedily instruct the mind, and strongly confirme the memorie beyond any thing else.

—Henry Peacham, *The Compleat Gentleman*, 1622

CAST OF CHARACTERS

Florrie Fox
    Veronica Fox—Florrie's sister
    Professor John Maxwell—Florrie's boss
    Mr. DuBois—Professor Maxwell's butler
    Bob Turpin—employee of Color Me Read
    Norman Spratt—crazy about Florrie

Regular patrons of Color Me Read
    Zsazsa Rosca—retired professor
    Professor Goldblum—retired professor

Percy McAllister—estate sale manager

Lucianne Dumont—Director, Dumont Foundation for the Arts

Jack Wilson

Mike—man in the park

Members of Hues, Brews, and Clues coloring club
    Dolly Cavanaugh
    Olivia and Priss Beauton—sisters
    Nolan Hackett—real estate agent
    Edgar Delaney—grad student

Maisie Cavanaugh—Dolly's daughter

Frederic van den Teuvel—antiques dealer

Sergeant Eric Jonquille

Chapter 1

"No one wants paper books anymore."

I bristled at the thought. I looked across the tables of yard sale items to see the nitwit who had said that. As the manager of a bookstore, I was horrified. I wished I were the kind of person who could give a stranger a piece of my mind. I'd love to tell him what I thought.

He was slender and medium height. Not particularly athletic. He wore his hair short in tight mocha curls. And every garment he wore was emblazoned with a designer label. He looked like a walking billboard.

He'd said it to a woman in a chic suit. Her hair was the color of peanuts, styled in short waves that were intentionally messy. She wasn't wearing much makeup. It was eight thirty in the morning, and her weary eyes suggested she hadn't been sleeping well. She wore a Bluetooth earpieces in her ear and said angrily, "How is it possible to lose a shipment that's only going from Washington, DC, to New York City? I could have driven it there myself in four hours."

Even though I knew she was talking to someone on her phone, she looked like she was speaking to invisible people.

She turned her attention to the man in front of her. "Okay, go."

He fingered his sparse mustache for a silent moment. "Oh! You're talking to me now. Ms. Dumont, all children think their parents have a treasure that will fetch millions at auction. They never do. I have handled a lot of these estate sales and I promise you, everyone has the same worthless junk. No one wants old furniture, china, crystal, silver, or tchotchkes, and they especially don't want ancient books. They're impossible to move. Tastes have changed."

The woman to whom he spoke appeared as horrified as I felt. The name Dumont rang a bell with me. Color Me Read, the bookstore I managed, was hosting a reading by the author of *From Fame to Infamy: The Dumont Family Curse.*

"Some of these books are probably out of print," she said. "There may even be first editions."

"If they're out of print it's for a reason—no one wants them. Besides, everything is on the Internet these days. If it's worth reading, you can find it there, usually for free."

He was really annoying me. I shuddered as I imagined how cold his apartment must look devoid of books.

"Mr. McAllister, I hired you to take care of this so I would not have to. The last thing I need from you is lectures. The books are for sale. And for your information, this is my grandparents' estate, not my parents'."

McAllister snickered. "I hope you have a van to remove the books after the sale is over. I don't deliver. What's left will go into the trash." He strode away.

Ms. Dumont squinted at his back as though she were sending evil thoughts in his direction. I got the feeling she wasn't used to being spoken to in that manner. Looking straight at me, she demanded, "Who recommended McAllister? He's a complete jerk."

I hoped she was speaking into her phone again.

I looked around for McAllister. *Oh no!* He had zeroed in on my sister, Veronica, a long-legged blonde who attracted the wrong men.

Veronica and I were opposites. She was gregarious, blond, and athletic. I barely hit five feet, two inches, had long chestnut hair, and preferred reading and drawing to bars and nightlife.

No, no, no. Veronica could not get involved with a man who thought books were trash. I hurried over to her. Too late. He was introducing himself.

"Percy McAllister."

My sister tilted her head coyly. "Veronica Fox."

He grinned. "I didn't expect to have a fox shopping here today."

Ugh. I cringed. There wasn't a thing I liked about him. Just then, I heard a woman call my name. "Florrie! Over here, darling."

I turned. Not too far away in the alley, Dolly Cavanaugh and Zsazsa Rosca waved at me and beckoned me over.

Dolly had been the first person to sign up for the Hues, Brews, and Clues coloring club at Color Me Read. In her early sixties, she was on the chubby side, but looked great. Not a single gray hair dared to invade her golden-brown tresses. Like a lot of Southern women, she wore a good bit of foundation that covered any blemishes. Her plumpness filled out wrinkles that might have lined her round face. She had taken great care with her eye makeup and wore a thick streak of perfectly applied liquid eyeliner on her upper eyelids in the latest fashion. Azalea-pink lipstick brightened her face. Dolly had told Veronica and me about the yard sale not far from the bookstore in the Georgetown section of Washington, DC. She had cautioned us to be there early on Saturday morning because all the best items would be gone by noon.

Zsazsa Rosca and Dolly had met at the coloring club and quickly become fast friends. One of my favorite regulars at the store, Zsazsa was a retired professor of art history. Named after the famous Hungarian actress, Zsazsa was as round as Dolly, but had confessed to me that to avoid jiggles she wore Spanx so tight she had to lie on her bed to pull them on. She wore dramatic eye makeup with black liner swooping at the outer edges of her eyes much like Dolly. I could pick Zsazsa out in a crowd in a second, thanks to her blazing tangerine hair.

They stood at a table laden with tchotchkes. The assortment of objects accumulated during someone's life was now being offered up in a yard sale for next to nothing. Zsazsa whispered, "Did you see the old Pyrex bowls at the next table over? They're highly collectible!"

Dolly added, "Look for the ones in the best condition and snap them up before someone else realizes what they're worth. You can sell them online for a nice little profit."

"Thanks for the tip. First I need to get rid of that guy who has latched on to Veronica."

Dolly gazed around. "Percy McAllister? The bane of my existence and yet a gift of good fortune. Don't antagonize him." She lowered her voice to a whisper. "He's a dolt who wouldn't know a valuable collectible if it fell on his head. He runs the best sales because he has no clue as to the real value of anything. Nevertheless we should rescue Veronica. Take it from me. I had four lousy husbands. Now that I'm older and wiser, I know trouble when I see it."

Without another word, Dolly hustled over to Veronica. "Sweetheart! I've found something you simply must buy. Excuse us, Percy." Dolly looped her arm through Veronica's and practically pulled her away from Percy. I couldn't help smirking. She was doing what I would have liked to do. But I wouldn't have been successful at it. Somehow, it was difficult to say no to Dolly.

Dolly steered Veronica toward a table of figurines. I wound my way through the tables to join them.

"Can you pick out the most valuable item on this table?" asked Dolly.

Veronica and I stared at a collection of Hummel figurines, Staffordshire jugs, and assorted bric-a-brac.

"This one," said Veronica with confidence, pointing to a Staffordshire jug.

"Very nice. A good pick, Veronica. Highly collectible. You could sell it for at least forty dollars more than Percy is asking."

Veronica beamed. "I like this! Shopping that will earn money. Two of my favorite things."

"Unfortunately, dear, it is the incorrect answer. Stick with me, darlings, and you will learn." Dolly picked up an eight-inch-tall statuette. It was coral-colored and had an Asian look to it. Dolly shook her head and tsked. "Two dollars. You would think Percy would know better. This is carved coral. Five scholars are playing with a dragon. It's worth at least a thousand, maybe more."

Veronica's wide eyes met mine. "Are you going to buy it?"

Dolly smiled and held it out to Veronica. "A gift to you. You buy it. Keep it on a shelf or sell it on eBay and treat yourself to something special."

"Dolly, we can't take that," I said. "You should buy it."

"You girls enjoy it. Didn't I tell you this would be fun?" Dolly winked at me. "I'm off to peruse the books. Maury Dumont was an ambassador who traveled the world. You never know what you might find. You girls should take a look at the furniture, too. Maury's wife had an eye for good pieces. I know they're not trendy, but those pieces are solid wood that will last your lifetimes and beyond, not sawdust pressed with adhesive that will fall apart. If you don't like the dark color, you can paint it."

She bustled off. I watched as she pawed through the boxes of books. It was sad to see Mr. Dumont's possessions strewn on tables outside of his house. They represented his life and now all those little pieces were being discarded like last week's left-overs. I felt like a vulture.

I gazed up at his home, shocked to see someone, probably Ms. Dumont, peering down at us from the semicircular window at the top of the house. There was no reason to imagine anything sinister, but the brownstone with the eyebrow window that extended beyond the roof was an ominous presence on the street of elegant historical homes.

"Creepy, isn't it?" Veronica tilted her head up to stare at the towering building. "It's probably worth a fortune but you couldn't pay me to live here."

"Did you see the face in the top window?" I asked.

Veronica shuddered. "Eww. No!"

I checked my watch. "I'm going to Color Me Read. See you later."

On my way, I paused briefly at a bakery to buy a package of pecan honey buns. They were so fresh the pastry box warmed my hands as I carried it.

The bookstore was only five blocks away, located on a busy street. An ideal location, actually. An awning hung over the front of the building, and show windows on both sides of the front door displayed books. I unlocked the door, flipped the closed sign to open, punched in the alarm code, and deposited the honey buns by the coffeemaker. After starting the coffee, I flicked on lights as I walked through the store. The building had been someone's home once. The parlor with a lovely fireplace was furnished with comfortable couches and chairs where customers could pause and relax. The owner made sure we carried a good selection of international newspapers to draw in the diplomatic community. Even though many of them were available online, a surprising number of people preferred the paper editions.

Coloring books were located on a back wall of the parlor. I

was proud that my adult coloring books were featured among them. While I managed the bookstore by day, I drew adult coloring books at night. I straightened our selection a little bit.

At the moment I was working on a book about gardens and flowers. I was thinking of calling it *Color My Garden*. It was the middle of the summer, so I was spending my spare time in beautiful gardens around the city. I was far from a botanist, but I was learning about the parts of plants as I sketched them for the book.

I turned on classical music at a very low volume, and opened the box of honey buns.

I carried a mug of coffee and a honey bun up to the third floor to my boss, John Maxwell. He hailed from a wealthy family that was well-known in Washington, DC. Once a professor, he now spent his days pondering the mysteries of the planet and often went on adventures in search of famous objects that had been lost. One of my favorite things about working in his bookstore was eavesdropping on conversations between the professor and his intellectual friends who dropped by.

The colors of Professor Maxwell's hair always fascinated me. His neatly trimmed beard and mustache were white as snow. But toward his ears they morphed to pepper, only to change back to snow again. Yet the top of his head was solid pepper. He wore the lines of age in his face with grace. Altogether, he was still a handsome man. He was also the most fascinating person I knew, with interests that varied from the location of the Holy Grail to aliens from outer space and whether Hitler actually died in his bunker.

While he was brilliant, he loathed confrontations. And he had the most peculiar habit of being oblivious about the time of day, which was something I couldn't comprehend. I was a stickler for being on time and couldn't resist collecting clocks that I found interesting.

He sat at his desk, holding a section of the newspaper in his hand. "Florrie, my dear! Thank you." He eagerly accepted the coffee and drained it by half. "Look at this."

He handed me the newspaper. It was folded to a tiny article that most people wouldn't even notice. The headline read "Orso Released."

Chapter 2

Professor Maxwell grimaced. "Over two decades ago, Orso Moschello drove a van that was picking up priceless items to be delivered to a local museum."

"Like an armored truck?"

"Quite the opposite. He was a trusted man who understood the value of antiquities. The belief is that it's far safer to transport such items in a regular vehicle that doesn't call attention to itself." Professor Maxwell grinned at me. "Every day there are vehicles passing this bookstore that contain amazing things. But only a handful of people know that the driver isn't just an ordinary fellow off to work. There are priceless and sometimes even dangerous items hitching a ride. For instance, if I had a couple of gold bars to be delivered to the bank, I might ask you to drive them over because no one would think a thing about it."

"You're not sending me anywhere with bars of gold are you?"

He laughed. "Not today. Anyway, after the precious cargo was received and unpacked, it was discovered that four items had gone missing. Among them was a small sunflower painting by van Gogh that my father was lending to a museum for an exhibit. It has never been found. Everyone hoped Orso would tell us what he did with the stolen goods but he kept his mouth shut."

"It was insured, wasn't it?"

The professor became grim. "Human error. The museum was supposed to insure it during transit, but the gentleman who should have signed the insurance document was out with the flu, so it was never processed. As you might imagine, there was a big legal fuss. The museum paid a token amount with the caveat that should the items be found, they would be returned to their rightful owners."

"Which would be you. You're hoping this Orso fellow will talk now?" I asked doubtfully.

"He has served his time. If he were a good man, he would reveal the whereabouts of the items. Of course, if he were a good man, he wouldn't have stolen them to begin with."

Uh-oh. If I knew the professor as well as I thought, he would embark on a search of his own. "So what are you going to do?"

He took the newspaper from me and slapped it on the desk a few times. "That is what I have been contemplating this morning. What would you do if you had been released from prison?"

I thought for a moment and understood where he was going with that question. "I guess I wouldn't have any money, so I would collect the goods from where I stashed them and sell them."

"Precisely. After all those years in the slammer, he probably doesn't have any funds. Not to mention the difficulty of getting a job. He'll be headed wherever he hid them."

"Please don't tell me you intend to follow him."

"No, my dear. I intend to wait until he offers them up for sale. A pity really. The sale of stolen goods will land him back in prison."

I left him contemplating the life and fate of a thief and hurried down the stairs.

Veronica walked in, beating the first customers by two minutes, and the store began to get busy.

An hour later the buzzer at the back door sounded. Probably a book delivery on the alley side of the store. I trotted down the stairs, unlocked the door, and opened it.

A man I didn't know fell partly inside the bookstore and lay crumpled on the ground. Streaks of blood ran down his face.

I glanced around quickly. There was no one in sight. The alley was calm. Not even a cat slinked by.

He looked to be about thirty years old. I kneeled on the floor. "Are you okay?"

It was a stupid question. The blood on his face was clear proof that he needed help.

He was on his elbow, struggling to rise. Reaching his hand out to me, he asked, "Could you help me up?"

"Of course." I said it with confidence that I didn't feel. But I wanted to assist him. I scurried to his other side. "Sling your arm around my neck."

He complied quickly. Between pushing off the ground with his right hand and holding on to me with his left, he was able to stand. "Do you see anyone?" he asked.

I assumed he was worried about the person who had attacked him. As we shuffled inside the store, I glanced around again. "Nope. All quiet back here."

He moved faster than I had expected. I wondered if fear of someone was motivating him. In minutes we were inside and the door was closed. I took care to lock it in case the person who clobbered him came back.

He sagged a little bit. Breathing heavily, he leaned against the door. "Thanks."

I fetched a chair. He perched on the edge as though he thought he might have to flee.

"Do you think you can walk up the stairs?" I asked.

"What's upstairs?"

"This is a bookstore. You'd be more comfortable there while we wait for 911."

"You don't have to go to that trouble. I'll be fine."

Maybe he didn't know he was bleeding. He needed medical help. "Rest here. I'll be right back."

He grabbed my hand. "No 911. Please don't make a fuss. I just need a few minutes to catch my breath and then I'll be on my way."

I bent toward him. In the gentlest voice I could muster, I said, "You appear to have a head injury. I think you'd better have someone look at it."

His brown eyes met mine and he reached up to touch his head. He lowered his hand and viewed the blood on his fingers. Unlike me, who would have been upset, he didn't even wince. He said calmly, "I'll get checked out by my doctor. Thank you for your concern."

"Head injuries can be serious."

He smiled at me. "I'll be okay. Maybe you could get me a wet paper towel? I don't want to scare people."

"I'll be right back."

"Uh . . . I don't know your name."

"Florrie. Florrie Fox."

"Jack Wilson. Florrie, I'd appreciate it if you didn't mention my presence to anyone else."

I studied him for a long moment. He dressed like a preppy in a blue button-down shirt and khakis. Brown hair the color of chestnuts waved in a well-behaved manner. His lips were thin and serious, but there was a spark of humor and kindness in his eyes. I didn't know what was going on with him, but he appeared to be thinking clearly.

Still, I hesitated to promise anything of the sort. I dodged his request. "I'll just get some hydrogen peroxide."

I dashed up the stairs and could hear Veronica at the front desk. I recognized the voice of a customer asking for the book he had ordered on seventeenth-century witch trials in Norway.

In haste, I grabbed paper towels and hydrogen peroxide. I carried them down the stairs guardedly, half expecting that he might not be there.

Jack had cracked the door and was peering outside. At the sound of my footsteps, he glanced back at me with wary eyes.

He closed the door, flipped the bolt, and sat down. "Thanks for helping me, Florrie."

"So what happened to you?" I dabbed at the blood on his face and worked my way back toward his wound.

"I'm not quite sure. I'm still trying to figure that out."

I looked into his eyes. "Someone clobbered you, but you don't know why?"

He smiled. "I realize that must sound strange, but I'm a little confused about it."

His primary injury was near the top of his head, well hidden by his thick hair. I saturated a paper towel with hydrogen peroxide and pressed it against the wound.

Jack squeezed his fingers into a fist but didn't complain.

"I'm putting some pressure on this to try to stop the bleeding," I said. "And if I were you, I'd stay away from that guy."

"That's exactly what I intend to do." Jack tilted his face up at me and grinned. "I don't mean to sound unappreciative, but are we done?"

I lifted the paper towel. "Your head is still bleeding. I don't know where you're off to, but you have blood on your shirt and khakis."

"Guess I'd better go home and change. Thanks, Florrie. I owe you one."

I grinned. "I'm hoping I won't ever be in the same situation. Stop by sometime and let me know how you're doing. Okay?"

He flashed me a thumbs-up and opened the door two inches wide. He stood quietly, as if he was depending on his hearing as much as his vision. And then, in a flash, he was gone, leaving only the bottle of hydrogen peroxide and soiled paper towels as evidence of his presence.

After the drama of finding Jack at our door, I was a little bit jittery. Just before noon, the members of the Hues, Brews, and Clues coloring club filtered in for their coloring session, including Zsazsa. I longed to join them to calm my nerves. As the founder of the group, Veronica handled most of the details, but newcomers approached me at the checkout counter to ask where the group was gathering. It seemed like additional members joined each time they met.

Our favorite pizza parlor down the block, Twisted Toppings, delivered seven pizzas for the group. I paid for them and hoped seven would be enough. It was hard to gauge how many we would need.

Olivia Beauton, one of the original members, barged into the bookstore without a word. She carried her favorite Polychromos colored pencils and made a beeline for the coffee.

She was followed by her sister, Priss, who smiled at me. "Hi, Florrie."

Olivia and Priss were in their sixties, only a year apart in age. The family resemblance was uncanny. They had the same lively hazel eyes and their noses were identical, right down to the slightly elongated tip and delicately flared nostrils. Even the little laugh lines around their mouths had formed in the same way. Olivia was plump and clearly the bossier of the two, while Priss was thin and fidgety but laughed easily. Olivia wore her hair in a short cut, while Priss's blond hair curled in loose coils around her shoulders. She had a tendency to wrap a strand around her finger. It seemed to me that Priss was always a step or two behind her sister.

The moment Nolan Hackett walked by, the Beauton sisters turned their attention to him. A firecracker could have gone off behind them and they wouldn't have torn their eyes away.

Personally, I failed to understand the attraction. Tall with a receding hairline, Nolan always looked exhausted. Two deep horizontal creases ran across his forehead. Pronounced bags hung under his eyes. Yet with all his wrinkles, there were no laugh lines around his mouth, only creases from age. A local real estate broker, Nolan had also been one of the original members of the coloring club, but he always seemed grumpy about it.

Olivia and Priss tittered like schoolgirls when he joined them.

Zsazsa whispered to me, "I don't know what they see in him." I grinned at her and shrugged. I didn't know, either.

I carried the pizzas to the long table where the group gathered. The scent was heavenly.

A group of them clustered around a member who demonstrated new shading pencils she had bought.

Zsazsa smiled at Edgar Delaney, a quiet graduate student studying for his master's in German and European Studies. "*Guten Tag,* Herr Delany. *Wie laufen Ihre Studien?*"

Edgar looked at her in surprise. Using his middle finger, Edgar pushed browline-style glasses upward on his nose. The glasses seemed rimless at the clear bottoms. The dark upper part matched his eyebrows and hair, a shade that made me think of used coffee grounds. A dark brown, but so close to black that it was difficult to reproduce and shade correctly with colored pencils. "I'm looking forward to coloring."

Someone touched my shoulder. I turned around to find Dolly clutching a tote bag to her chest. A carmine-red leather Coach purse hung from her arm.

"I need your professional opinion," she breathed in a low voice.

Her complexion was pale, but she was smiling.

"Sure. Is everything okay?"

"I might have won the yard sale lottery."

Chapter 3

Dolly opened the bag she held and thrust a book at me. A leather cover the color of cinnamon covered the pages. There was no title or author's name on the leather. I opened it and realized immediately that the leather wasn't bound to the pages. It was only to preserve the pages inside. They were fragile and yellowed, almost an ochre. On the top one, the title had been written in capital letters, *THE FLORIST*.

My heart beat faster. Surely this couldn't be the earliest known adult coloring book? Breathlessly, I glanced up at Dolly. "Where did you get this?"

"I bought it at the Maury Dumont yard sale. Do you think it could be the real thing?"

I gently felt one of the mustard-tinged pages and turned it carefully. There was no mistake. The pictures were botanical images of flowers. Piony, double violets, and something called persicaria. "It looks real to me. I'll have to check it out, Dolly."

She nodded and took a deep breath. Flapping her hands in front of her face to cool herself, she said, "I need a drink. What do you think it's worth?"

I smiled at her. "A bundle if it's the real thing. Of course, that will fluctuate depending on how much someone wants it. May I take it upstairs?"

"Yes, of course."

Carrying the book as though it were the most precious thing in the world, and if it was real, it was definitely the most valuable thing I had ever touched, I walked up the stairs to the third floor, passed the rare book room, and stepped into Professor Maxwell's office. Setting it on the desk, I looked the book up on his computer. It didn't take long to find a photo of the title page. Published around 1760, there were fewer than ten known volumes in the world, most of them owned by museums.

Touching it gingerly, I carefully compared the words on the title page to the photo to be sure they matched. A person trying to forge a copy might have misspelled something, particularly since some of the words were old English. The *S* in many of the words was the ancient form of a long *S* that resembled a lowercase *f*. If I recalled correctly, it went out of vogue just before the 1800s. That would certainly jibe with the age of the real book.

Sketches of vines and delicate blooms rose on the right and left of the title and a perfect ornate script which read,

> *Containing Sixty Plates of the most*
> *beautiful Flowers regularly dispos'd*
> *in their Succefsion of Bloming*
> *To which is added*
> *an Accurate description of*
> *their Colours with Instructions*
> *for Drawing & Painting them*
> *according to NATURE:*
> *Being a New Work intended*
> *for the use & amusement of*
> *Gentlemen and Ladies*
> *Delighting in that Art.*

LONDON
Printed for Robt. Sayer in Fleet Street
F. Bowles in St. Pauls Church Yd. &
John Bowles & Jen, in Cornhil
Price 6J, & Colour'd 1L 1J 0d

I didn't see any errors. I checked the physical description. Sixty leaves of plates. Robert Sayer and John Bennett, publisher. Doing my level best not to touch the pages more than necessary, I counted them. Sixty plates exactly. It appeared they were all there. I hadn't examined each thoroughly, but hadn't noticed any scribbles or torn pages. Out of curiosity, I looked up persicaria on the computer. The flowers were known as knotweed. I had definitely seen them before but hadn't given them much thought.

The book contained a lovely introduction that began with:

PAINTING having already had fo many eloquent and powerful Advocates, it would now feem impertinent to tire the Reader in endeavouring to prove that Art noble and delightful. That it is fo, the Ingenious have always, in the ftrongeft Manner confefs'd, by their conftant Attention and Encouragement: Therefore, the only Ufe here made of an Introduction, will be to inform the Purchafers of this Work, of the Plan on which it is executed.

It went on to speak of shadowing and light, and then described the "COLOURS ufed in FLOWER-PAINTING." They included reds such as lake, vermillion, and carmine; blues of ultramarine and bice; and the most curious description of brown as Gall-Stone. I shuddered to imagine why gallstones would have been common enough for everyone to know what color they were.

We would need to get a second opinion from an expert, but as far as I could tell, Dolly had found the real thing.

As an adult coloring book artist, *The Florist* held special interest for me. I had read that coloring sketches of plants was a popular pastime hundreds of years ago and a precursor to adult coloring books.

I carried the book downstairs. Dolly jumped up as a hush descended upon the other people gathered there. All faces turned toward me.

"Well?" Dolly's chest heaved with each breath she took.

"We should get confirmation from an expert, but it appears to me that you have stumbled upon the real thing."

Someone gasped sharply.

Dolly reached for the pages, and stopped. Her hands still midair, she asked, "Should I wear gloves to handle it?"

"That's not necessary. You can, of course. But the trending thought regarding white cotton gloves is that they do more damage than good. We have some oils on our fingers, but nothing compared to the culprits that do serious damage like water, pollution, or extreme humidity. Besides, cotton gloves make it very difficult to handle a page. You're likely to get a better gentle grip if you use your bare fingertips. Cotton gloves lead to tears."

Nolan rose from his seat. "Are you serious? It's really from the 1700s? I thought Dolly was exaggerating."

Even shy Edgar Delaney drifted toward us. He approached the book with interest. "May we see it?"

When Dolly placed the book on the table to show everyone, Edgar wedged in between her and Zsazsa. His slight frame made Dolly's figure appear even more generous.

The members of the coloring club clustered around, oohing and aahing about the book.

Nolan clapped his hand against Dolly's back. "You're gonna be a millionaire, Dolly. What say I find you some new digs worthy of your status?"

Priss gasped and Olivia's eyebrows tanked over her nose.

"Dolly!" said Zsazsa, "what a wonderful discovery. I'm so pleased for you."

Dolly giggled. "I hope it's worth as much as you think, Nolan. Wouldn't that be fantastic?"

"You'll be living the lifestyle of the rich and famous," Nolan blathered, pulling out Dolly's chair for her.

I returned to the front desk to ring up some adult coloring books for newcomers to the group. Nolan followed me and waited quietly until I had finished.

Leaning against the tall counter, he asked quietly, "So just how much do you think that old coloring book is worth?"

"I can't put a number on it, Nolan. It will probably go to auction and the price will depend on how much someone wants it."

"Museums?"

"Probably, but there could even be a private individual with an interest in it."

He gazed away from me, his mouth shifting from side to side. "Could it be a million?"

"I honestly don't know. As far as I can tell on a cursory search, there are very few left in the world, and none have been up for sale to the general public."

He nodded. "Real estate can be like that. There's always a house that's extraordinary but not for everyone. Find the right buyers and they'll pay a hefty price. But put it on the market at the wrong time and it will just sit there and languish. You never know."

I grabbed pots of regular coffee and decaf and followed Nolan back to the coloring group.

I refilled Dolly's mug. She sipped her coffee, clearly too excited to color. "Wait until my daughter hears about this. Maisie was always embarrassed by my scavenging. That's what she called it. She equated it to digging through strangers' trash." Dolly closed her eyes and shook her head. "She just didn't understand that I had to pinch pennies after her father died." Her eyes opened wide and she threw her hands in the air. "But now she'll see that it pays off. Maisie will finally be proud of her mama."

"What happened to your husband?" asked Edgar.

In a flirting tone, Dolly asked, "Which one?"

"Just how many have there been, Dolly?" Nolan ignored his coloring book. He didn't take his eyes off Dolly as he gnawed on a slice of pepperoni pizza.

"Four. I married the first one at seventeen. Young love is so blind. I dropped out of high school to marry him because I was pregnant. Inside of two months, I was already thinking the marriage had been a mistake. He'd punched me a couple of times, and I wasn't having any more of that. On the day that I miscarried, he was killed in a bar brawl. Can you imagine? He was out at a bar. What kind of man doesn't stay by his wife's side when she's going through a miscarriage?"

"Good for you," said Zsazsa. "Women should not tolerate such abuse."

"After that, I went overboard in the other direction. My second husband was a lovely man." She smiled at the memory.

"He was an artist, so sensitive and warm. They say artists are never appreciated in their time. Unfortunately, his work wasn't appreciated during his life or after his death, either. I think I still have some old paintings of his around the house somewhere. I worked two jobs trying to keep us afloat. During the day I sold women's clothes at a department store while he painted. On my days off and in the evenings, I helped feed people at a nursing home. Unfortunately, I stopped by our apartment at lunchtime one day and found him being entirely too familiar with one of his models. I threw him out, of course. The next day a cop showed up at my door to tell me my husband had perished in a motel fire caused by faulty wiring. He had been with the model at the time."

"Ouch!" Nolan's mouth pulled back in horror. "Surely you received some money for that death."

"Really?" asked Olivia. "That's where your mind went? Not to the fact that he shacked up with the model?"

Nolan raised his palms as though he was giving in. "Of course. I've had three wives, but I never stepped out on any of them."

"Nolan, I didn't receive a dime," said Dolly. "I admit I felt some guilt. If I hadn't tossed him out, he might not have been in the motel. Then again, maybe he would have been. I'll never know but it has bothered me my whole life. I would hate to think I was the catalyst that sent him to his gruesome death."

"But Dolly," cried Priss. "You couldn't anticipate where he would go. If he hadn't been fooling around, he would still be alive today."

"I agree with Priss," said Zsazsa. "You didn't send him into the arms of another woman, nor did you force him to go to that particular motel. His death was not your fault."

"Third time is the charm they say." Nolan raised his eyebrows. "That wasn't the case for me. How about you, Dolly?"

Edgar colored a little bit on a sailboat in churning waves but seemed engrossed in Dolly's stories.

"The third time I *thought* I was getting smarter. He is still the most charming man I have ever met. I thought I had finally gotten it right. He was a traveling salesman, which suited his gregarious personality. My goodness but we had fun together. I have never laughed as much since then. But it turned out that he was also laughing with two other wives, one of whom stabbed him to death when she discovered the truth."

Several people gasped.

"Dolly!" exclaimed Zsazsa. "You never told me. This is terrible."

"I've said it all my life. I was blessed with beauty and cursed with lousy husbands."

Olivia gazed at her, and Priss giggled.

"But you bought the brownstone. Even years ago, that couldn't have been cheap." Nolan frowned at her. "Insurance proceeds of some kind?"

"Ah." Dolly sipped her coffee. "The brownstone came from my fourth husband, Harry. He wasn't much to look at, bless his heart. No charm, either, to tell you the truth. He looked a lot like Florrie's old boyfriend who comes in here. What's his name again, honey?"

I groaned at the thought.

"Norman," Veronica supplied helpfully.

I hastened to add, "But Norman was never a boyfriend. I just went out with him to make our mothers happy."

"That's the one. Pale and not unlike an egg with thinning hair. Harry looked a lot like Norman, but with wrinkles. Still, he was a kind man. Harry was an accountant who dabbled in antiques on the side. He taught me most of what I know about antiques. When we married, we bought the brownstone where I live today. But when Maisie was a toddler, Harry got into some kind of financial argument with a man. At the time, guns weren't legal in Washington, you know. When Harry went across the river to Virginia and bought one for security, I should have realized that he was in trouble. The day that man showed up at our house, Harry sent me upstairs with Maisie. I could hear them arguing. That guy managed to wrest Harry's gun away from him and shot him dead in our front parlor with Harry's own gun."

Everyone had stopped coloring to stare at her. But Dolly spoke as if it was all matter-of-fact and delicately shaded the mane of a lion. There wasn't even the slightest bit of drama in her voice.

"How can you be so calm?" asked Zsazsa.

"Goodness. It's all old hat. My life hasn't been exactly scintillating. It's a dreary story of struggling to get by. The narrative of man, unless you were born to wealth, like Professor Maxwell. Besides, I've had years of lying awake at night to think about it." Dolly sucked in a deep breath of air. "I should have called the police right away instead of waiting until I heard the gunshot. But it all happened so fast that I have come to the conclusion that I couldn't have prevented Harry's death no matter what I might have done. My greatest regret was that Maisie didn't have a daddy. I don't think she remembers Harry at all. But I have realized that even though she didn't know her daddy, Harry's death influenced her more than any other thing in her life. Everything would have been different if he had lived."

"Now, Dolly, don't you go kicking yourself. Priss and I lived in that brownstone with Maisie from the time she was just a grasshopper. You were a wonderful mother to her."

"Thank you, Olivia. I did my best. Of course, I had to do something to provide for her. Paying the mortgage and staying in our home seemed of primary importance to me, so I used most of Harry's life insurance proceeds to chop the brownstone into apartments. Poor Maisie. Even at that age she really resented giving up her pretty lilac bedroom on the second floor."

"Is that my bedroom now?" asked Priss. "I never knew it was lilac once. I think I would like that."

Dolly nodded. "I did what I could for Maisie. The parlor on the first floor became her bedroom. She loathed it. Meanwhile, I slept on a sofa in our family room so she could have a bedroom of her own. Privacy is so important to preteens."

"But she never appreciated it," said Olivia as though it was a fact. She outlined a castle in a coloring book.

Dolly sighed. "Children have such small worlds. Everything revolves around them. Most of them don't see beyond their own needs and wants. In retrospect, it may have been a mistake to stay here in Georgetown. I thought she would get a better education here and feel more secure in the only home she had ever known, but the real result was that she resented me because she didn't live like the wealthy children who were her friends." Dolly's face brightened. "But *The Florist* will change everything! Now she'll see that her old mama knows a thing or two."

Nolan leaned back in his chair, his legs outstretched in front of him. He hadn't colored a thing yet. "You could make a mint off your house, Dolly."

"It's amazing what they're worth these days. Maybe years from now when Maisie inherits my brownstone she'll be proud of her mama."

Nolan's mouth twisted. "What if her mama used the money from the rare coloring book to buy a new house? One that would impress Maisie?"

Olivia and Priss looked up from their coloring, clearly concerned. Not that I could blame them. They were Dolly's tenants. What would happen to them if she sold her house?

Nolan sat up and leaned toward Dolly. "There's a fabulous house on S Street. You don't have a garage, do you? This house does. And the garden in the back is among Washington's finest. You'll think you're in Williamsburg. Four bedrooms, four and a half baths, and the most amazing two-story sunroom you've ever seen. What do you think? Want to take a look at it?"

Dolly flushed the color of a ripe persimmon. "Do you think I dare? I suppose it couldn't hurt just to have a look."

Nolan grinned, and his fist hit the table. "I'll make an appointment for tomorrow morning. Excuse me, please." He left the table in a hurry, focusing on his cell phone.

I returned to the desk near the front door. Nolan stood outside on the stoop with his phone to his ear.

Moments later, voices behind me in the hallway caused me to turn around.

Olivia held on to Priss's forearm. "For heaven's sake, get a grip, Priss."

Nolan bounded back inside clearly pleased. He winked at me. "This would mean two nice commissions. One for selling Dolly's house and another for selling her the new house. I may not even need to color anymore."

Chapter 4

Olivia must have overheard him. "Need to color? That's a peculiar thing to say."

Nolan seemed a little bit embarrassed. "I'm under a lot of stress. My doctor prescribed coloring. The jerk actually wrote it out on a prescription pad."

"Don't most people just take a pill or something?" asked Priss.

"Hah! That's what I thought. I should probably change doctors. He thinks people take too many pills. So I joined this coloring group in an attempt to bring my stress level down."

Olivia raised an eyebrow. "But you don't color! All you do is chat and drink coffee."

"Don't you think that's the point? To get out and talk about something other than real estate?" Nolan smoothed his hair back.

Olivia clucked at him. "I thought you were smart. They've done studies that show coloring lowers stress and anxiety. There's something about it that is healing for your brain. It calms you."

Nolan shrugged. "If I sell Dolly's house my stress level will be just fine."

Priss's eyes opened wide. "You can't do that!"

"Priss, stop it." Olivia appeared annoyed.

"And why not?" asked Nolan.

Olivia snapped her fingers at him. "She's worried about where *we'll* live. We've been there for nearly twenty-five years. It's our home, too, you know."

Nolan studied the two of them for a moment. "I don't suppose I could interest you two in a condo?"

Olivia snorted. "We work from home tutoring online. If we could afford a condo in Washington, we would have bought one years ago. Maybe you could find us another rental."

Nolan nodded. "Sure."

Olivia appeared relieved and they returned to the coloring group.

"It's hard to find a reasonably priced rental in Georgetown. I looked for years," I said. "If Professor Maxwell hadn't offered me his carriage house, I would still be on the hunt for a place to live."

"I know." Nolan sighed. "I don't do rentals. They're not worth my time."

He returned to the coloring table. I watched as he picked up a fancy green pencil. Sitting up straight, he made several tiny strokes with it as though he was thinking about something else.

When they left around four in the afternoon, the members of the coloring club were all still talking about Dolly's discovery of *The Florist*. A few of them were pondering what they would do if they received a monetary windfall.

Veronica waved to Dolly and Zsazsa as they left together. When the door closed she asked, "Will Dolly really be wealthy?"

"I don't know. I hope she won't be disappointed. There's no telling what it might sell for."

Veronica strode toward me. "Maybe we should hang with Dolly more often. I had no idea you could find such valuable things at those yard sales. Did you see the gorgeous purse she was carrying?"

"I wouldn't count on getting that lucky."

At five o'clock, Dolly phoned Color Me Read. "Florrie, would you be a sweetheart and check to see if I left my handbag at the store? I'm at the Blackberry Tea Room with Zsazsa, celebrating. I was so excited about *The Florist* that I think I left my bag behind."

While Veronica looked for it, Dolly babbled excitedly. "You wouldn't believe how much attention my Facebook post about *The Florist* has received! Zsazsa says it's going viral. I guess a lot of people dream of something like this happening to them."

I wished she hadn't posted anything. It would only draw attention to her. I didn't want to put a damper on her fun, though.

Happily, Veronica discovered the purse behind a chair in the parlor.

"We have it. Veronica can bring it up to the tea room."

"That's a relief. But don't bother bringing it up here. Zsazsa is picking up the tab today. We're having champagne to celebrate! Would you mind dropping it off at my house on your way home?"

"Not at all." I was still on the phone with Dolly when Ms. Dumont entered the store and marched up to the desk where I stood.

I smiled at Ms. Dumont, and said to Dolly, "We'll see you then." I hung up.

"May I help you?" I asked Ms. Dumont.

She wore the same earpiece she'd had on in the morning. "That's not funny." She paused and stared at me. "I saw you earlier today."

"Yes. At the yard sale."

"Estate sale," she corrected. She looked straight at me and shouted, "Kansas! What's it doing in Kansas? Call them right back and tell them I expect them to hire a courier at their own expense and deliver it to New York *today*. I don't care what time it is. So help me, if they don't get it to New York, I will have their jobs. Get their names. I would like the address of one Dolly Cavanaugh."

I assumed she was now speaking to me. "I'm sorry but I can't give out customer information."

"Why is *everyone* so difficult? Look, on very poor advice, I hired a colossal idiot to run the sale of my grandfather's estate. He assured me that there was nothing of value, but it turns out that my grandfather was in possession of a valuable coloring book which the idiot sold by mistake."

How could she know that already? There were so many things I wanted to say to her. After all, *she* was the one who had hired Percy. In my opinion she most certainly had a legitimate beef with him. But that was something she should take up with Percy. She may have wished she had kept the book and sold it privately, but Dolly had bought it fair and square. Dolly had rescued the book. If Dolly hadn't recognized it as valuable, it would have landed in the trash and been lost forever.

Most of all, though, it really wasn't my problem. I wasn't responsible for Percy, or Dolly, or anything that had happened.

I said simply, "I don't think you would like it if I handed out *your* address to strangers."

"You don't have *my* address. And I am not a stranger. I am Lucianne Dumont. Perhaps you have heard of me."

Since her grandfather had been an ambassador, I assumed she was related to the infamous Dumonts. But I didn't really care who she thought she was. "I'm sorry. I can't help you, Ms. Dumont."

Her eyes narrowed. "You know where the book is, don't you?"

I didn't respond.

"Apparently you don't realize that I have connections in very high places. Am I making myself clear? The most important people in this country take my phone calls. I can have you fired from this store in two seconds."

I was beginning to understand why the professor loathed confrontations so much. She was acting like a bully. It was mean of me, but I couldn't help saying it. "Good luck getting that package to New York."

"I demand to speak to your superior."

I was fairly certain the professor was not upstairs in his office. But that didn't matter. Ms. Dumont's problems weren't his concern, either. "I'm sorry. He's not here at the moment."

"Angie, take this down," she spat. "What's his name?"

"John Maxwell."

"Maxwell?" She looked around. "This is Maxwell's bookstore? I had no idea. Well, I'll be having a word with him about you. I am a very close friend of Maxwell's." Her eyes narrowed. "Miss . . . ?"

I couldn't help grinning. It was tempting to give her a fake name. But at that moment, Helen barreled through the front door, asking, "Florrie, can I switch days with you?"

Ms. Dumont, for whom I no longer felt sorry, even if she did appear to be exhausted again, said in an evilly smooth tone, "Florrie. Did you get that? How would I know how to spell it? Can't you do anything on your own?" She turned and left the store, still muttering to poor Angie.

Helen's mouth dropped open. "Was that Lucianne Dumont?" she whispered.

I nodded.

"What did she want here? I would love to work for her."

I seriously doubted that but kept my opinion to myself. I pulled out the work schedule to see if I could accommodate Helen's changes when the phone rang.

"Good afternoon," said a voice with a British accent. "This is Frederic van den Teuvel. Have I reached Florrie Fox?"

Who on earth? "Yes. Speaking."

"Wonderful. I hope I have not phoned you at an inconvenient time, but I felt the need to reach you as soon as possible. It is my understanding that you have a copy of *The Florist*?"

"Actually, I am not in possession of the book."

"No? Oh my! I apologize. I was told that you have a newly discovered copy."

"It . . ." For absolutely no good reason, my wariness antennae shot up. I felt like they were glowing red with alarm. "How may I help you?"

"Now I am confused. Do you have the book?"

"Not in my possession. Are you interested in acquiring *The Florist*?"

"Very much so. What is the price which you are asking?"

Why did I feel so suspicious? "May I have your name again?"

I grabbed a periwinkle-blue pencil and a notepad. I wrote as he spoke. *Frederic van den Teuvel.*

"Your phone number, please?"

He gave me his number as well as an address in Aachen, Germany. "I am representing an interested party."

"I see. You are an antiques dealer?"

"Something like that. When can I see the book?"

"It hasn't been authenticated yet, but I will be happy to call you when the owner is ready to sell it."

After a long moment of silence, Frederic said, "I shall only be in Washington for a matter of days. Perhaps we can arrange a time for me to view the book?"

Why did I feel pressured? I didn't like this Frederic guy, but that wasn't fair to Dolly. For all I knew he was representing someone who would pay more than our wildest dreams. "Perhaps you could telephone me tomorrow. At this point, I am not able to schedule a viewing."

His tone grew testy. "But you do have the book? It seems that you are unsure."

Hadn't I already explained that? Maybe his English wasn't as good as it sounded. "I do not have it in my possession. I am not the seller of the book, so I cannot make any representations at this time."

"Very well. I shall phone you in the morning to arrange a viewing of the book."

He hung up, and I was confused. I stared at the book a customer handed to me. How had Ms. Dumont and Frederic van den Teuvel already heard about *The Florist*? Was it a more valuable commodity than I had imagined?

I forced myself to concentrate on customers. Saturday night diners, moviegoers, and revelers kept us busy through the dinner hour and beyond.

It was after ten by the time we had rung up the last sales of the day and shooed everyone out of the store. Veronica and I split the floors, each of us doing one last sweep, to make sure no one lingered behind. We turned off lights as we went. We finally flipped the sign on the front door to *Closed,* set the alarm, and locked up.

It was a beautiful summer night. Veronica and I admired the gorgeous historic homes as we walked. Lights shone in Victorian-style turrets and bay windows, depending on the architecture of the house.

Dolly lived in a brownstone, a tall old building that stood out by virtue of its unusual shade of cream. The front door was recessed. The first and second floors, as well as the basement, were built out a few feet in a rather boxy construction. Light beamed from the large arched window that graced the first floor. The matching glass arch over the front door shone, too. Outdoor lights on each side of the front door illuminated the concrete steps that led up to the stoop.

A wrought iron picket fence and ornate gate marked the tiny front yard of the property. The leaves on the tree just inside the fence were completely still in the balmy night. The second floor, where the Beauton sisters lived, didn't appear to be quite as glamorous, but lights shone in a sizable square window that faced the street, where I imagined their parlor must be.

The top floor was actually an attic, and the roof took a steep angle. The blue slate fish scale tiles appeared to be black in the dark of night. I had noted before that they interestingly matched the roofs on several homes on the street as though they had all been installed at the same time. The tall dormer window at the top of Dolly's house was dark.

The gate swung open easily. I carried Dolly's purse up the stairs. While I knew that the front door was generally un-locked during the day, I expected it to be locked given the late hour. I rang the bell, but Veronica tried the doorknob. The door swung open.

I cringed. "I hope the doorbell didn't wake anyone."

A narrow passage was now the foyer of what had once been a single-family home. Four robin's egg blue mailboxes that resembled tall birdhouses were mounted on the wall in a row over a narrow table. An old-fashioned chandelier with sparkling prisms added a touch of glamour. Matching well-worn red oriental runners covered the floor. One ran from the entrance to the foot of steep stairs. The other ran alongside the stairs to the door of Dolly's apartment on the first floor.

Dolly's door stood open a few inches, as though she ex-pected us. I rapped a knuckle against the door and called out, "Dolly! It's Florrie and Veronica with your purse."

She didn't respond, but I peeked inside anyway. "Dolly?"

And then I saw her. She lay on her side on an oriental car-pet, one hand outstretched.

Chapter 5

"Dolly!" I shouted. I dropped her purse and rushed to her. Kneeling, I bent over her. "Dolly, what happened? Are you okay?"

I could hear Veronica calling 911 behind me.

Dolly's lovely face was contorted as if she was in pain. Her eyes were open, but they didn't appear to see anything.

While Veronica spoke to the dispatcher, I gently massaged Dolly's arm, unsure whether she could feel my hand.

"They want to know if she's breathing," said Veronica.

I watched Dolly's chest but couldn't tell if it was moving. "Dolly! Dolly, can you hear me?" I grasped the hand close to her chest, "Squeeze my hand if you can hear me."

Her fingers twitched so imperceptibly that I wondered if I had imagined it. "Veronica, I think she moved."

"They want me to stay on the line with them," said Veronica. "No, I don't see any blood."

I watched her chest for any sign of movement. "I can't tell. Dolly? Can you give me a sign? Can you blink?"

Veronica spoke softly but there was an urgency in her tone. "The door. It's open!"

The French door leading to the backyard was open and

moved gently in a breeze. Beyond it, a lantern flickered on a table on the enclosed patio.

I jumped up and looked outside. I didn't see anyone. The romantic light from the lantern revealed three champagne glasses and a bottle of bubbly. I stepped out and checked the latch on the gate. I opened it and by the light of the moon, I could see the dark shadow of a figure running in the alley.

I was not a runner at all, but I tried. As I loped along, I knew full well that I wouldn't make it to the street in time to see the person before he disappeared into the night. Veronica, who thought sports involving running were fun, might have been able to catch up to the person. Panting like a worn-out dog, I stopped when I reached the sidewalk. I looked to the left. The street lay peaceful and quiet. Shade trees lined the sidewalks and beautiful old homes stood in a stately row.

Still trying to catch my breath, I stumbled back to Dolly's house in haste. I banged my knee on the gate and limped into Dolly's living room. She hadn't moved.

Veronica crouched beside her, murmuring comforting words of encouragement. I kneeled on the other side of Dolly.

Veronica whispered to me, "I saw her eyelids flutter. I know I did."

I didn't want to, but I slid my hand under the collar of her blouse and felt for a pulse. I didn't find one. "Her skin is warm," I uttered hopefully.

I leaned toward her. "Dolly? Dolly!" Ever so gently, I shook her shoulder.

A commotion at the front door caused me to look up. Three emergency medical technicians strode in. Veronica and I rose and moved away from Dolly, making room for the two EMTs that immediately assessed her.

The third one asked us what happened. I was explaining when I heard my name. "Florrie?" Even without seeing him, I knew immediately who it was. My relationship with Sergeant Eric Jonquille was still new enough for me to tingle at the sound of his voice. I turned in haste.

The first time I had seen Eric, I was certain he was out of my league. After all, I was sort of mousey, not a bombshell like Veronica. But for some reason, I had gotten lucky with Eric. His chestnut hair tumbled in loose curls, and he had the most vibrant blue eyes I had ever seen. They were truly the shade of delphinium flowers.

"Eric!" I explained to both of them how we happened to be there and that we had found Dolly.

Eric and the EMT looked over at the purse I had dropped, and I realized that a tiny thing like that verified our story.

One of the EMTs on the floor was doing CPR on Dolly.

Eric coaxed Veronica and me out of the way of the EMTs. "Are you two okay?" Eric asked.

Tears welled in my eyes. "We will be if Dolly is all right. What on earth could have happened to her?" I wiped my tears away ferociously but more sprang up in their place. I sniffled, and Eric wrapped an arm around me. He slung his other arm around Veronica.

"The doors were open," Veronica said, pointing toward the French door. "The front door was open and the door to the garden was open."

"I ran outside and saw someone running along the alley. He turned the corner at the end of the alley."

"Did you recognize the person?"

"I couldn't even tell if it was a man or a woman. Whoever it was turned left."

Eric frowned at me. "Did you see him leaving Dolly's garden?"

"No. He was pretty far away."

"So you don't really know that he had been here?"

The EMT who had been doing CPR looked up at us and shook his head. "It was probably a heart attack."

Another EMT rose to his feet and handed something to Eric. "She was holding this in the fingers of her outstretched hand."

It was a brittle scrap of paper that was yellowed with age.

Eric shrugged.

"May I see?" I asked.

He pulled a tissue from his pocket, laid it on his palm, and placed the scrap of paper on top of it.

It was a tiny triangle, maybe two inches on the longest side. It appeared to be the bottom corner of a page that had torn off. I knew instantly what it was—a corner of a page from *The Florist*. I sucked in a sharp breath and peered at it more closely to be sure.

"Does this mean something to you?" asked Eric.

I told him about the valuable coloring book Dolly had scored at the Dumont yard sale.

"Published in 1700? Are you kidding me?" His brow furrowed, and he gazed around. "Do you see it? Is anything out of place?"

He was scanning the room, taking in every little detail.

Dolly's apartment was decorated to the hilt. A stranger might have called it fussy. But I knew the truth. The items that cluttered the room so that the eye didn't know where to land were all Dolly's treasures. Louis the fifteenth and sixteenth chairs bore mismatched upholstery, yet they seemed to fit together in Dolly's eclectic style.

Bookshelves lined two walls. Books packed the shelves, standing and in piles. More books stood in stacks on the floor. Paintings hung all the way to the high ceiling and even on the woodwork between the bookshelves. The zebra pattern settee was where I usually sat when she insisted I stay a few minutes for a cup of tea and a pastry. She used a round tufted ottoman as a coffee table, moving it about as needed. The ivory velvet fabric of the ottoman was a calm oasis in the middle of the cacophony of colors and patterns in the room.

As far as I could tell, it didn't look any different than it usually did. That didn't mean a book or some other new tchotchke that I didn't know she had acquired wasn't missing. She had amassed an astounding number of objects, but the only two I knew much about were the rare coloring book and the piece of coral. "Veronica, do you have the coral?"

"It's in my bag." Veronica sounded defensive. "She gave it to us, remember?"

I tried to smile at my sister. "I'm not accusing you of anything. I'm just making sure that no one stole it."

To Eric, I said, "Maybe her daughter would be able to tell you. Nothing jumps out at me."

"I'm sure she was a nice woman," said Eric, "but her shelves are so cluttered with stuff that it would be nearly impossible to tell if a piece were missing here or there."

"Dust," Veronica uttered.

"What?" he asked.

"I'm just guessing that she probably doesn't dust those shelves constantly," Veronica clarified. "You could tell if there were a spot that wasn't dusty."

"Eric"—I looked up into his lovely eyes—"I have a bad feeling that the missing item is *The Florist*. She posted about it on Facebook earlier today. In fact, we had an odd call from a Frederic van den Teuvel who . . . gave me the creeps. I didn't know what to think of him. He was quite insistent about wanting to see the book."

Eric shook his head like a wet dog. "Why do people blab on Facebook about valuables or vacations? It's like sending an invitation to burglars. Not a good idea."

"Do you think someone attacked her for the book?" Veronica asked.

It seemed obvious to me. "That makes perfect sense. Some-one tore the book away from her and caused her to have a heart attack."

"Not so fast, ladies," Eric said in a kind tone. "Except for the paper, which could have torn because she fell, there's no outward sign of an attack on her. We'll know more after the medical examiner has a look. Of course, it's worth noting that she had that piece of paper in her hand." He cocked his head sympathetically and looked at me. "But the book could still be around here somewhere. This might just be a scrap of paper."

A cluster of people arrived at that moment.

Eric said, "Sorry, ladies. I'm going to have to ask you to step outside so they can collect evidence."

"Evidence of what?" asked Veronica.

"Evidence of what happened to Dolly."

The newcomers said hello to Eric as they passed us and started their work in Dolly's apartment.

When we walked into the foyer, Dolly's tenants were clus-tered on the stairs, watching in horror.

Eric motioned to them. "Everyone follow me, please?"

He led the way out to the sidewalk.

Priss bawled. She pulled the sash tighter on her silky pink robe. Edgar removed his glasses and rubbed his eyes. He wore a gray T-shirt and jeans as though he had thrown them on in a rush.

"Florrie!" cried Olivia. "What happened?"

"I'm so sorry. Dolly died. She left her purse at the book-store. When we brought it to her, she was on the floor."

"I saw her eyelids move," said Veronica.

"Are you sure she's dead?" Priss ran to the gate and gazed at the house. "Maybe she's alive but not able to move? I've heard about that happening."

"I'm sorry, Priss. I don't think so. We were hopeful, but . . ."

I wanted to join her at the gate, but Eric asked her to move away so the investigators could get in and out.

"Nooo," she sobbed.

Edgar appeared to be stunned. He wiped his eyes with the back of his hand. "She was so happy this afternoon."

"Who will call Maisie?" asked Olivia.

The words were barely out of her mouth when Eric asked who Maisie was.

"Dolly's daughter." I introduced him to everyone. It wasn't like a social introduction, though.

He took each of them aside and asked them questions. When he was through, he joined the rest of us. "I gather Dolly wasn't married," he said. "How many children did she have?"

"Just the one daughter," said Olivia. "Can we go into Dolly's apartment? She kept Maisie's phone number on her desk."

"Sorry, I can't let you in there yet. I'll look for it when the evidence technicians are through."

"What's Maisie's last name?" asked Eric.

"Cavanaugh. Just like her mom," said Olivia.

Priss sniffled as she said, "Maisie was engaged once very briefly, but it didn't work out."

"I don't understand," blubbered Veronica. "If she died from a heart attack, what are they looking for?"

Eric wrote a note to himself as he answered her. "Sometimes there's a cause of death that isn't readily apparent. An injection site, for instance. And sometimes insurance companies ask for information after a death. So we have to be thorough."

We watched silently as they brought Dolly's body out of the brownstone on a gurney. I felt as though we were already part of a funeral procession as we followed Dolly's gurney to the waiting ambulance.

The evidence technicians were still at work. Eric told us to remain outside, but he entered the building.

Neighbors began to collect and ask questions. Tears flowed from everyone. Dolly had been much loved.

Eric finally returned. "Thanks for your help. You can all go home now. They're still working in Dolly's apartment, but they're done with the foyer. I found the phone number, by the way. I dread making this call."

Olivia dabbed her nose with a tissue. "Don't sweat it. Maisie wasn't close to her mother."

We said good night to Olivia, Priss, and Edgar, before setting off on foot with Eric.

"We don't need an escort, Eric." Veronica pulled her cross-body bag over her head.

"I don't mind. Besides, it's two in the morning."

I gasped. "It didn't seem like it took that long. Poor Dolly. It's such a cruel twist of fate for her to die right before life would have gotten easier for her."

"It's so unfair," wailed Veronica. "Which just goes to show that we should all live each day as if it's our last—because it could be."

Eric waited until Veronica was safely in her car and pulling out of the estate driveway before walking me to the front door of the carriage house and kissing me. "Are you going to be all right? I go through this a lot, but I usually don't know the person. It must have been a big shock to you."

"I can't quite grasp that Dolly is gone. Just a few hours ago she was fine and happy."

"I'm sorry I can't stick around. I have to file my report."

"No problem. I'm sure you still have a lot of work to do."

"Maybe I'll see you tomorrow?"

"Veronica and I are supposed to meet our parents for brunch before work. In the evening, maybe?"

After one last long kiss, I shut the door. Through the window, I could see that he waited to hear the bolt drop in place before he walked away. Cops! They saw danger everywhere.

My cat Peaches yawned as she stretched.

"Hungry?" I asked.

She moseyed over to her bowl and looked up at me sleepily.

I filled the bowl with beef cat food. "Sorry about the late dinner."

She didn't seem too upset about it.

I changed into an oversized T-shirt in the colors of the rainbow that said, *Color your cares away!* I returned to the kitchen and contemplated a stiff drink. Wasn't that what people did when they'd had a rough night? It didn't appeal to me, though. I fixed myself a mug of steaming English Breakfast with milk and sugar, and curled up on my sofa with my sketchbook. What had Dolly said? She was blessed with beauty. Drawing Dolly's face was simultaneously sad and cathartic for me.

As I drew, I realized that her face was quite oval, not round as one might have thought. Her likeness came together well, and I realized that she hadn't been boasting. She must have been beautiful when she was young. Except for her few extra pounds, she had been remarkably pretty in her sixties as well.

She had amazingly symmetrical features. Her large eyes seemed too happy when I drew them, but that was how I had known her. They matched her bubbling personality. Through it all, the four husbands and the struggle to make a life for herself and Maisie, she had remained cheerful and optimistic.

I doodled the shape of the scrap of paper she had held at the time of her death. Was she holding on to it while someone ripped it away from her? Or had she fallen while looking through the book and accidentally torn the page? I itched to see the scrap again. Could a scientist tell what had happened by the way the margin had been torn? Probably not. A tear was a tear.

I paused to sip my tea and when I began to doodle again, I found myself drawing Jack Wilson's face. With all the excitement about *The Florist*, I had nearly forgotten about Jack.

It was his sharp jaw that I recalled most vividly. Thick walnut-brown eyebrows topped serious hazel eyes that canted down just a bit at the outer corners. I had trouble getting his nose right, but his thick hair was easy.

It had been a strange day. I wondered if he had made it home okay.

I finally drifted off, only to be awakened by the telephone at four in the morning. In my entire life, I had never received good news from a phone call between midnight and six a.m. Immediately alert, I seized the phone and said hello.

Chapter 6

The voice on the phone said, "This is Steve Goolsby from Goodwinkle Security Systems. The alarm on Color Me Read is going off. We have notified the police."

"Thank you. Thank you very much." I hung up and dialed Professor Maxwell's number as I ran upstairs, limping just a tad from the bruise on my leg. I was holding the phone with one hand and pulling on a pair of pedal pushers when his elderly butler Mr. DuBois answered in a very grouchy tone.

"Do you know what time it is? Of course you do. You have a hundred clocks."

I slid a blue short-sleeved top over my head. "The alarm is going off at the store. I thought Professor Maxwell should know." I rushed downstairs, holding the phone to my ear. Peaches recognized my panic and ran along with me as I dashed through the carriage house.

While I popped the top on a can of cat salmon and dumped the contents into Peaches's plate, I realized there had been a long silence from Mr. DuBois. "Hello? Are you there?"

"*I* am, but Maxwell is not."

To Peaches I whispered, "I'll be back later, but I don't know when."

Still on the phone, I grabbed my purse, and locked the door behind me.

"Okay. No problem. I'll have to handle it. Where is he?"

"Miss Florrie! How many times do I have to tell you that I do not gossip?"

I was too worried about the store to laugh. Mr. DuBois loved to gossip. Maxwell had recently rekindled his relationship with his ex-wife. She often stayed over at the mansion. "I'm sure Jacquie knows where he is."

"I doubt that. Jacquie is off at some romance writer convention in Las Vegas. I'm quite concerned about Maxwell. I don't like him staying out all night. It's not like him."

While I would have been happy to learn more, it just wasn't the right time. "When he comes in, tell him what's going on." I said goodbye and hung up. And for the second time in twelve hours, I did my best to run. The streets of Georgetown were still sleepy. Few houses had lights on yet. I hadn't run an entire block when I slowed to a rapid walk, which probably was about the same speed as my inept running had been.

I tried to calm myself by thinking Professor Maxwell had probably arrived at the office in the middle of the night and simply forgotten to shut off the burglar alarm. He hadn't done it before, but it was certainly possible.

I heard the alarm blaring as I power-walked closer. When I rounded the corner and saw two police cars parked in front of the store and no sign of the professor, those hopes faded fast. A uniformed officer casually walked toward me. "Are you the manager?"

"Yes. What happened?"

"We got a call from your alarm company. The front door is locked." The name on his uniform said *Petrocelli*.

"That's odd. Unless"—I hated to even imagine this possible scenario—"the owner arrived and something happened to him so that he couldn't turn off the alarm."

The officer looked at me askance. "I doubt that. Not many people would arrive at their place of work this early."

"He does. Professor Maxwell doesn't seem to have an internal clock."

Another officer joined us as we walked up the few stairs to the entrance.

When we reached the top and I pulled out my key, Petrocelli said, "I want you to unlock the door, but you stay out here on the sidewalk while we go inside. Understand?"

"No problem." I had no desire whatsoever to encounter a burglar. I unlocked the door for the officers and scampered down to the sidewalk.

Petrocelli opened the door. The two officers entered Color Me Read.

I waited outside with adrenaline pumping through me. I reasoned that the burglar had probably left as soon as the alarm blared. There was nothing to be nervous about. He was probably long gone.

To see above the awning that ran across the front of the building, I backed up as far as I could go without stepping into the street.

The beams of flashlights flicked by the display windows on the first floor as the officers swept the building. Seconds later, someone ran out the front door. I moved closer, thinking it was a cop, but he or she wore a ski mask that covered his face.

I shrieked in surprise and shock. Those ski masks were some kind of scary! The person looked straight at me for what must have been seconds but felt like minutes. He turned right and hightailed it along the sidewalk. I yelled, "He's running down the street!"

The cops must not have heard me over the alarm that was still ringing.

I backed up to the street again and waved my arms in case one of them looked outside.

The second-floor windows were tall French doors that opened to a tiny balcony that ran the width of the building. They were dark, as were the windows on the third floor.

Suddenly, one of the French doors on the second floor opened and someone stepped out. Thinking it must be a police officer, I yelled, "He went that way!" And I pointed to the right.

The person jumped onto the awning, slid off it, and landed feet first in a squat. He was dressed all in black, definitely not one of the officers. I couldn't see his face. He touched the sidewalk briefly to stabilize himself and took off running.

It happened in a matter of seconds. I ran up the stairs to the front door. Remaining outside, I yelled again. "They're out here!"

Over the blaring alarm, I could barely hear footsteps on the bookstore stairs as Petrocelli ran down. I stepped aside and pointed in the direction the people had gone. Even with the showroom lights of the stores that lined the street and the prominent streetlights I couldn't make anyone out. They had disappeared into the night.

Petrocelli jogged along the sidewalk but he was too late. He trudged back to me, calling in on his radio. I hoped another squad car in the area might intercept the burglars.

When he put his radio away, he said, "Come inside and turn off that blasted alarm."

I entered the bookstore and gazed around in horror. The burglars had done a number behind the checkout counter. All the special orders that were waiting to be picked up now lay haphazardly on the floor. They had torn a framed poster off the wall that said *Good friends, good books, and a sleepy conscience: this is the ideal life. —Mark Twain.*

"I would assume that your visitors don't have a sleepy conscience," quipped Petrocelli.

He watched while I punched in the code. The sudden silence was almost deafening after the blare of the siren.

"Stay out there where you were while we finish," said Petrocelli. "We need to make sure there wasn't anyone else."

It irritated me not to have my watch on. How could I have skipped putting it on? I estimated that it only took them another ten minutes, though it felt like hours before they appeared on the stoop. Petrocelli asked, "Would you please come inside?"

I returned to the store and walked to the middle of the mess behind the checkout counter. "It doesn't look like they tried to break into the cash register."

"How can you tell?" asked Petrocelli.

"They were pretty brutal with everything else, but there aren't any scratches or obvious attempts to break into the cash register."

"Don't touch anything. We'll need to check for fingerprints."

I nodded and stepped into the parlor. The furniture hadn't been slashed or turned over, but the cushions were on the floor. They didn't come to destroy the store. They hadn't come looking for cash. They had been looking for something else, and I thought I might know what it was.

I turned to Petrocelli. "I think they may have been looking for *The Florist*. It's a rare book. The woman who discovered it . . ." I paused, unsure how to phrase what had happened to Dolly. Should I say she was murdered? They hadn't decided that for sure. I kept it simple. "The woman who found the book is now dead."

After that, of course, it seemed prudent to tell them the whole story.

Petrocelli stepped away and made a phone call.

The other officer smiled at me. "It's probably just a coincidence."

Really? I didn't think so. What kind of burglars ignored the cash register and ripped cushions off a sofa in a store? I didn't think for one minute that they were hoping to find loose change that had fallen out of pockets. Nope. Those guys were looking for something. Something that someone would have hidden. I wondered if they had torn apart the rare book room on the third floor. With any luck, they hadn't known that we had a rare book room or maybe they hadn't made it up to the third floor before the cops arrived.

I peeked into the children's book room. It was in surprisingly good shape, which I thought supported my theory.

Then it dawned on me that while I didn't live that far away, it must have taken me at least ten minutes to get to the bookstore. I whipped around. "When did you arrive?"

The cop looked at me in surprise. "Just before you did."

"So those guys heard the alarm going off and were willing to hang around anyway for ten minutes?"

"The pros figure they've got a couple of minutes."

They figured right. I guessed they might have been walking up the stairs or checking the basement when the police cars pulled up. "You didn't have your siren on?"

He shook his head. "Not for something like this. We thought it might be a silent alarm and didn't want to scare away the perpetrator."

I guessed that made sense. Still, it had to take some very serious guts to search while an alarm was going off and everyone was being notified. I wouldn't have been able to concentrate. It did explain, however, why they were so sloppy. There wasn't time to do anything but run through the store slinging things around.

"Did you check the basement?" I asked.

The cop looked annoyed.

Thankfully, at that very moment, Eric dashed into the store. He grabbed me by the upper arms and looked into my face. "Are you all right?"

I couldn't help smiling. He looked so sincere. "I'm fine. I

was at home asleep when the alarm went off. How did you hear about it?"

He took a deep breath. "I was at home asleep, too. But I got a call from the station. Something about a connection to Dolly's death."

"That's my fault. I think the burglar was searching for *The Florist*."

I explained my reasoning to Eric but the whole time I talked, I could see the cynical expression on the other cop's face.

"So," said the other cop. "Some old lady died, and you think that someone broke into your bookstore in search of her book? Sheesh."

Eric squeezed my hand, and I knew he didn't agree with the other guy.

"If I don't touch anything, may I look upstairs?" I asked.

"Yeah. Be my guest."

The second I started up the stairs, I could hear the other cop say, "What a crock. Does she really think we're going to chase down a couple of two-bit burglars for breaking and entering a lousy bookstore?"

I wanted to cut him some slack. Maybe he was tired of his job. Maybe he was jaded from having seen too many truly terrible things. Maybe he didn't care about crime anymore and was waiting for his time to run out so he could collect retirement pay. But my efforts to justify what he had said didn't work. I was ticked off with him for not caring more about the people who counted on him. Maybe this was a two-bit bookstore to him, but it mattered to a lot of people. Not to mention that he might have been a little more sympathetic about Dolly's death. She wasn't just *some old lady*.

The second-floor rooms were a disaster area. If I was correct and the burglars had been looking for *The Florist*, then I could understand why they couldn't delicately look at every single book. But did they have to knock them all on the floor?

It was six in the morning by the time the police collected fingerprints. Thankfully, Petrocelli and the other cop were gone. Eric and I sat outside of the store on a bench sharing a takeout breakfast of lattes and freshly baked ham croissants.

"Do you think we'll be able to open the store today?" I asked.

"Sure. Florrie, I'm personally going to follow up on the fingerprints, but I don't want you to be disappointed if they don't lead anywhere."

I swallowed a sip of the bracing latte. "I've been thinking about it. You're not going to find anything. If they were smart enough to know how much time they had before anyone arrived, then they probably wore gloves."

"Did you notice gloves on either of them?"

"It all happened so fast. I hate to admit it, but I was so astonished that I didn't notice much of anything. But I think the burglars might have done this before."

"Broken into Color Me Read?"

"I mean I think they were professionals. That sounds weird. Can you be a professional thief? Is that an oxymoron? I heard that cop minimizing the importance of the break-in, but here's what I think. The burglars had the confidence and guts to look for something in the store with the alarm ringing. They knew people were being alerted. A common thief would have left immediately. It wouldn't have been worth it to him to be caught. The alarm would have scared him away. But these guys knew they had about eight to ten minutes, maybe more, before anyone arrived to check things out. They didn't stop at the cash register, try to get into it, and leave. They didn't just vandalize the store, either. They were looking for something specific. They knew what they were after, and it was something worth enough to them to take the risk of searching even though an alarm was going off the whole time."

Chapter 7

Eric leaned over the food between us on the bench to kiss me. "I think you're right. But not everyone will agree with us."

"Was that kiss supposed to soften the blow of the truth? You're trying to tell me that the burglary won't be a priority for the police department?"

"Sorry, Florrie. Probably not. Break-ins like this aren't unusual. And in this case, nothing appears to be missing. Unless we can prove that the person meant to commit an additional crime in the bookstore, all we have is the misdemeanor of unlawful entry."

"Breaking in isn't enough? It's not like they did it for a lawful reason. Clearly anyone who breaks into a business in the middle of the night is up to no good."

"That's true. But it's still just a misdemeanor."

I huffed a little. "I can't say I like that, but I do understand that there are more important crimes to investigate. Like Dolly's death."

Eric stared at me silently. "Would another kiss help?"

"Eric! They can't just sweep Dolly's demise away like it's nothing."

"It will depend on the medical examiner. If she had a heart

attack, then obviously, as tragic as her death was, she died of natural causes. I know you think the paper in her hand was from a valuable book, but, Florrie, we don't know if she was still in possession of the book. She could have given it away, or hidden it, or left it with someone for safekeeping. So far, we don't really know that it's missing. All we know for sure is that the one person who knew where it was has died."

"When will we hear from the medical examiner?"

"Depends on their backlog. Hopefully today sometime. I promise I'll call you when I hear."

Professor Maxwell strode up to us. Wherever he had spent the night, he hadn't gotten much sleep. His eyes were their usual violet, but his eyelids hung low and he had dark circles under his eyes. He paused for a moment, taking in the police vehicles and commotion at the store. "What's going on?"

"Didn't you see Mr. DuBois?"

Professor Maxwell turned his head toward me fast, as though I had asked the wrong thing. "No."

Eric and I filled him in on everything from Dolly's discovery of *The Florist,* to her unexpected death, and the burglars at Color Me Read.

The professor listened intently. "I have a few underground contacts. I can put out the word that I'm looking for *The Florist.* If it has landed on the black market, I may hear about it."

He strode up to the bookstore and entered it.

Eric scowled. "He has underground contacts? I don't like the sound of that."

I thought I'd better switch the subject before the professor landed in jail again. "I need to call Veronica, Bob, and Helen. It will take us a while to get the store in order."

An hour later, the police were gone. Veronica and Bob had shown up to help shelve books. Helen hadn't answered her phone. Bob took one look at me and his eyebrows tanked over his nose. "Are you okay?"

A long breath shuddered from my mouth. In a whisper, I said, "Dolly is dead. They think she had a heart attack."

"What?!" Bob shrieked so loud that it echoed up the stairwell. "What a cruel fate. She finds something worth a lot of money, enough to change her life, and she dies that night?"

I told him about the scrap of paper she held between her fingers.

"Do you think someone threatened her and stole it?"

"I hope that wasn't the case. Maybe they'll find it on the floor."

We all did our best to focus on cleaning up the store. I worked with the professor in the second-floor room dedicated to philosophy and what he liked to call *books by and about great thinkers*.

I was slightly amused by his lack of urgency. He examined almost every book he handled as though he wanted to read it. Meanwhile, I was just concerned about getting them back in order so we could find them.

When the bulk of them were back in place, I left him to his musings and went downstairs. Bob was just finishing with the special orders.

"Everything is in good condition. I don't think we'll need to reorder any of these."

"Great. I needed some good news."

"I'm broken up about Dolly." Bob reached out to hug me. When he stepped back, he wiped tears from his eyes.

Veronica walked up, dusting off her hands. "We have a couple of hours before the store opens. Do you think that's enough time to meet Mom and Dad for brunch? They might still be there."

"I forgot all about that. I'm kind of grubby. I'd rather run home and change clothes."

Veronica suggested that Bob go with her. I would go home to change and stop by the restaurant if time permitted.

It was a glorious summer day, but now that the burglary crisis was over and the adrenaline had worn off, I dragged along the sidewalk thinking of Dolly. My feet felt like they had turned to lead. Nothing would bring Dolly back. I imagined horrible scenarios of someone viciously fighting with her over the book.

Lucianne Dumont! What if she had managed to obtain Dolly's address? It was probably available through land records. The invisible Angie on the other end of Lucianne's earphone might have even found it online.

Peaches was glad to see me when I unlocked the door. She mewed nonstop as though she was trying to tell me she had been worried by the disruption of our normal schedule.

I showered and changed into a sleeveless dress the color of sea glass. It would be cool for the hot day ahead, and I always thought it gave me an air of professionalism. If more people like van den Teuvel had heard about the book, I might need to look cool and collected, even if I was quivering inside. Who would have thought running a bookstore could put me in this kind of position? I had thought it would be a very calm and peaceful job.

I apologized to Peaches for leaving her at home again. If the press got wind of the story, it could be a zoo at Color Me Read today. Peaches might be better off at home. I filled her bowl with her favorite tuna to make it up to her.

I wouldn't have much time with my parents, but the restaurant wasn't far away. Walking back slowly, I thought about Dolly's last minutes. Heart attacks weren't uncommon. They could come on quickly, too. But the piece of paper Dolly held in her fingers gave me pause. I was fairly sure it came from *The Florist*. If Dolly had been looking at the book, maybe even turning a page when the heart attack hit her and she fell to the floor, she could have easily ripped it. But if that was the case, wouldn't the book still be on the floor or the sofa? I hadn't noticed it when I looked around. It could have slid under a piece of furniture, I supposed. Even if the scrap of paper came from something else, wouldn't the rest of the document be somewhere near Dolly's body?

I didn't want to think about it, but I couldn't help going there in my mind. It was the logical conclusion. If the rest of the torn document wasn't in the room, then someone had ripped it away from Dolly and taken it.

The crowds grew dense as I approached the Georgetown Flea Market, which was doing a brisk business. I didn't have the time to pause and peruse their wares today, but I saw something that made me stop in my tracks. Across tables laden with china, knickknacks, and paintings, gawky Edgar appeared to be negotiating with a gentleman.

There wasn't a reason in the world to be suspicious. Edgar was just a student. A guy from out of town taking in one of Georgetown's fun weekly events.

So why did I feel the need to spy on him? True, students were notoriously poor, but I didn't know anything about him. He could come from a wealthy family who was footing his expenses. Besides, even if he was in need of money, it didn't mean he had killed Dolly and stolen *The Florist*. Maybe he was buying a desk or a reading lamp. Keeping an eye on him, I circled through the tables and tents, drawing ever closer.

At the table where Edgar stood, the vendor was selling books. My heart beat a little bit faster. I scolded myself. Edgar could be in the market for used textbooks, or books in German.

I backed as near as I could in an effort to eavesdrop.

"Sorry, son, I'm afraid I can't help you."

Were they were talking about *The Florist*?

"Florrie! Florrie!"

Why? Why now?

Norman. Pink, flaccid Norman bumbled toward me. I thought of him as walrus pink, but today he was pinker than usual, almost a flamingo, probably due to the heat. He caught up to me and leaned toward me for a beefy kiss.

In the nick of time, I spun away, avoiding those rubbery lips, ever so reminiscent of plump erasers. "Norman. What are you doing here?"

"We saw you from the restaurant. You looked like you were going in circles, so I offered to show you the way."

Great. Just great. I glanced toward Edgar, but he had moved on. "Lead the way."

Reluctantly I followed him into the restaurant to the large table overlooking the flea market where my parents sat with his parents. The last I heard, his mother didn't want him involved with me, which suited me just fine. Alas, something must have changed her mind. Maybe she couldn't find anyone else to go out with him.

Veronica was wolfing an omelet and Bob was busy with a breakfast steak and fries.

"We ordered eggs Florentine for you." Dad pointed at a plate with a cover on it. I slid into the chair next to him, prepared to eat fast.

Norman lifted the cover off my food as though he was waiting on me.

His mother shot me a stern look. "Veronica and Bob have been telling us the most horrific stories about burglars. I thought you Fox girls were through with criminals."

My eyes met Veronica's. Why wasn't Norman infatuated with her like other guys? And then I realized this was my opportunity to get Mrs. Spratt to discourage Norman from being interested in me. I did my best to make it sound terrible. "I'm afraid not, Mrs. Spratt. Did Veronica tell you that we found one of our customers murdered last night? And the killer was still there, hiding in the garden!"

My mother gasped, and I felt a twinge of guilt. I would have to make it up to her later.

"And one of the men who broke into the bookstore during the night very nearly attacked me," I said. "He jumped from the second floor. If the police hadn't been there, I don't know what would have happened."

Bob and Veronica quit eating and stared at me. But I ate ravenously, keeping an eye on my watch.

"This is what comes of dating a policeman," said Mrs. Spratt. "It wouldn't happen with a nice man like our Norman."

That was entirely unfair, of course. I had to say something. What kind of girlfriend would I be if I didn't? "Eric had nothing to do with it. Those things would have happened anyway."

"He did come to her rescue, though. That's one of the perks of having a boyfriend who's a cop." Veronica smiled at me.

"Maybe you should think about finding employment elsewhere," suggested my mom. "The store is so lovely, but odd things happen there."

They all spoke at once.

In the din, my dad leaned over to me and whispered in my ear. "Was that for the benefit of Mrs. Spratt?"

"You bet."

He shook his head. "And to think that you're my quiet, bookish daughter." But a slight smile crept over his lips, and I knew he was teasing me.

Veronica, Bob, and I apologized to everyone, excused ourselves, and rushed out the door.

I was very glad to leave Norman behind, but I tried to send Veronica and Bob ahead.

Veronica folded her arms over her chest. "No way. What are you up to?"

I looked at my watch. "Okay then come with me, but we'll have to hurry."

They followed me through the crowd to the vendor who was selling old books. I was frantically trying to figure out how I could get him to tell me what Edgar had wanted. I couldn't exactly come right out and ask him that, could I? I smiled at him as brightly as I could. "Hi! I'm looking for a book called *The Florist.*"

The portly guy looked at me in surprise and I feared I had done the wrong thing by asking about the book.

"The coloring book?" he asked.

"Yes."

"Funny, you're the second person today to ask about it. I'm gonna have to find a copy of that book."

"Oh?" I positioned my purse so that it hid my left hand and nonexistent wedding band. "That might have been my husband. Slender with old-fashioned glasses?"

"Now look here. I'm not spoiling a husband's surprise. I've been married forty years, and I know better than that." He winked at me. "Let's just say I'll be looking for a copy."

I thanked him and walked away with Bob and Veronica, who promptly asked, "Your husband? What was that about?"

I explained about having seen Edgar speaking with the man. "At least it tells me one thing. Edgar was asking about the book."

We rushed through the Sunday morning brunch crowds on our way back to Color Me Read.

The store was silent and a little bit creepy when we opened the door. But within half an hour, it became a different world. Sunday browsers clustered inside, children ran by me clutching books, and the ever-present classical music played soothingly in the background. It was as though nothing untoward had happened. I felt as though a cloud of gloomy gray surrounded me as I strode through the happy bustle.

But word had begun to spread and it wasn't long before members of the Hues, Brews, and Clues coloring club began to filter in looking for confirmation of the rumors they had heard.

Nolan arrived first. He gazed around and helped himself to

a cup of coffee. "I heard about Dolly. I know it's not our regular coloring day, but I'm too restless to sit around my office, and I don't feel like being alone today."

"That's understandable. Everyone grieves in different ways. We're happy to have you hang out here with us."

"I never imagined anything like this. She was younger than me. Far too young to die."

He had barely finished speaking when Edgar loped in. He took off his glasses and wiped his eyes with his sleeve. "I didn't know Dolly for very long. How can I feel such a loss? I've been wandering around Georgetown all day. It's just too depressing to be at the brownstone right now."

Edgar must not have seen me at the flea market. Or was he acting like he didn't know I had been there? He certainly hadn't been teary then. "You're both always welcome at Color Me Read," I assured them, leading them to the parlor. "We're all depressed about Dolly, too."

Other members of the group filtered in one by one. They spoke softly and the mood was somber. Not the best thing for the store, but I felt we owed it to Dolly.

I sent Bob out for pastries that people could nibble on while they talked.

Veronica joined me behind the counter. "Did Dolly have a history of heart problems?"

"That's a good question. I don't know."

She intercepted a little boy and his mother before they wandered into the parlor. "Do you like giraffes?" She led them past the parlor to the children's book room.

I had just answered the phone when a gaunt man walked into the store. The skin on his face was so taut that it was concave beneath his cheekbones. His blue eyes flitted around, as if he was taking stock of the store.

When I completed the call, I asked, "May I help you?"

"I am looking for Florrie Fox."

His British accent clued me in. "You would be Frederic van den Teuvel?"

"You recognized me by my voice, no doubt. I am here about *The Florist*. My client is very eager to make an offer, assuming the book is in acceptable condition."

"I'm so sorry to tell you that the owner of *The Florist* died unexpectedly."

"So I have heard. May I see the book?"

Hadn't I been perfectly clear with him about that? "I don't have it."

"How can that be?"

"Excuse me, but our friend has died. I don't know where she put it."

"I see." He shot me a perfectly evil sideways glance.

Chapter 8

"Did Orso beat me here?" asked van den Teuvel.

Orso? I hardly knew how to respond. So many thoughts ran through my head. Could he mean the man who had gone to prison for stealing the Maxwells' painting by van Gogh? Orso had only been out of jail for a few days. Why would van den Teuvel think Orso would have the money to make an offer for *The Florist*? I frowned at him. Did he mean he thought we had made a deal with this Orso or could he mean that the said Orso had killed Dolly for the book? Could Orso have been the burglar? I tried to phrase my response carefully to learn more from him. "Orso is interested in the book as well?"

"I assume so."

Well that didn't help. I stared at him in silence, hoping he would blather and spill some information.

He flipped his palms up in a gesture of frustration. "Of course he is! You don't seem to understand. A rarity like this is a coup. *The Florist* hasn't been for sale in our lifetime. Not in the last century as far as I know."

"Is it worth killing for?"

"You Americans are always so dramatic. Perhaps you can arrange a meeting for me with the owner?"

Hadn't he heard me? "I'm sorry. She is dead."

He placed a hand on the counter and his eyes narrowed. He took a deep breath and rubbed his mouth with a bony hand. He spoke slowly, as though I wasn't capable of understanding. "She must have an heir. *He* would now be the owner."

"Possibly."

"Ms. Fox, I do not intend to leave Washington without this book."

I relaxed. That meant he hadn't stolen it from Dolly. But he might have hired the person who ransacked the store. "Just how much are you willing to pay for *The Florist*?"

He gave an ugly snort. "Are you representing the seller?"

"No."

He tapped his fingers on the top of the counter. "I would rather negotiate with the seller, if you don't mind." He withdrew a business card from his wallet. "Have the heir phone me. I await his call."

He stalked toward the door but turned to face me before he left. Holding up his forefinger, he said, "Do not make a deal with Orso without speaking to me. No matter how much he offers, I can beat his price." Holding his head high, he left the store.

I was reeling from his attitude. Part of me thought I wouldn't want to sell him anything. He struck me as an arrogant jerk. But it wouldn't be my decision. Dolly's daughter would have to deal with him.

I felt the presence of someone behind me. I whipped around, only to find Professor Maxwell standing there, looking at the closing door. "Was that van den Teuvel?" he asked.

"You know him?"

"I know of him. The poster child of parasitic symbiosis."

I was going to have to look that up.

Professor Maxwell smiled at me. "One organism benefits while harming the other organism. That's van den Teuvel.

He's always ready to take advantage of people and leave them to die."

I gasped. Maybe I had jumped to conclusions. "Do you think he would have killed Dolly?"

"I thought she had a heart attack. I am very sorry about Dolly's untimely death. She was a charming woman."

I nodded. "Everyone is broken up. Apparently van den Teuvel has a client who is interested in purchasing *The Florist.*"

Maxwell snorted. "Watch out for him, Florrie. He'd cheat his own mother."

"He said something about not selling to Orso."

"Well, well. When it rains, the worms do come out."

"If Orso has been in prison for almost two decades, how would he have that kind of money?"

"That's the question, isn't it? How indeed?" He gazed at the group in the parlor. "Are you okay? It's not easy to happen upon a dead person. Especially one you knew and liked."

"I'm all right," I lied. "It's good for me to have to work and not dwell on Dolly's death."

Another member of the coloring club burst through the door. "Is it true?"

I showed her to the parlor and then helped an elderly gentleman who was looking for an autobiography by Winston Churchill.

Color Me Read closed at six o'clock on Sundays. Even though I did my best to keep busy, my thoughts rarely strayed from Dolly. Her death took a toll on all of us. I almost wished we would stay open late that night. But promptly at six o'clock, Bob, Veronica, and I closed the store and headed to our respective homes instead of picking up some dinner as we usually did.

When I came home, Peaches opened one eye to look at me before flipping over and curling tight with one paw over her eye. I got the message. *Go away.* I had interrupted her catnap.

I paced around the carriage house, too restless to cook dinner or do anything productive. I finally grabbed my sketch pad, tucked some pencils into my purse, and locked the door behind me. I wasn't sure where I intended to go. Maybe one of the beautiful gardens I had spotted around Georgetown. There were lovely garden nooks everywhere.

I ambled along the streets and discovered Book Hill Park. Broad concrete stairs led to a circular stone patio with benches. A few people sat under trees and on the lawn reading. It was surprisingly quiet, probably because of the time of day. From where I sat, I didn't see any children's playground equipment.

I settled on a bench and began to sketch a rosebush with bright pink blooms that cascaded over a small stone wall and onto steps.

It was a relief to be able to draw and momentarily think about something other than Dolly. My concentration was so intense that I jumped when I heard a man's voice.

"Pardon me. I didn't intend to frighten you." He gestured toward the bench. "Do you mind if I join you?"

I scooted over to make more room for him. "Of course not."

His age was hard to gauge. He moved like someone with achy bones, somewhat slow and careful. His eyes were bright with crow's feet so deep and perfectly spaced that they reminded me of half-spent daisies. His lips were so thin they had almost disappeared, but he had no trouble smiling.

He sat down licking an ice cream cone. "Butter pecan," he said. "One of the simplest things in the world, but what a treat."

I smiled at him.

"That's very good." He gestured to my sketch. "Are you an artist or is this a hobby?"

I told him about my adult coloring books.

"I heard they were popular." He raised his chin and inhaled deeply. "It's such a beautiful evening. I never knew this park was here. It might become my favorite."

He reached a hand to me. "I'm Mike."

"Florrie."

He appeared surprised. "You don't hear that very much. It means you are like a flower. Like the Roman goddess, Flora, who represents spring."

"That's a lovely thought. Where did you learn that?"

"From a book. Amazing things, books. You never know what you might learn."

He sat quietly for a few minutes, methodically licking his ice cream cone. "Do you believe in forgiveness?"

His question took me by surprise. Was he trying to convert me to his religion? "Are you a minister?"

He laughed heartily. "No one has ever mistaken me for a man of the cloth."

I thought about his question for a moment. "Yes, most definitely."

He raised his eyebrows and studied me. "You sound so certain."

"I am. Most of the time, people don't mean to hurt us. Maybe it's a matter of degrees. We forgive little things every day. But if someone hurt a member of my family I might feel differently. Are you trying to forgive someone?"

"A man who did me wrong. He changed my life. If I had never met him, my life would have been completely different."

"Better?" I asked.

He snorted. "In every conceivable way."

At that moment, an elderly woman walked down the stairs I was sketching, tripped, and fell flat on her face.

"Oh!" I jumped up and dashed over to her. "Can you stand? Should I call for help?"

It took some doing to assist her to her feet. Her palms were bloody from putting out her hands to break her fall. "Maybe you could call my daughter?"

"Of course." I pulled my phone from my pocket. "What's the number?"

I reached her daughter, who promised to come immediately.

I turned back to look at Mike, but he had disappeared. His ice cream cone lay on the bench, dripping onto the stone floor.

At the sound of footsteps, I expected to see the woman's daughter, but it was Jack Miller.

"Hi. How's your head?"

"Florrie Fox! My head is great, thanks to your expert nursing care." He took a long look at the woman. "Need help?"

"Her daughter is on the way. She didn't want me to call 911."

He smiled at me. "Do you always turn up when someone is bleeding and in need of aid?"

Why wasn't I quick with quips? "I try."

The woman's daughter arrived and started to fuss over her. "Good grief, Mom. What have you done now?"

"Do you need help?" I asked.

"Thanks. I think she can walk to the car. But I might swing her by the emergency room."

She helped her mom to her feet and as they walked away, the daughter turned back to me. "Thank you so much!"

Jack winked at me. "Another successful rescue. See you around." He ambled off.

The sun had begun a slow departure from the sky. I returned to the bench to retrieve my sketch pad.

On the top page was a quick sketch of my face.

Chapter 9

Peaches purred nonstop when I came home. I cuddled her until she couldn't stand it and leaped from my arms. It wasn't late but the lack of sleep the night before was catching up with me. After changing into the nightshirt that looked like a green crayon, I made a ham sandwich for myself and scooped duck cat food into Peaches's bowl. She snarfed it and ran to me meowing, determined to have a taste of my dinner. I gave her a pinch of ham to try.

I settled on the sofa with my sketch pad intending to draw Lucianne Dumont, but as I began to sketch, the face that I couldn't get out of my head was that of Frederic van den Teuvel. I'd thought it was his skin dipping under his cheekbones that gave him a dour expression, but as I drew, I realized it was his mouth that made that impression. His lips were very thin and turned downward at the edges. Worry lines rippled across his forehead just above his eyes. He had a sizable nose, but it suited his face. I sat back and examined my drawing. I didn't trust the fellow one bit.

I set aside my sketch pad and pulled out the iPad to look up Orso. There was precious little about him that I didn't already know.

In spite of myself, I fell asleep on the sofa.

At four o'clock on Monday morning, I woke with a start. Dolly's face and *The Florist* kept me from dozing off again. There was no point in fighting it. I got up and showered. Peaches was overjoyed to be up early. She chased a toy mouse around the bedroom while I pulled on shorts and a T-shirt. I walked downstairs and put on the kettle for tea.

Normally, I would have taken my tea out into the lovely walled garden behind the carriage house, but the darkness outside the French doors didn't beckon me. I longed to be able to call someone to talk about Dolly, but it was just too early. Instead, I peered in my refrigerator for something to bake.

Plump indigo blueberries were just waiting to be used. I took out butter, eggs, and pecans for a blueberry crumb cake. If nothing else, it would be a delicious breakfast. I preheated the oven.

I considered using the food processor, but this morning chopping the nuts with a cleaver appealed to me. They wouldn't be as fine, but there was something very satisfying about mincing the nuts with a giant knife, while I contemplated the extremely rude Frederic van den Teuvel and aggravating Lucianne Dumont.

Peaches zoomed around underfoot. She batted her toy mouse under furniture, retrieved it, and batted it across the room again.

The carriage house had been built by John Maxwell's second wife. Originally a true carriage house, it had been part of the underground railroad, helping slaves escape to freedom.

An author, John's ex-wife Jacquie had created her dream writing space while preserving parts of the ancient carriage house. The kitchen, dining room, and living room were all one large open space. The inside wall on the side toward the mansion was covered with bookshelves that displayed not only my favorite mysteries, but some of my artwork and my clock collection. A stone fireplace flanked by giant columns was at the end of the room. On the other side, a line of French doors opened to the tranquil garden. One bedroom and the bathroom were upstairs. I never could have afforded anything this wonderful in Georgetown. But my boss, Professor Maxwell, had been in a bit of a pickle and needed a tenant fast.

I had been lucky to be able to move in. Only blocks from the bookstore, my life had simplified considerably. Plus I loved the atmosphere in Georgetown. It was an upscale historic area with a wonderful mixture of students, academics, diplomats, and families. I wasn't involved in the active nightlife, though. I wasn't much of a clubber. I never had understood the beauty in standing around with a bunch of strangers and drinking.

My mom and sister made fun of me for that. It was okay with me if they thought that. At twenty-nine, I was old enough to pass on social conventions that didn't appeal to me.

As I beat the butter and sugar in my fire engine–red KitchenAid mixer, my thoughts returned to Dolly and *The Florist*. If there really were people interested in paying a lot of money for it, and Maisie could find it, then life would change for Dolly's daughter. I was only sorry that Dolly wouldn't benefit from it herself. Dolly had been a lovely woman, warm and fun, but life had been hard for her. I couldn't think of many people who had deserved a break like this more than Dolly.

But I couldn't help wondering if that break had led to her death. Was it possible that she would be alive today if she hadn't found the book?

Frederic van den Teuvel still bothered me. Somehow news of Dolly's discovery had made it all the way to antiques dealers and opportunists in less than a day. I supposed that thanks to social media, that wasn't an impossibility. Every post on Facebook or Twitter had the potential to be seen almost anywhere in the world instantly. Still, among the millions of Internet users, what was the likelihood that the right person might have seen it this fast?

I added the other ingredients, watched them spin, and then poured the batter into a rectangular baking dish, scattered the blueberries on top and sprinkled the pecan streusel over them. Just as I slid it into the oven, there was a knock at my door.

I looked at it in fear, as though the mysterious Frederic van den Teuvel had managed to find my home already.

I scolded myself for being ridiculous. I was still jumpy from the murder of Professor Maxwell's nephew earlier in the summer.

Still, I approached the door with caution, flicked on the outside light, and held my breath when I peered out.

"Miss Florrie? Is that you? Is everything okay? If someone is holding you captive, knock once."

I burst out laughing. I could only see the top of Mr. DuBois's head, but I certainly recognized his voice. I swung open the door to Professor Maxwell's butler.

The wizened little man lurched inside on crutches. He waved one around and whispered, "Shall I call the police?"

I closed the door behind him. "That's not necessary. The only other person here is Peaches."

He glanced at my sweet kitty and shuddered. "I fail to understand why anyone would adore a creature who cares about nothing but itself."

"Peaches is very sweet. You just have to give her a chance."

He swung toward me. Having broken his leg earlier in the summer, he was quite adept with his crutches. "I smell a cake baking. What are you doing up so early? You have completely destroyed the structure of my day."

Little did he know that I saw him as someone I could talk to about Dolly and van den Teuvel. "May I offer you a cup of tea?"

"English Breakfast?" He raised one eyebrow.

"Of course."

"Hmpff. There may be hope for you yet. One teaspoon of sugar and just a splash of milk. I hope you have decent milk."

"Two percent?"

Both eyebrows rose. "Not in some garish mug with a saccharine saying."

I opened a cabinet and withdrew a breakfast-sized teacup and saucer made of porcelain and painted with roses in pinks and reds. "Will this do?"

He sighed. "I find it highly annoying when people exceed my expectations."

Chapter 10

While Mr. DuBois made his way over to the sofa, I put the kettle on again and made him a cup of tea. I carried tea for both of us over to the coffee table on a tray.

He graciously accepted his cup and sipped his tea, nodding his approval. "So?" he demanded. "What nature of life crisis prohibits you from sleeping?"

"The untimely death of Dolly Cavanaugh."

He nodded. "Yes, I heard something about that. A heart attack, I believe?"

I told him about Dolly's stroke of luck in finding the book and the demands of Lucianne Dumont and Frederic van den Teuvel.

He looked around nervously. "You didn't bring that book here, did you? That sort of thing attracts barbaric crooks. They'll think nothing of killing you to obtain the book."

I tried to hide my smile. Professor Maxwell had warned me that Mr. DuBois watched too much true crime TV. "You needn't worry. It's not here. Actually," I said, "now that I think about it, I would have refused to keep it in my possession even if Dolly had asked me to take it. I wouldn't want to be responsible if something happened to it. As it is, no one knows where it is." I told him my belief that someone had taken it from her.

"You see? You see how something like that attracts lowlifes?" Mr. DuBois sniffed the air. "Your cake will be done soon."

The heavenly scent of baking blueberries wafted our way.

"You must be very careful, Miss Florrie. A criminal broke into the Medford's garage the other day. And now the bookstore? We could easily be next."

"Where did you hear that?"

"From their housekeeper."

"I don't think you have to worry. Why would someone break into a garage? Who keeps valuables there?"

"The house will be next. They start small but grow brave when they're not caught. You just wait and see. That person will be back looking for more things to steal and sell."

"Maybe the thief found exactly what he wanted and he won't be back."

Mr. DuBois ignored my teasing. "You are quite right to be troubled by this van den Teuvel fellow. In the first place, it means people think you have this valuable book in your possession. Whether it's true or not is irrelevant. Your name is out there and associated with the book. Secondly, how do you know this man isn't watching the mansion now? Miss Florrie! How do you get us tangled up in these things?"

"That's not fair. I was only doing my job. If the book is found, I think the best thing to do is hand it over to an auction company immediately. They can have it authenticated and they are in the business of handling rare and expensive items. They'll know how to store it until it's sold."

"An excellent idea. They'll go public with it right away and no one will come snooping around here for it."

I didn't hide my smile this time. "I honestly don't think you have to worry about that."

"Naïveté, Miss Florrie. The young always have it in abundance. You cannot imagine the lengths to which evil people will go to satisfy their own base needs."

"Excuse me. I think the cake is ready. Will you join me in a piece for breakfast?"

Happily, the fresh blueberry streusel cake cheered up Mr. DuBois. He even took a piece home to the mansion for the professor's breakfast.

After he left, I showered and slipped into another dress that gave me confidence. I didn't wear it often because it was cherry red and somewhat eye-catching, which wasn't my style. I was perfectly happy to blend into the background. I had bought it on a shopping expedition with my mom and Veronica, who had loved it. They had said it made me exude courage, something they both thought I was short on. Today, though, I had a bad feeling that I might need to look poised even if I wasn't.

After breakfast, Peaches waited by the door. I put her harness on her, and explained that she needed to walk like a dog, not a cat. I didn't think she cared what I was saying, she just wanted to go to the bookstore instead of staying home alone.

To my surprise, she did walk like a dog—almost. She stopped a few times to check out scents and sounds, but overall, she appeared to have learned the route and was eager to get to the store. She nearly raced up the stairs to the door.

I unlocked it, closed the door behind us, and took off Peaches's halter. She leaped up on the checkout desk and gazed around like she owned the place.

Meanwhile, I went through my morning ritual of turning off the alarm and switching on lights and music.

For the first half hour of my day, I was reassured by the simple routine of life. It didn't bring Dolly back, but it was oddly comforting to just go about business, putting out new books on a table for our customers to see when they walked through the door.

Unfortunately, at four minutes past eleven, a grumpy male customer arrived. He stomped through the store and proceeded to inform me that he could buy books cheaper elsewhere. As he left the store, he bumped into a woman nearly my age. She glared at him and brushed off her dress.

Bob was right behind her, carrying boxes of goodies for customers. They almost toppled out of his hands. The woman who entered before him turned and caught the top box. She set it on the counter for him.

"Honestly!" she said. "People in Washington used to be so polite."

Bob looked over at her. "Thanks for giving me a hand." To me he said, "What was his problem? He nearly bulldozed me."

I shrugged. "He didn't like our prices."

"Are you Florrie?" asked the woman.

Her eyes were red-rimmed. Her hair was a warm blond shade with a tinge of apricot that was most likely dyed. Although she had her mother's generous figure, it was her pretty mouth that gave her away.

"Maisie?" I guessed.

"How did you know?"

"You resemble your mom. I'm so sorry, Maisie. We loved Dolly."

"Really? I didn't think anyone liked her, much less loved her." I was stunned. "She was a lot of fun and so nice to everyone."

"That doesn't sound like my mother at all. I didn't think anyone would miss her."

"She spoke of you often."

"You're just saying that to be kind."

"Nope. She loved you, Maisie." I wasn't sure what happened between them, but she needed to know. Dolly would never be able to tell her.

Tears brimmed on her lower eyelids. "I didn't expect this to happen. I thought she would be around for a long time, annoying me and pestering me." She sniffled and tears ran down her cheeks. "I'm sorry. I never thought I would cry about losing my mother. She was such a pain. I suppose that sounds cruel, but we were estranged. You can't imagine the things she did to me."

"Did she set you up on a date with the most boring man on the planet?" I asked, thinking of Norman.

A whisper of a smile emerged. "She set me up with a guy old enough to be my grandfather."

"Oof! That must have been awful. What was she thinking?"

"She was determined to break off my engagement to the only man I ever loved." Maisie took a deep breath. "And she did it. She broke my heart, but that didn't matter to her."

"I'm sorry." There wasn't anything else I could say. Dolly had been wonderful to me, but maybe as a mother she had been domineering.

"I got in late last night and stayed at Mom's house. It was surreal being back there again. Especially without her. The newspaper ran an abbreviated obit this morning and that brought out the vultures."

I frowned at her. "What do you mean?"

"People who sell estates. People who auction things. Real estate agents. Everyone was looking to make a buck. Do you know"—she pawed through a Gucci purse—"a Nolan Hackett? He told me he was very close to Mom and she had been thinking about selling her house."

"They were in the bookstore coloring club together. He was planning to show her a property."

"How odd." She shook her head. "Mother was probably just flirting with him. She didn't have any money to buy a house. That was just like her. Well, what brings me here are my mother's books. I don't know beans about the value of books, but I do know my mother and it wouldn't surprise me in the least to find some books of value. I found a bag from your store at her house yesterday. I wondered if you have any-one on staff whom I could pay to go through her books."

"Did anyone mention *The Florist* to you?"

"Why do people keep talking about the florist? I haven't had a chance to think about the memorial service yet. Do you have a florist you want to recommend?"

I grinned in spite of myself. "I mean the book *The Florist.*" I told her about the book and her mother's amazing discovery.

"Ohhh! So that's what Ms. Dumont was talking about. She probably thought I was insane because I didn't have a clue. I thought she dropped by to express her condolences, which surprised me because I didn't think my mom ran in her circles. She kept saying *The Florist* belonged to her. Out of context, that's just crazy talk."

"I'm no lawyer, but I think Dolly bought it fair and square. Did you see it in her apartment last night?"

"To tell the truth, all I could see was that there's a lot of stuff in my mom's house. So many little pieces of bric-a-brac. Would you be willing to go through her books? Perhaps you know where the ones of little value could be donated?"

I had some ideas about that. Dolly would have liked to do-nate them to the library for their annual fund-raising sale. "I'm not an expert on valuable books. But maybe I could go through and pull the ones that could have some value. At least narrow them down for you."

"I'll pay you, of course. What do you charge?"

"Dolly was a dear customer, more of a friend really. I'm happy to do it for her."

"That's very kind of you. I know she would appreciate it. *I* certainly do. My head is just spinning. Her death was so unex-pected. I didn't know she had a heart condition. But that was Mom—always keeping secrets and finagling things."

We arranged for me to go to her mother's house the next

morning and Maisie left the store. I wandered to the glass front door and watched her.

Frederic van den Teuvel loped up to her. He stood a full head taller and said something that made her smile. They walked away together.

Had he waited outside for her? If she knew him, surely he would have mentioned *The Florist,* wouldn't he? But Maisie had acted as though she knew nothing about Dolly's lucky find. What had the professor called him? Some kind of deadly parasite.

Would Maisie resent me if I told her what the professor had said about van den Teuvel? Maybe I should just mind my own business. Or I could play it by ear when I went over to look at Dolly's books. If the opportunity came up, maybe I could warn her.

In the afternoon, a florist delivered a giant bouquet of flowers to the store. Rich golden sunflowers contrasted with dark violet gladioluses, fuchsia Gerbera daisies, and pink Stargazer lilies. He set it on the desk, and said, "Have a good one."

"Veronica!" I called.

She ambled in. "Oh my! They're so beautiful."

"Are you dating someone new?"

Veronica tensed, which made me very suspicious.

"Who would have sent me flowers?" She delicately plucked a card out of the elaborate arrangement. "They're for you!"

"What?" I took the tiny card from her. "Eric must have sent them."

The card bore my name and the words "with thanks" but no sender's name. I flipped the card around. "There's no name."

Veronica snatched it out of my hand and examined it. "Why wouldn't Eric have signed his name?"

That night, I settled on the sofa with my sketch pad fully intending to work on the coloring book I had been neglecting. Peaches played with her favorite mouse again. She would sneak up on it, lower her head, and wiggle her hind end before pouncing on it and batting it across the room again.

But my mind was on Maisie. Instead of working on a garden scene like I should have been, I drew Maisie's face, plump with pronounced cheeks. I was pleased that I managed to accomplish the resemblance to her mother.

I stared at her face, melancholy about Dolly's passing. I wished that she and Maisie could have made amends before her death. It would have meant so much to Dolly, and it would have been better for Maisie, too.

I certainly had spats with my mother, but I couldn't imagine being estranged. She meant well even when she did things that I considered outrageous.

Staring at my sketchbook, I thought about *The Florist* and how different my own adult coloring book would be. *The Florist* was accurate enough to be a precise guide to plants, while the images I was drawing were from a greater distance. They were garden images with mixtures of plants and benches. Some even included little hedgehogs and chipmunks. As I compared the two, it dawned on me that maybe the simple title *The Garden*, would be appropriate for my book.

It was still light outside. The garden in back of the carriage house was surrounded by a tall fence that was barely visible through the dense flora. In the middle, the koi pond had grown dark now that the sun no longer hit it directly.

I opened the French doors. Peaches shot outside and headed directly to the pond. She could spend hours perched on the edge watching fish glide by.

My attention turned to the beauty of the garden as we neared twilight. The greens of vines and trees darkened as the sun faded, but the daisies, white fronds of astilbe, and the white edges of hostas seemed to come alive at twilight, almost as though they were lighted from behind. I had bought solar fairy lights and strung them on the pergola over the outdoor dining table. They came on as darkness fell and while they offered no significant illumination, they gave the garden a sparkle that I loved.

Peaches perked up and looked back toward the house. She dashed inside and a second later, I heard a knock on the door.

I followed her into the house and heard Eric calling, "It's me, Florrie."

Ugh. Why was I wearing a crayon nightshirt? I was sorely tempted to race up the stairs and primp. Sadly, there was no time. I opened the door and smiled at him.

"Cute outfit! Did I come by at a bad time? Neither of us got much sleep last night."

"I was just sitting out in the garden. Would you like a drink?"

"If you're having one."

I quickly mixed lemonade with a little vodka. We carried the drinks out to the garden.

Eric looked over at my sketchbook. "I *am* interrupting. Sorry, I should have called first." He took a sip of his drink and leaned toward me. "I wanted to tell you this in person—"

Chapter 11

"Dolly was murdered," I said flatly. I had feared it all along, but the police explanation had been so much more palatable.

"I'm sorry, Florrie."

"How did she die?"

"The medical examiner was suspicious because she was in pretty good health and there was no sign of a heart condition." The muscles in his jaw tensed, as though he was saying something unpalatable. "She was poisoned by ethylene glycol."

"Antifreeze?" I didn't want to be melodramatic but antifreeze poisoning sounded like a terrible way to die. I swallowed hard imagining it. "Is that as awful as it sounds?"

Eric squeezed my hand. "They tell me it tastes sweet."

I noticed that he skipped how sick she must have felt before she died. Poor Dolly! I must have swayed a little bit because Eric reached for my hand.

"Are you okay?" he asked.

"It's just so horrible. Was there any liquid?" I asked. "When I found her, there wasn't a glass or anything on the carpet." I searched my memory. "But there were glasses outside with a bottle of champagne. Three champagne glasses. I thought maybe she intended to celebrate her good fortune with Veronica and me."

"I don't remember any liquids inside, but I can check the photos. No one removed anything from the scene—unless you did before we got there."

"No, of course not. Everything was exactly as we found it. Believe me, the last thing we were concerned about was cleaning up. Veronica and I thought she was still alive."

"That happens a lot. The body can twitch and make little sounds that lead people to think the person isn't dead yet."

"I wish we had gotten there sooner. I don't know what happened but maybe if we had arrived sooner . . ."

Eric winced. "You can't go there, Florrie. You didn't do anything wrong. You had no way of knowing that something was going awry at Dolly's house. Not to mention that you and Veronica might be dead right now, too, if you had timed it differently."

I shivered at the thought.

"Did anyone find the rare coloring book?" he asked.

"No. I'm going over to Dolly's house tomorrow morning to go through her books. I'm hoping I might find it there. Will they test that tiny bit of paper? I think they'll be able to tell approximately how old it is by examining the fiber content."

He nodded. "It won't be my case, of course, because I'm not in homicide, but I'll pass that along."

I sagged at the thought of dealing with homicide again. They were completely unreasonable when I encountered them before.

"Do you know anyone who would have wanted that book enough to kill Dolly for it?" he asked.

"No!" The word popped out of my mouth. I didn't want to think I knew anyone who would be so cruel. But only a moment later I had to reconsider. "Maybe. I'm surprised by the number of people who are interested in it. Dolly bought it at the Dumont yard sale. Lucianne Dumont came by the store and asked for Dolly's address. She claimed that it had been sold by mistake. And there's an antiques dealer named Frederic van den Teuvel who is dying to get his hands on it. Now maybe the police will believe that the intruders at the bookstore were searching for it."

Eric took a deep breath. "Are you certain Dolly had it? She didn't give it to someone for safekeeping or sell it?"

"When she left Color Me Read, she and Zsazsa went to a tea room to celebrate. I have no idea what she did between then and the time Veronica and I found her. Dolly seemed very protective of it, but that doesn't mean she didn't hand it over to someone she trusted. I'm almost positive that the scrap of paper in her hand was from the coloring book, though. If that's true, then someone must have taken it from her. On the other hand, it would have been easy for a cop to overlook those pages as just an old book."

"Are you saying that we cops are not sophisticated?" he teased.

I laughed. "It would be very easy to mistake as worthless."

Before Eric left, I remembered the flowers. "You must think I'm horrible. With all that's been going on I forgot to thank you for the flowers. They're beautiful!"

Eric stiffened. I'd never seen him look quite like that before.

"I didn't send you flowers. Of course"—he looked down at his shoes before meeting my gaze—"now I wish I had." Before my eyes, he turned into a sheepish schoolboy. "Who sent them?"

I couldn't tell if he was serious or teasing me. I went with teasing. "Very funny."

"I'm not joking. Maybe it was a customer? Did you go

above and beyond to get someone a special book that's hard to find?"

"Not recently." I grinned at him. "Are you pulling my leg?"

"No. I truly wish I had thought to send you flowers. Now I'm a little worried. Sounds like you have an admirer."

Eric left soon thereafter, still teasing me about the flowers. The sad thing was that I truly couldn't imagine who had sent them.

Later on, when I was snuggled up in bed with Peaches it dawned on me that they might be from Norman.

In the morning, I pulled on cropped jeans and a sleeveless cotton top. Pawing through Dolly's books would probably be a dusty undertaking.

Peaches snarfed her meal of chicken stew while I sipped my tea and ate a fried egg and avocado toast. When I was ready to leave, Peaches sat by the door, as though she wanted to go to the bookstore with me again.

I scooped her up. "Not today, sweetie. But maybe I'll take you to work tomorrow."

When I set her on the floor, she scampered over to the French doors and watched the birds in the garden, which made me feel better. I locked the door behind me, but before I made it down the driveway, Mr. DuBois swung open the back door of the mansion. "Florrie! Florrie!" A wisp of newspaper fluttered in his hand as he lurched toward me on crutches. He handed it to me. "I fear this has something to do with Maxwell's mysterious hours. I found it in his dustbin."

Search of Morrissey Site

A collection of newspaper clippings
about the 1970s disappearance of two

local children has turned up in a search of Ayres Morrissey's home in Maryland, prompting the father of one of the girls to request a more thorough search of the site. The papers were discovered pursuant to a search warrant issued after Morrissey's arrest on charges of surveillance with prurient intent.

The articles chronicle the investigation of the disappearance of Caroline Maxwell, heiress to the Maxwell fortune, and Bonnie Beaulaurier. The girls vanished from the birthday party of a friend in Washington, DC, and have never been found.

At the time of the party, Morrissey worked on a construction crew in the neighborhood. Beaulaurier's father has requested a search of the grounds of the Morrissey home by cadaver dogs as well as ground-penetrating radar. Authorities say an excavation is likely in the event that the dogs or the radar indicate the presence of human remains.

I heard my sharp intake of breath. "They might have located his daughter! The professor must be beside himself. I wouldn't know whether to be relieved that she may have been found or sad to know she was probably dead."

"Not so fast. Stories like Caroline's are perennial fodder for newspapers. I fear we are all mesmerized by unsolved mysteries. Maxwell saved the first few articles about possible leads, but there came a day when he threw them all out. I suspect he couldn't take it anymore. Each time hope springs anew, only to be dashed again in the end. Now he tosses them, and I retrieve them from the dustbin and add them to a bundle in my closet."

"It must be cruelest kind of misery for the professor and Jacquie. No wonder he's acting out of sorts."

I thanked Mr. DuBois and headed for Dolly's house, wondering if finding Caroline's bones would be a blessing or torment for her parents.

Tall trees provided some shade from the sun as I strolled along the sidewalks admiring the beautiful homes. It was so quiet that I could hear birds singing.

I walked up the steps to Dolly's house and knocked on the front door while opening it. Everything looked exactly the same. I half expected Dolly to answer the door to her apartment when I rapped on it.

Maisie swung the door open. "Hi. Thanks for coming."

I stepped inside. Dolly's organized clutter had devolved into a wild mess. "What happened?"

"You sound like the police. They were here late last night." She wiped her eyes. "Apparently Mom was murdered. I don't know why that should come as a surprise to me. Mom was obnoxiously pushy. There's no telling who she aggravated."

"I'm so sorry, Maisie."

"The police were pretty miffed when they saw what I had done here. What did they expect? That I would sit around doing nothing? If they were on the ball, they would have known sooner that she had been murdered. They asked me a million questions, like they think I killed her! I have an alibi, though. I was way down in South Carolina at the time. I'll admit, there were times when she did things that, well, that ruined my life."

Maisie shuddered. "I can still hear her saying, 'Honey, this

is for your own good.' But it never was. At this point, all I want
is to get rid of her junk, get out of here, and never come back.
But first, I have to go through everything. You knew my mom.
She was likely to hide something of value. I have a limited
amount of time off from work, so I have get it done."

"What do you do?" I asked.

"I'm a buyer for an upscale women's clothing chain based
in Charleston, South Carolina. You'd think they would give
you weeks to take care of everything when a parent passes
away. Instead, they call me every five minutes with questions.
Anyway, I thought I'd better have a look around before I turn
everything over to a stranger to sell."

Her cheeks flushed in embarrassment. "I didn't mean you,
of course!"

I believed her. The books hadn't been touched. "Have you
found *The Florist* yet?"

"Olivia and Priss were telling me more about it last night.
I'm sick that I don't know what Mom did with it." She
glanced around. "That's part of the reason I'm tearing her
house apart. It has to be here somewhere, doesn't it?"

I wondered how much she had been told about her mother's
death. Should I mention that it might have been stolen?

A knock on the door cut my thoughts short.

When she opened the door, a woman's voice sang, "Maisie!"

As far as I could tell, she was a childhood friend who had
learned of Dolly's demise. Leaving them to catch up, I set to
work, neatly separating contemporary books from those that
might have greater value.

It wasn't as though I was eavesdropping. After all, I happened to be in the room where they were speaking.

"Mother was always such a pack rat," said Maisie. "I never
gave any thought to the fact that getting rid of all her junk
would fall to me. You can't even imagine what a pain this is. I
don't want anything of hers."

"I know how you feel," said her friend. "I'm not into clutter. But my sister collects Hummel figurines. Looks like your mom had quite a few."

"Help yourself!"

"I wouldn't be so quick to give them away, Maisie," said the friend. "They're very collectible. Have you hired someone to clean out the house?"

"Not yet."

"I'll send Percy McAllister by."

I turned to look at them, wondering if I should say something. Dolly would come back to haunt the house if she knew that Percy was selling her things.

"You remember him, don't you?" asked the friend. "Percy went to high school with us."

When Maisie didn't respond, the friend said, "How could you forget him? Percy is the one who set off firecrackers in the school library."

I shuddered at the thought. That probably resulted in a terrible fire.

Nevertheless, the two of them laughed at the memory.

"I do remember him. I had no idea that Percy still lived around here," said Maisie. "I haven't had any breakfast. How about we grab a bite and catch up?"

"Absolutely!" In a low tone that I could hear perfectly well, her friend asked, "Can you trust her here alone?"

My back was to them, and I was kneeling on the floor. I smiled.

"Oh sure. There's nothing here of any *real* value anyway."

Nothing but *The Florist,* I thought.

Maisie walked over to me. "I picked up some boxes yesterday. Maybe you could put the books in them so they can be removed? There are more books in the studio on the third floor." She handed me a key. "I'll be back in a couple of hours."

The two of them gabbed nonstop as they walked out the

door. I was glad that Maisie had made contact with an old friend, but I felt worse than ever for Dolly.

The second the door closed, I got to my feet and examined the rug where Dolly had lain. I sighed. In my mind's eye, I could see her there. The rug bore a faint buff color where it should have been white, but the stain could have been there for years. I touched it. It wasn't damp. That was probably just as well for Maisie. Would she have felt differently if she had seen her mom outstretched on the rug? Would she have been more sentimental about her mother's passing?

Maisie seemed to swing back and forth. I had seen her tears, but she had tried to sound nonchalant in front of her friend. Maybe her mother's death was harder on her than she had expected.

I walked over to the door and snapped the deadbolt so no one would walk in and surprise me. I returned to the spot where Dolly had fallen, dropped to my knees, and peered under the sofa and chairs.

My hopes shattered. There was nothing under the furniture. Not even dust. I crawled around the room anyway, checking under everything. No luck. If the police had found *The Florist,* surely they would have mentioned it to Maisie.

A movement in the corner of my eye caught my attention. I turned to find a little gray mouse staring at me, as appalled to see me as I was to see him. We watched each other warily for a few seconds, neither of us moving. The mouse gave in first and scurried off into another room.

Dusting off my jeans, I stood up and gazed around. Where would I have hidden a priceless book?

Unfortunately, sometimes the best hiding place was right out in the open among other similar objects. No one would have noticed the plain leather which surrounded the pages if it stood between other books. I returned to work.

An hour later, I had found a very early copy of *Winnie-the-Pooh* but didn't know the original copyright date off the top of my head. I set it aside with a few other older books. The boxes were filling rapidly with mysteries, romances, and popular fiction. Dolly had loved to read.

After two hours, I paused and stepped out in the backyard for some fresh air. It had turned into a hot, humid summer day. The champagne glasses still stood next to the lantern where they had been the night Dolly died. The bottle of champagne had disappeared, though.

Dolly had collected cute yard art that was no doubt an embarrassment to Maisie, but the gnomes, goat, dachshund, and mule made of wire and tin made me laugh and reminded me of Dolly and her sense of humor.

I returned to the house, took the key Maisie had handed me, and left Dolly's apartment. I climbed one flight of stairs. Olivia and Priss had decorated their front door with a wreath covered with artificial flowers that were azure as the summer sky and the rich yellow of butter. A little bench next to their door sported a needlepointed pillow in matching colors.

I continued up the stairs to the top floor. It wasn't spooky, but lacked the warmth of Olivia and Priss's door. I slid the key into the lock. When I turned it, a bolt groaned as though it didn't get much use.

The hinges squealed when I swung the door open. The attic was dark as an underground basement.

Chapter 12

I felt the wall for a light switch before entering. Hadn't I seen a window from the outside?

I touched a wall switch and flicked it. An overhead light flickered as if the bulb might burn out soon. It was a Tiffany-style fixture that didn't offer much light. I wondered if Dolly had scored it at a yard sale.

The ceiling had a steep pitch, which I had suspected from the roofline. The wall in the rear of the room was brick. To the front, the walls cut into the ceiling as though they led to a dormer window. But black plastic had been taped over the spot where a window should be. A corner was coming loose. I probably should have left it alone, but I pulled on it gently. The plastic gave way, and I could see a lacy curtain that had probably been white once. It was now buff, almost the color of parchment. It felt stiff in my hands. I suspected it had been there for a long time, and had been discolored by the sun. I stuck the tape back up as well as I could. Dolly had probably wanted to keep the cold out in the winter.

I turned around. The unit had clearly been a studio apartment at one time. A refrigerator, tiny stove, and cabinets lined one wall. A leather sofa in a warm ombre cognac thick with dust stood in the middle of the room. At the rear, the aged brick wall gave it a bohemian feel. An old library ladder was attached to a rod on bookshelves that ran across part of the brick wall.

It was actually a very cool studio apartment. I wondered why it wasn't rented. Maybe it was too cold in the winter? I glanced around for radiators and spied an ancient one.

I ventured toward the ladder and tested it to be sure it would hold my weight. If the dust was any indication, no one had been up here in quite a while.

I climbed the ladder and began at the top. Dust filled the air when I blew at it. One thing was for sure, I wouldn't find *The Florist* up here. Dolly would have disturbed the dust had she hidden it in this room.

Shelf by shelf, I unloaded books and set them in piles on the floor, differentiating between those of possible interest and plain old paperbacks that had been issued en masse.

As I emptied the third shelf, which was about three feet off the ground, I accidentally hit the back panel with my hand. It wobbled as though it wasn't very strong. I made a mental note to be careful. I certainly didn't want to damage anything.

I worked my way down the wall, clinging to the ladder and bringing down armfuls of books. Maybe Maisie could pay some neighborhood kid to pack them into boxes. The floor looked a mess with my finely curated stacks. While many of the books were old, few appeared to be of value.

I was getting tired and thinking about continuing after work the next day, but I climbed the ladder one more time and loaded my arms with books. As I leaned back a bit to make my way down the ladder, I swayed and in a desperate attempt to avoid falling, I rocked forward. Heavy books spilled out of my arms and crashed through the thin wall of wood backing the bookcase.

I grabbed the ladder with both hands to stabilize myself. What had I done? In horror, I peered at the damage. I would have to pay to have it repaired. Who would put such a flimsy backing on a bookcase in the first place?

There was a space between the brick wall and the back panel of the bookcases. I had read about secret hiding places along those lines. To the uninitiated, the bookcase appeared to be flush but there was usually a panel that slid open for access to a secret compartment.

I carefully dismounted the ladder, stood back, and examined the wall. Could Dolly have hidden *The Florist* up here without disturbing the dust? She surely hadn't anticipated her sudden death, but might have thought it would be safe from anyone who would want to steal it.

I examined the floor. It didn't show the same kind of dust that was on the shelves so there weren't any tracks of shoeprints.

I studied the wall again. I hadn't emptied all the shelves yet, but if there was a special door or moving panel, it should be accessible with most of the shelves loaded. Otherwise it would be a huge hassle to open it.

Stepping closer, I pressed the panel where I had emptied the shelves. The key to opening a secret compartment could be hidden by books on one of the other shelves. If a person knew which one, it would be a small task to move them.

For the next hour, I continued taking down books. When the entire shelving system was empty, I didn't see anything that looked like a latch. For that matter, there wasn't anything at all on the back panel.

I tried pushing against it in the hope that something might slide. It did. The panel I had damaged moved, and I was able to slide it across behind the other panel and see all the way to the brick wall where a skeleton looked at me, not six inches from my face.

Chapter 13

I screamed and fell backward onto the floor. Shudders rippled through me, and I screamed again.

I scrambled to my feet, ran out of the room, and slammed the door behind me. My breath came heavy and hard. My heart pounded. I wasn't usually such a sissy, but this time my knees gave. I sat on the top step, trying to pull myself together.

I glanced back at the door. I knew perfectly well that it couldn't open by itself, but I still kept a wary eye on it.

Maybe the skeleton was a fake. Maybe the person who built the bookcase thought it would be a funny gag? Or a deserved shock to someone who snooped and managed to open the panel? I had read about people hiding things when they built houses. But they usually hid letters or photographs, not skeletons.

I pulled my cell phone out of my pocket. I needed reinforcements. Eric would be the perfect choice. Or Veronica.

But they would make fun of me for being afraid of the skeleton. And what if it *was* a stupid Halloween gag that someone hid there as a joke? I would never hear the end of it.

There was only one thing to do. Go back inside and look

at the thing. After all, even if it had been a person once, it couldn't hurt anyone now.

I sucked up all the courage I had and opened the door again. I propped it open with a couple of heavy books, which I knew was silly, but it gave me some degree of comfort that I could leave in haste.

Walking slowly, I approached the skeleton. The skull leaned to the left where it was propped against a brick column. Bits of old yarn clung to the ribs. A moldy, greenish-colored fabric was fastened at the waist. The bones in its feet bore the ancient plastic of decayed sneakers. I was no expert, but I didn't think the skeleton was a fake.

But now that I had looked at him a second time, I wasn't as frightened. I was still shocked, but he wasn't as scary as when I first saw him. Poor guy. At least I assumed it was a guy. I guessed it would take a doctor to make that determination. Women wore sweaters and sneakers, too.

"Is that a skeleton?"

I screamed again and heard two more screams behind me. Obviously, my nerves weren't quite as stable as I thought. I whipped around to find Nolan, Olivia, and Priss standing behind me. "I'm afraid so. I lost my balance and books slid into the back panel and, well, this is what I found."

Olivia and Priss gazed at the skeleton with the same kind of horror that I had felt.

Priss crossed her hands over her mouth. "I think I'm going to be sick." She raced from the room. We could hear her rushing down the stairs.

"Aww, rats!" said Nolan.

"What?! I saw a mouse, but I haven't seen any rats."

Olivia gasped. "Whatever you do, don't mention the mouse to Priss. She's scared out of her wits by them. We don't have rats in this building." She crept closer for a better view of the skeleton.

"No, no. I mean it will be a problem to sell the house now. There will be a huge delay while they figure out what happened here, and then no one will want to buy it. You know, ghosts and all." He glanced at Olivia. "You haven't experienced anything ghostly, have you?"

"Don't be ridiculous," she growled as if she was offended by the question.

Nolan fell silent for a moment. "I don't suppose you would be amenable to putting everything back up and pretending you never saw it?"

"I would not! And I'm sorry to say that this is something I will never be able to un-see. Covering him up again would be almost as bad as hiding him there to begin with." On that note, before Nolan could make more stupid and probably illegal suggestions, I pulled out my phone and dialed Eric's private number.

He answered immediately.

"I have a little problem. Could you drop by for a minute? You'll know what to do."

"Sure. Are you at the bookstore?"

I gave him Dolly's address. "The front door is open. I'm on the top floor."

"Isn't this the address of Dolly Cavanaugh's house?" he asked.

"Exactly the same."

"Please tell me that no one else died."

How to answer that? "Sort of. But it's way too late for an ambulance. You'd better come see for yourself."

I hung up and considered going downstairs to wait for him, but decided it might be better to keep an eye on Nolan. I certainly didn't want him tossing the skeleton out a window and pretending it had never been inside the house.

Nolan couldn't take his eyes off the skeleton. But he spoke in a totally matter-of-fact tone, as though he saw walled-up skeletons on a regular basis. "I never would have thought Dolly had it in her. Do you think it's one of her late husbands?"

The thought hadn't even crossed my mind. "I hope not. It would have to be the fourth one, because she didn't own this house when she was married to the others. But really, Nolan, I hardly think she would talk so lightly about him if he were upstairs in her attic! Besides, we don't know how old it is. It might have been here when she bought the house." I made a mental note, though, to warn Maisie. If it was her father, it would be devastating.

"Florrie?" My name echoed up the stairwell.

I dashed out to the top of the stairs. "Up here, Eric."

The top of his head emerged as he walked up. "Cool house."

He was wearing his Metropolitan Washington, DC, Police uniform. His vibrant blue eyes made the police blue of his crisp short-sleeved shirt seem positively dull.

I showed him into the attic room.

For a long moment, he said nothing. "Well, this is a new one on me. Hi, Nolan, Ms. Beauton."

Nolan nodded at him. "Sergeant."

Olivia simply said hi.

I launched into an explanation of my klutziness.

"Maybe it was fortunate that you lost your balance." Eric walked up close to the skeleton and peered at it. "I'd have to guess that it has been here for a long time. They say you can't take it with you," he quipped. "Looks like that applies to secrets, as well. Too bad Dolly isn't around anymore to explain this." He looked over at Olivia. "Do you know anything about the skeleton?"

Olivia's eyes widened. "No!" She sounded indignant.

Eric scanned the room while he called in his location and explained the situation.

Nolan grinned at him. "No police code for skeleton?"

"This isn't something we run into on a regular basis."

Nolan shook his head. "Dolly, Dolly, Dolly, how little we knew ya."

At that moment, Maisie walked in and shrieked. "Is that what it looks like?"

Eric shifted into his formal police mode, identified himself and asked who she was. His demeanor was appropriate but businesslike.

Her hands tented over her nose and mouth, she asked, "Who is that?"

"I was hoping you could tell us," said Eric.

"How on earth would I know? Oh no!" Maisie wailed. "What did Mom do?"

"Mom?" Eric sounded so calm and personable that Maisie didn't clam up.

"Of course! This is her house." Maisie staggered backward. "It's like she's reaching out from the afterlife and cursing me even though she's dead. Will it never end? What's next? What other horror will I find?"

Maisie ran from the room.

"I'll make her a cup of tea," I said.

Eric nodded. "It's probably better if she's not up here when the crime scene investigators arrive."

"She wasn't happy with the cops who questioned her earlier." I scurried out, but it was too late. Police and plainclothes personnel were hiking up the stairs.

I could hear Maisie trying to get by them in the foyer. In a hysterical tone she cried, "Excuse me. Please! Let me pass!"

I stood aside while they trekked by me and into the attic room.

Nolan joined me. "The sergeant threw me out. You seem to know him quite well."

I smiled. I still felt awkward when people asked me about Eric. Why couldn't I get used to saying I had a boyfriend? I choked a little bit when I said, "We're dating."

"Your parents must be happy."

I shot him a quizzical look. "I suppose they are."

"Don't be so sensitive. I just meant that he's a nice guy. Most parents would be very happy if their daughter dated him."

"Sorry."

"Did you notice how Maisie immediately assumed her mother had something to do with the skeleton?" he asked.

"Maisie and Dolly had issues. I'm not sure it means anything."

He nodded as we started down the stairs. "The parent-child relationship is a difficult one."

"Do you have kids?"

"Four children and three ex-wives. They all think I'm a twenty-four-hour ATM."

"You don't mean that."

"But I do. Don't get me wrong, I make a decent living. And I love my kids. My ex-wives, not so much. But they all think money magically multiplies in my wallet. They only call or come by when they need to pluck some more green off me." He sounded bitter.

I felt for him. "Would that have anything to do with your membership in the coloring club?"

He snorted. "I work all the time. It's what I like to do. That's why I was here today. I want to land the listing on this house before anyone else does. But my doctor has been telling me I need to cut back. Frankly, I don't think my work is as stressful as my kids and lousy ex-wives."

"You came to talk to Maisie about selling the house?"

"And to see what kind of shape it was in. It's not a bad rental property, though I suspect that Dolly wasn't charging what these units are worth. And you know what they say about real estate—location, location, location. This house has got that in spades. Of course, the skeleton is going to throw us off now.

It'll draw attention to the house, but a lot of people will shy away because of that crazy skeleton."

From the door to Dolly's apartment, we could hear Maisie inside crying.

"Why don't you go in first? I'm terrible with sobbing women."

Nice guy, I thought sarcastically. I didn't mind, though. I knocked on the door as a courtesy and walked inside.

Maisie was seated on the zebra settee. She sniffled and looked at me. "What now?"

"I thought I'd make you a cup of tea."

Her cell phone rang. She glanced at it and winced. "I don't drink tea. Besides, you have done quite enough. If you don't mind, I would like to be alone." She held the phone up to her ear and said, "Just a moment, please." To me she asked with annoyance, "Is there anything else?"

My first instinct was to defend myself. It wasn't as though *I* had hidden the skeleton in Dolly's house. But I thought better of it. Her mother had just died. She had a ton of things on her mind and now she was surrounded by boxes of books and there was a skeleton upstairs. I would probably be testy, too.

As kindly as I could, I said, "The books in the boxes by the fireplace are the ones that could have some value in my opinion. And just so you know, I did not find *The Florist.*"

"Huh? Oh, I don't care about some stupid book my mother found in a bin at a yard sale. Close the door on your way out."

I had been dismissed. I would have felt slighted, but Dolly had said Maisie didn't appreciate her yard sale hobby. Nothing Maisie was doing should come as a surprise to me.

As I walked toward the door, I heard Maisie say, "My mother just died, and I am totally bereft. How dare you demand payment when I'm dealing with such a crushing event?"

I glanced back at her. People reacted to loss differently, but she didn't seem heartbroken to me.

Chapter 14

I did as Maisie requested and closed the door behind me.

Nolan raised an eyebrow. "I have a kid like that. Everything is always wrong, everyone is always against her, and her parents are nothing but an embarrassment."

"Teens are difficult," I said.

"My daughter is thirty-three! I thought she might outgrow it, but she likes to blame everyone except herself. Given what Dolly said, I'm thinking maybe Maisie is like that."

We stood in the vestibule. I eyed Nolan. "You seem to know a lot of people around here. Have you ever met Frederic van den Teuvel?"

"Doesn't sound familiar. Is he selling a house?"

"Not that I know of."

Nolan jingled coins in his pocket and gazed around as if he was taking inventory of the woodwork. "How come it's always the rotten kids who inherit these grand houses and sell them? This place is something special. But someone will buy it and rip out the incredible original woodwork. Pity."

"I hope that won't happen."

He sighed. "I'm going to hang out here a few minutes,

then knock on the door and see if she'll talk to me about listing the place."

I nodded. "Good luck. I'm headed upstairs to let Eric know I'm leaving. Assuming they'll let me in there. See you later." I started up the stairs.

At the top, no one paid any attention to me. It was fascinating to see them photographing the skeleton. It was wedged in between brick columns pretty well. I assumed it would collapse and fall apart as soon as they tried to move it.

Eric spied me and walked over.

"I snuck in," I whispered. "No one chased me away."

"They're focused on their jobs. This is highly unusual. I'm hoping we can get a handle on how long it has been here. What do you know about the other residents?"

"You met them last night. They're all members of the coloring club, but I don't know them very well. Olivia and her sister Priss tutor online for a living. They've lived here a long time. Edgar Delaney is a grad student. I think he's new to town."

Eric slung his arm around my shoulders and squeezed. "Just think, if you hadn't stumbled into this, it could have been hidden here for decades."

"I suspect it would have been discovered when someone renovated the house. Maisie doesn't want anything of her mother's. The house will be sold, though Nolan says the skeleton will discourage some potential buyers. Not that I blame them. I don't know how I would feel about living in a house where someone had been hidden in a wall." I wrinkled my nose.

"Florrie Fox! Are you afraid of ghosts?"

Even though he was teasing me, I thought about it for a minute. "The rational part of me acknowledges that a skeleton can't hurt anyone. But knowing that something bad probably happened to him in this house is kind of creepy."

Eric nodded. "But a lot of bad things have happened everywhere we go. We just don't know about them as we're living our lives and going about our business. I think I could get past that."

"How do you know Nolan?" I asked.

"He's sort of a fixture in this neighborhood and knows a lot about it. When a house goes up for sale, Nolan is likely to be involved. He usually lets me know when a house is empty so we can help him keep an eye on it." His eyes narrowed. "So you've been going through books all day?"

I nodded and dusted off my clothes. I gazed around at all the people working. They were so intent on their jobs.

Eric glanced at the piles of books on the floor. "Were these books like this?"

"No. They were on the bookshelves. I went through all of them and took them down. There was nothing on the floor when I came in. But I did notice the plastic over the window. From the outside, you can't tell that it's sealed off. When I first saw it, I thought maybe Dolly was trying to keep out the cold, but now I wonder."

"Looks like Dolly had a very big secret." He glanced at me sideways. "Makes a person wonder what else she might have done."

"We don't know that Dolly killed this person," I said without much confidence.

"If we can figure out who it was, maybe we'll have a better grasp of what happened. It appears that the skeleton had a broken neck. It's in better condition than most of the bones I've seen."

A woman passing by us looked at Eric. "It depends on the microclimate of the place where the skeleton is found. This one wasn't subject to water or sunshine, but it would have gone through cycles of heat and freezing as the temperature changed."

It was almost overwhelming. Dolly's death, and now an

unidentified person who died heaven knew when? I asked Eric to keep me posted and walked down the stairs slowly.

I hadn't even made it to the second-floor landing when I heard a muffled crash and a scream. I was ready to dash to someone's aid, but I wasn't sure where the sound came from. I knocked on Olivia and Priss's door.

Olivia opened it.

"Are you okay?"

"Sure. Seeing that skeleton was certainly a shock. But we'll be fine. I can't believe that Dolly would have done something like that."

"You didn't hear a crash?"

"When?"

"Just now."

"No. Not a thing."

"Okay. Sorry to disturb you."

I walked down to the first-floor landing. A door in the foyer was open, and I could hear moaning.

The front door opened. Priss stopped short and eyed the floor, scanning it from one side to another. She looked up at me, and her face flushed. "Mice." She shivered and her shoulders twitched. "I saw one here the other day. Are you all right? I thought I heard a crash."

"So did I." I flicked the switch for a light, but it didn't come on. "Is someone down there?"

"Florrie?" It was Nolan's voice.

In a loud voice that I hoped he could hear, I said, "We're coming."

I grasped the railing, and walked down carefully, step by step. "Nolan? Are you okay?"

"Be careful, Florrie. One of those steps is slippery."

I made it to the bottom where a light illuminated Nolan on the carpeted floor.

Priss was right behind me. "Oh, Nolan! You poor thing!"

"I think I twisted my ankle."

I pulled up his trouser leg a little bit to get a look. It was already beginning to swell. "You'd better have it x-rayed."

"Nonsense. Help me up. Forty years of selling houses and this is the first time I have ever fallen."

He was tall, but Priss and I managed to get him on his feet.

"Man, but that's painful. He leaned against the wall and pulled a cell phone out of his pocket. "Whew. Looks like it still works." Nolan dialed a number. "Of course, my daughter's phone would roll over to voicemail."

"I can take you to the emergency room," offered Priss. "We just have to figure out how to get you up the stairs to the car. I'll get my car keys."

"While you're upstairs, why don't you ask Sergeant Jonquille to give us a hand?"

"It's lucky that he's still here!" Priss walked up the dark stairway carefully.

"They need to replace that light bulb," grumbled Nolan.

"I guess Dolly was the one who kept up with things like that."

"One of those stairs is slippery as all get out, too. Didn't you notice it?"

I hadn't. "I walked down very carefully."

"Aww. This is just what I needed."

The sound of someone flicking the light switch on and off caused the two of us to look up the stairs.

"Be careful!" yelled Nolan. "There's a slippery step."

Eric loped down to us. "What happened?"

After a short discussion, Eric called an ambulance. When Priss returned, she promised to meet Nolan at the hospital.

The EMTs made quick work of putting Nolan in the ambulance.

As soon as he was out of the building, I returned to the

stairs. I walked up them slowly in case Nolan was right about one of them being slippery. But none of them were.

Eric returned. "You should have been a cop. Did you find the slippery step?"

"Nope. I was talking with him not fifteen minutes before he fell, so I don't think he had been drinking."

Eric walked up and down the stairs, examining them. "I don't see anything. Sometimes people just slip. I'll have a word with Maisie about switching out the light bulb."

When I was leaving the building, I found that a small group of people had gathered outside. Two large TV vans had parked on the street.

A reporter holding a microphone rushed at me. "Are you a tenant?"

"No."

"Can you confirm that a skeleton was found in a wall?"

They already knew about it? I could have confirmed the existence of the skeleton, of course, but it felt wrong to do that. Eric or another police officer should tell them. I took the easy way out by saying simply, "No."

"Can you tell us if this was related to the murder of Dolly Cavanaugh?"

That stopped me in my tracks. How could they already know that she had been murdered? I had only learned the night before.

"Who left in the ambulance?" asked another reporter.

"I don't have any information. The police will be able to tell you more."

"Then what are you doing here?"

"A favor. I just came over to do someone a favor." I hurried away. Some favor. Exposing a secret wasn't exactly what I would call a favor. And now that Dolly was dead, she couldn't even defend herself. Everyone would assume she had murdered the person in the attic. Dolly would be blamed and the case would be closed. It wasn't as though the real killer would step forward. He would get away with murder.

I crossed the street and looked back at the big brownstone. I didn't think I had been taken in by an act on Dolly's part. She had been genuinely nice. I strolled over to the store to talk with Veronica.

Color Me Read bustled with patrons. It was an odd contrast to the glum atmosphere at Dolly's house.

Veronica and Helen were in the middle of a child's birthday party. The children laughed and giggled as Veronica read *Bats at the Beach* to them. Helium balloons floated in the air and a special bat birthday cake sat on a table in the corner, just waiting to be cut.

I trudged up the stairs in search of the professor, but I found Zsazsa in the second-floor reading room. She held a book about estate planning.

"Zsazsa?" I said in horror. "Are you okay?"

She closed the book. "I miss Dolly so much. We often went to estate sales together early in the morning, then grabbed some breakfast. She was frequently my companion for afternoon tea. Something precious is missing from my life now."

"You two were quite different."

"Our backgrounds and our education weren't in the least bit similar. Yet we were kindred spirits. We understood each other. Everyone needs a friend like that. I shall miss her every day as I would a sister."

She sighed and sucked in a deep breath. "But her death was good in one way. I need to put my matters in order. I won't have my nieces hiring a dolt like Percy. That's for certain."

Now that she'd told me Dolly was like a sister to her, I didn't know how to break the news about the skeleton. "There's a skeleton in Dolly's attic," I blurted.

Zsazsa gazed at me blankly for a moment. "Is that some kind of joke? I don't understand the humor."

I collapsed into the chair beside her. "It's not a joke. I found it this morning behind a built-in bookcase in her attic."

"This cannot be. I knew Dolly very well. She would never have done such a thing. It must have been there for a very long time, and she had no knowledge of it."

"I guess we'll find out. With all the amazing modern techniques, they can probably tell quite a bit about the skeleton."

"There you are." Professor Goldblum joined us. He plopped into a chair. "I've been looking all over for you two." He peered at us with inquisitive eyes. "Unless this is a private discussion?"

Zsazsa waved her hand. "Nonsense, you are most welcome. We were talking about Dolly."

Goldblum, a chubby little man who had retired from the university, sat back in his chair. "Her death was such a loss. Dolly was a pistol."

I was slightly amused to hear him describe her that way. "Did you . . . go out with her?"

He chuckled. "Gracious, no! I'm not the sort of man who interests women. And Dolly had her share of admirers. I'd have been at the end of the line."

"Oh?" I asked as casually as I could.

"For starters, I'm pretty sure that Nolan was attracted to her."

"Nolan?" Zsazsa pinched her nose. "I cannot fathom why women chase him. Like the"—she lowered her voice—"Beauton sisters. They practically salivate when they see him. If you ask me, he looks like a weathered sailor and has all the appeal of a shark."

Goldblum snickered. "All I can say is that women never look at me that way."

"Really," continued Zsazsa, "have you ever heard Nolan talk about anything except real estate? It's like watching a TV with only one channel. I find him painfully dull."

I didn't know how to break the news to them. Was there any good or kind way to tell someone about murder? Zsazsa and Goldblum were very smart. Maybe they would come up with ideas that could help the police. I closed the door to the room.

Zsazsa sat up in alarm. "What is it? What has happened?"

I told Goldblum about the skeleton.

"Fascinating!" Goldblum sat up. "I can't quite picture how one would do that. Do you have photos?"

"No!" I exclaimed. "What kind of pervert would take pictures of it?"

"I thought young people took pictures of everything these days."

That was probably true. I shuddered at the thought of a selfie with the skeleton. "Honestly, it didn't even occur to me, but the police are taking plenty."

"But *they* won't show them to me!" Goldblum smirked at me. "Didn't I say Dolly was a pistol? My, my! I never would have expected it of her. She was wilder than I thought."

"There's more. I'm so sorry." I reached for Zsazsa's hand and clutched it. "I'm afraid Dolly was murdered."

Zsazsa bounced on her chair like she had a spring inside her. "I knew it! I have said all along that she did not have a heart attack."

"She drank antifreeze."

The two of them fell into silent horror.

Zsazsa made the sign of a cross over her face and shoulders.

Goldblum rubbed his eyes with his thumb and middle finger. He sniffled a little when he said, "Could it have been related to the skeleton in her attic? Someone took revenge?"

"So if they figure out who the skeleton is, then they will know who murdered our Dolly?" Zsazsa looked down and shook her head. "I'm sorry, but I cannot believe that sweet

Dolly would have killed someone and hidden that person in her attic for eternity."

"Now, Zsazsa. Do not despair. There are several possibilities," Goldblum reasoned. "A previous owner could have hidden the body there. Or perhaps it was done by her husband who lived there for several years before he passed. A tenant might even have done it."

Zsazsa's eyes opened wide. "The Beauton sisters," she whispered.

"There is one other thing you should know," I said. "*The Florist* appears to be gone. When I found her, she held a small scrap of paper between her fingers. I think it's from the book."

"That changes everything," said Professor Goldblum. "Obviously the thief murdered her to steal the book."

"Not so fast." Zsazsa held up a finger. "How would a thief manage to get her to drink something with antifreeze in it?"

Chapter 15

"At gunpoint?" I suggested. "Or the thief poured it into something delicious. Something he knew Dolly would never be able to refuse."

"Like chocolates." Goldblum frowned. "I don't think you could put enough antifreeze to kill someone in a chocolate. Must have been a drink. But why kill her? Why not just take the book and flee?"

"Clearly, so she could not report the identity of the thief to the police. She was very protective of that book." Zsazsa shook her head. "After the coloring club meeting, Dolly and I went out for tea and pastries. A late afternoon tea. She kept the book by her side every moment. I should have insisted she place it in a bank for safekeeping. Of course, it was a Saturday night and no banks were open. It is too late for such thoughts now. But we can still help our beloved Dolly. We must find the person who did this terrible thing to her."

I understood exactly how Zsazsa felt. But there wasn't anything we could do. "The police are already on it, Zsazsa."

She winked at me. "Your Sergeant Jonquille is so handsome. Nevertheless, it is the least we can do for Dolly. I shall not stand by and watch as her death is boxed up and put away like some inconvenience."

That wouldn't happen, would it? I wanted to think that Eric wouldn't allow it to happen, but the truth was that he didn't have that kind of power. Professor Maxwell had once said to me *even those of us who are timid face times in our lives when we must brace our shoulders and stand our ground*. I didn't have to be Wonder Woman. Maybe if we put our heads together we could figure out who killed her.

A knock at the door took us by surprise, though it shouldn't have.

Veronica peeked inside. She flapped her hand. "Oh, it's just you guys." She looked over her shoulder as she swung the door open. "Come in, please. Florrie, this gentleman is in search of *Leonardo's Notebooks*. It's in here, right?"

Goldblum rose and beckoned to the man. They launched into a discussion about great thinkers.

Veronica whispered to me, "Lucky break finding Goldblum in here. I had to look it up. I thought it would be with art books."

Speaking quietly, Zsazsa and I filled her in on the news about Dolly.

"A skeleton?" Veronica whispered. "Who do you think she killed?"

And that was exactly what worried me. Everyone would believe Dolly had murdered someone.

I had planned to go to Dumbarton Oaks to sketch for my garden coloring book in the afternoon, but my heart wasn't in it. I forced myself to take my sketchbook and head in that direction, but it wasn't long before I found myself across the street from Dolly's house, watching the commotion.

A woman's voice said, "It's such a shame what happened to Dolly."

I looked around. A gaunt woman in sunglasses and a stylish sun hat stood up from her garden work and waved a trowel at me. "It could have been any one of us. Were you a friend of Dolly's?"

I debated how to answer that. To say that I ran Color Me Read didn't begin to describe our relationship. It seemed simpler to say, "Yes."

"Poor Dolly, she was so young when she was widowed. My husband passed last year. You know, I had always assumed she was doing fine without her husband. It wasn't until mine died that I understood her struggles. I don't know what I would have done in her shoes. I have to admit that I wasn't happy when she took in tenants, but now I wonder if I wouldn't have done the same thing. Of course, there are no skeletons in *my* walls."

I was tempted to ask how she could be so sure, but decided that might be rude and it could make her clam up. "Did you see or hear anything unusual the evening she died?"

She lowered her sunglasses for a better look at me, revealing aged eyes with harsh crow's feet. "Are you with the police?"

I introduced myself. "I found her."

"You poor dear! That must have been just awful for you. I didn't hear a thing. Of course, I don't know exactly what time she died. Let's see, that day I was up early to work in my garden in back of the house. I like to get an early start before it gets too hot." She adjusted the long white sleeves of her shirt. "I was probably indoors with the air-conditioning running when she died. But I didn't hear any screaming or arguing or anything like that." She pointed to my sketchbook. "Are you planning to sketch her house?"

I told her about the coloring book I was drawing and showed her some of my sketches.

She immediately invited me into her backyard. I followed her along the side of her house and entered a fantasy garden. Grass grew between large white paving stones that were set in a huge rectangle. Two chaise lounges rested on it with an umbrella offering shade just behind them. I could imagine tall, frosty drinks on the little table between the chairs. Vines grew on the wooden fence walls, creating a small oasis of privacy. Birds bathed at a fountain at the back wall, probably oblivious to the arch of vibrant violet roses that framed them.

"Would you mind if I sketched your fountain?" I asked. "It's stunning."

"I would be honored. If the neighbor's cat comes over, would you shoo him away? I don't want him eating my beautiful bird guests. There was a time when we had so many"— she lowered her voice to a whisper when she said the word, "rats" and then raised it again—"around here that everyone had cats. We used to joke about it. We called it the year of the rat, and said the Chinese zodiac must be wrong because it was actually the year of the goat. But they're long gone, and it's my birds that I'm concerned about now."

She left me to sketch. I settled on one of the chairs and spent the next two hours sketching a bird wonderland of flowers and twining vines around the fountain. For that brief time, I almost forgot about Dolly. Almost.

Sketching had relaxed me and put me back into a more sensible frame of mind. I felt more myself again until I left the garden and rounded the house.

Jack Wilson, the guy who had shown up at the back door of Color Me Read with a head wound, stood on the sidewalk observing Dolly's house.

"Hi. How's your head?"

"Florrie Fox! My head is great, thanks to your expert nursing care. What are you doing here?"

I lifted my sketchbook. "Drawing."

"I suppose you heard about the murder?" he asked.

"I am all too acquainted with it."

"Really?" He looked at me with a gleam of interest. "You knew Dolly?"

It was my turn to be surprised. "I did. It sounds like you did, too."

"Not well, I'm afraid," he said. "There's a rumor that she was murdered."

I took a harder look at him. How many mysteries had I read where the killer returned to the scene of the crime? Some of them even buddied up with the cops to find out if they had any clues. Was he trying to get information? Speaking as casually as I could, I replied, "I've heard that, too. It's so sad. Dolly was a wonderful person."

His eyes narrowed as he regarded me. "Everyone says that when someone dies."

"That's a little bit cynical." He seemed like such a nice guy. It was the kind of remark I would have expected from Nolan.

"Sorry. I didn't mean to offend you."

"How did you say you knew Dolly?" I knew perfectly well that he hadn't told me, but I wanted to force him into a corner so he would have to be specific.

"It was a little business transaction. Dolly liked antiques."

That sounded plausible. But what if the transaction had gone wrong? Or what if he knew about *The Florist*? Just because he said something plausible didn't mean he was innocent. I looked up at him. He was so cute, though. It was hard to imagine him being a hard-hearted murderer. Nevertheless, I played clueless. "Did you buy something from her?"

"I wanted to."

I sucked in a deep breath. "*The Florist?*"

He frowned at me. "I'm not following."

"What did you want to buy from Dolly?"

"A drawing." He jammed his hands into his pockets.

"But she refused to sell it?"

"She died too soon for us to come to an agreement."

I felt the flush of embarrassment burning the tops of my ears. Thank goodness my hair covered them. I was as bad as Mr. DuBois, imagining everyone was an evil killer. "Her daughter might be willing to sell it to you."

"I was told she's giving everything to some estate company to sell."

"You're in luck, then. She may hire Percy McAllister, who apparently doesn't value anything correctly. You can probably get it for a steal."

He glanced over at me, but his eyes darted at something past me. "Thanks for the tip. That's very helpful, Florrie. Nice seeing you again."

Jack gave me a friendly nod and ambled away.

I couldn't help thinking that Dolly's house was very close to the bookstore. Surely it wasn't Dolly who had clobbered him the morning he appeared at Color Me Read. Probably not. She had been busy prowling through the Dumont estate sale.

I turned my attention to the forensics crews that still came and went from the house. How would I feel if someone found a skeleton hidden in the wall of my parents' house? Suddenly I felt very sorry for Maisie.

As I watched, Zsazsa exited the house. She spied me standing across the street and waved at me. There wasn't any traffic, but she looked both ways before jogging across the street to me.

"My goodness but it's hot today." Zsazsa fanned herself with her hand. "I was just visiting with Maisie, poor thing. She harbors such ill will toward her mother. It's a pity Maisie never matured enough to get to know Dolly as the delightful woman she was."

"I guess she knows now that Dolly was murdered?"

"Do you know what she said to me? 'Mother embarrassed me her entire life. And now she didn't even have the decency to die with class.' Who says that about their murdered mother? She acts as if Dolly chose to be murdered."

"I wonder if she knew about the skeleton," I mused.

"She *says* she knew nothing. I believe her exact words were, 'Mother didn't leave me a legacy, she left me a curse.' "

Maisie made it hard to feel sorry for her. Would I have said something similar in her shoes? I didn't think so. She assumed her mother had killed the person and had hidden him in the wall. "You don't suppose it was Maisie . . ." I hated to even suggest that Maisie might be the one who killed Dolly.

"My dear, I have had the same thought. Where was Maisie the day her mother died?"

Could she have been the person I saw running away? "She claims she was in South Carolina. Dolly would have been overjoyed to see her and wouldn't have thought twice about letting her in or sitting down to drink a beverage with her."

"Mmm," Zsazsa murmured. "I wouldn't dream of consuming anything that Maisie offered *me*." She gasped. "What a horrid woman I am to say such things! Besides, I have a second suspect in mind as well." Zsazsa nodded, looking to her right and over my shoulder.

I turned to see Edgar Delaney slowly walking toward the house.

"He claims to be a graduate student of German and European Studies, but on Saturday, when I addressed him in German to ask how his studies were going, he clearly did not understand a word."

"Is it obligatory to speak German in that field?"

"I imagine so, especially for someone doing graduate work. German is a very difficult language, but I would have expected him to understand my simple question."

"We should find out where he went after he left the bookstore. But maybe that doesn't matter. If he was at home, he could have gone up to Dolly's apartment and been back at his own place in minutes."

Zsazsa checked her watch. "I believe I'll pay a little visit to my friends at the university. Perhaps I'll learn something more about our Edgar Delaney."

Zsazsa bustled off in the direction of the university. I was about to go home when I realized I must have left my purse in the garden. I returned to collect it and found it on the table, exactly where I had placed it.

As I walked along the side of the house and approached the street, I saw Edgar do a quick about-face in front of Dolly's house. He hurried along the sidewalk, going back in the direction he had come. I was almost at the gate when I realized someone was watching Edgar.

Chapter 16

Jack Miller had made a U-turn.

I ducked back into the passageway a little bit, hoping some of the gorgeous climbing roses on the house would help hide me. But I peered around them enough to be certain that Jack was tailing Edgar. He strode by the police vans looking straight ahead as though he was completely unconcerned by their presence. He was totally focused on Edgar.

For a long moment, I argued with myself about following them. Part of me longed to go back to the carriage house and curl up in the safety of my home. But another part of me wanted to know the connection between them and why Jack would be following Edgar. Had Edgar seen him? Did he know the man? Was that the reason he had turned and walked in the other direction?

In the end, I decided that I was being silly. It was broad daylight. I was on a public street, and they weren't paying any attention to me.

I strolled casually along the other side of the street, keeping both of them in view. *Curiosity killed the cat,* I reminded myself. Nonsense. I was being ridiculous! There was something peculiar about Edgar and Jack. Nothing would happen to me if I followed them. If they turned into an alley or something, all I had to do was go in a different direction.

Edgar stopped in front of a narrow two-story shop. On the sidewalk in front of it, three oversized clocks leaned against a white wicker settee and matching table. The name written in graceful script on the show window read *Time and Again*.

I reminded myself that I didn't need any more clocks. How had I managed to miss this little place?

Edgar went inside.

Jack ambled toward the store and gazed through the show window before he backpedaled a little and leaned casually against a wall. If Edgar left the store, Jack would certainly see him.

There weren't many places to hide on my side of the street. I darted behind the trunk of a large tree and hoped that Jack was so focused on Edgar that he wouldn't notice me.

When someone tapped me on the shoulder, I screamed and whirled around.

Eric grinned at me and whispered, "Screaming will give you away every time. Who are we spying on?"

"What are you doing here?"

"I work in this neighborhood, remember?"

"Well, thanks for giving me away."

"You're really tailing someone?"

"I just happen to be walking in the same direction," I replied defensively.

"And trying to hide behind a tree."

He was so annoying! And I was thoroughly humiliated. "Edgar, who was Dolly's tenant, is being followed by a guy. I thought I'd amble along on the opposite side of the street to see what they were up to."

"Who is the good-looking fellow watching us?"

I glanced in the direction of the store. Jack Miller was staring at Eric and me. "This is so embarrassing."

"A friend of yours?"

"That would be an exaggeration."

"A customer?"

I didn't want to lie to Eric. Did it matter at all that he showed up at the store on the run from someone who clobbered him over the head? "Something like that."

Eric tilted his head and squinted at me. "Maybe I should have a word with him." Eric started to walk away.

I grabbed his hand. "No! He'll think I reported him."

"For what?"

I had dug myself into a hole. "He came by the store and was bleeding, so I helped him. No big deal."

"If it was no big deal, then why are you tailing him?"

"He's following Edgar. It's remotely possible that Edgar killed Dolly. He hasn't been in town very long. I'm not sure anyone knows much about him."

Eric's eyebrows jumped. "But you didn't think it was worth mentioning to me?"

"I would have, sooner or later. I happened to see Edgar, and then Jack seemed to be watching him, so I thought I would amble in the same general direction." I tugged on his sleeve. "There goes Edgar."

We watched as Jack deftly stepped into the doorway of another store. Edgar didn't appear to notice Jack at all.

Jack didn't give us so much as another glance. He focused on Edgar and fell in step a distance behind him.

Keeping his eyes on Jack, Eric touched my elbow. "Let's go. Why would Jack be following Edgar?"

"That's what I want to know."

"Did Jack know Dolly?"

"He said something about wanting to buy a painting from her. But now that he has seen us I think it's useless."

Eric shot a look at me and grinned. "They're almost finished with the skeleton."

"I'm sure all the tenants will be glad about that. Maisie, too."

"Do you know what happened between Maisie and Dolly?" he asked. "I can't imagine being so uncaring about my mom."

"Me, either. She said something about Dolly interfering with her relationship with the only man she ever loved. And Priss said Maisie was engaged once. So maybe Dolly did something that caused the wedding to be called off?"

"I can see how that would make for hard feelings. But it seems like you would get over it eventually."

I agreed with his logic. But a terrible thought hit me hard. None of the rest of us had known Dolly as well as Maisie had. What if Dolly had a dark side that Maisie had seen but Dolly kept well hidden from the world?

"Should I find out for you?" I asked.

"Think you can?"

I pretended to be appalled. "You doubt my abilities in the much-maligned field of gossip?"

Eric winced. "Yeah. Pretty much. The Florrie Fox I know is a straight shooter. You're not very good at being sneaky."

"I consider that a challenge," I teased.

"Don't get into any trouble."

"I'll call you if I do."

Glad I had the day off, I stopped by the market for mozzarella and tomato sauce. At home, I started pizza dough. While it was resting, I sliced onions and sautéed them over a low, slow heat before adding minced garlic and bits of red pepper. I rolled out the dough, spread the sauce and the onions, then sprinkled shredded mozzarella on top, and popped it into the oven. When it was ready, I wrapped it in heavy-duty aluminum foil, grabbed a bottle of red wine from the fridge, and hustled over to Dolly's house.

There was always the possibility that Olivia and Priss would take it and shoo me away. If they did, I would have to figure out another method of getting them to talk.

The police vans were gone. The people strolling along the sidewalks had no idea about the dramas that had transpired there over the last few days. Maybe Eric was right. Every day we walked by places where terrible things had happened. Especially in a town that had been around for a long time.

I walked up to the second floor and knocked on the door.

Olivia answered, surprised to see me. "I was afraid it would be another cop. The two of us fled the house today. It was craziness here."

"I thought you might be worn out. I brought you a homemade pizza."

Olivia blinked at me and reached for the pizza. "This is so thoughtful of you. Won't you come in? Priss! Florrie brought dinner."

"And wine!" I held up the bottle I had brought with me.

Priss flitted in. "Did I hear someone say wine? I hope it's not that nonalcoholic stuff. This has been the worst week of my life. If I ever needed a girls' night with wine, this is it."

I settled on the sofa and looked around while they retrieved wineglasses and plates. The massive wood surround on the fireplace was probably original to the building as were the parquet floors. Nolan was right about the magnificent moldings. They were the color of mahogany and had never been painted. They probably didn't suit most people's taste today, but it would be a shame to rip out all that hand-carved wood.

The Beauton sisters didn't have as much clutter as Dolly. But their walls were packed with art. One of them had an eye for balancing the diverse shapes and sizes.

I stood up for a closer look. There didn't seem to be a central theme or color. The largest painting was wildly abstract, either of giant multicolored fishes or spaceships. I wasn't sure which. Two ornately framed oil paintings showed girls posing with dogs on a beach. I gasped in surprise when I realized they were of Olivia and Priss.

I peered at a set of small mismatched frames. They held photographs of people dressed in formal attire from the 1800s.

"Our great-grandparents," said Olivia as she returned. "I love those pictures."

"The paintings of you and Priss are wonderful!"

"Thanks. At the time we complained bitterly. But now we're glad we have them. They bring back memories of carefree summers at the beach."

"Please don't get started on the beach, Olivia," whined Priss. "She loves the wind in her hair and sand between her toes. But I'm allergic to the sun."

Olivia shook her head. "You are not."

"I am if I say I am. I loathe the beach. Sand gets in everything and my hair frizzes like I stuck my finger in an electrical outlet." She touched her smooth curls. "Wait! I think it's starting to frizz at the mere thought of the beach."

I grinned. Veronica and I sometimes had that kind of conversation. "How's Nolan?"

"He's home with his leg elevated. I'm going over later to check on him."

Olivia poured the wine, grabbed a piece of pizza, and sat back on the sofa. "Thank you so much for bringing this. Losing Dolly was like losing a sister. We've been through so much together over the years."

"It's wonderful that you became friends. I have never understood how people can be neighbors for decades and not get to know each other at all."

Priss giggled. "There were a few tenants we didn't want to

get to know better. There was the woman who didn't shower. I'll never understand *that*."

Olivia snorted. "She was an oddball, for sure. Dolly said not to complain because it kept the water bill low."

I tried to steer my questions to Maisie. "How old was Maisie when you moved in?"

"Three? She was very little. Such a cutie." Priss poured herself a second glass of wine.

"What happened between Maisie and Dolly?" I asked as casually as I could.

Olivia waved her hand as though she wasn't interested in going there. "Dolly was right about Maisie being resentful. You know how children are. They want to be exactly like their friends."

"Maisie felt like the odd one out," said Priss. "Frankly, I think most children do. She was always a very pretty girl, but she made up her mind that she was different and that notion ballooned as she got older. And then she fell in love."

"She was positively giddy. She was in college then, as I recall," added Olivia.

Priss swirled the wine in her glass. "Dolly was furious. She had pinched and saved and worked all kinds of night jobs to put Maisie through college. Dolly's biggest regret was that she never went to college. She was determined that wouldn't happen to Maisie. And then Maisie came home and announced she was dropping out of school and getting married."

"If Maisie had wanted to upset Dolly, she could not have picked a better way to achieve it. Dolly said over and over again that she wasn't going to let Maisie ruin her life over the wrong man." Olivia took a bite of pizza.

"Like Dolly had," I said. "She wanted to protect Maisie from making the same mistakes. Sounds like a mess. So did Maisie break off the engagement under pressure from Dolly?"

Priss laughed. "If it had only been that simple. Dolly went to the boy's mother. Of course, *she* was offended that her precious son wasn't good enough for Dolly's daughter. There was a big brouhaha."

"His mother put her foot down. He was not going to marry Maisie." Olivia cut another piece of pizza. "Of course, it's not hard to see what would happen next. They planned to elope."

Chapter 17

"But Dolly was way ahead of them." Priss finally set her wineglass down. She picked little bits of cheese off her piece of pizza and nibbled on them. "Dolly called his former girlfriend and invited her to have dinner with him. Imagine this scenario, two angry mothers, and two girls vying for the same guy."

"He must have been very special."

"Just an average Joe," muttered Olivia.

"That's not true." Priss leaned toward me. "Percy is very good-looking. I still see him around town sometimes. If I had been younger . . ."

"Thank heaven you weren't," said her sister. "He was being torn in every direction. The last thing we would have needed was *you* chasing him."

"Percy? Percy McAllister?"

"That's the one," said Priss.

How odd. When her friend mentioned Percy, Maisie had acted as though she didn't remember him. "What finally happened?" I asked.

"He picked the other girl over Maisie!" Priss shrieked. She immediately clapped a hand over her mouth. "I hope she didn't hear me."

Ohhh. That explained Maisie's behavior. Maybe she was embarrassed to have been engaged to such a jerk. I might have acted that way, too, if I were in her shoes.

"Dolly was relieved, but Maisie was devastated."

"She blamed Dolly," said Priss.

"Maisie was so angry that she did the two things she knew would kill Dolly. She dropped out of school, and she moved away. For six months, Dolly didn't even know where Maisie was," said Olivia.

"She hired a private investigator to find her." Priss refilled her wine.

"For years, Dolly kept an eye on Maisie through the private investigator," said Olivia. "And then one day, she paid Maisie an unexpected visit. We weren't there, of course, but according to Dolly it all went very well at the beginning. Then Maisie told her she was planning to take night courses to finish her degree. Dolly was so thrilled that she offered to pay for the classes."

"That was all it took to set Maisie off. I thought it sounded very generous of Dolly, but Maisie saw it as Dolly being controlling," explained Priss.

"Did she ever finish school?" I asked.

Olivia burst into laughter. "We're too afraid to ask her!"

"So it was really all over a boy," I mused aloud.

Olivia frowned. "That was the breaking point. But it had been building for a long time. Dolly wanted a better life for Maisie, but Maisie felt stifled, as though Dolly wouldn't allow her to make her own decisions."

"And now she's gone, and it's too late to put their problems behind them." I thought about my own mom. "That's very sad."

"I think Maisie realizes that now." Priss burst into tears. "I just can't believe Dolly is gone."

"I can't, either," said Olivia softly.

The silence that followed was awkward and my cue to go

home. I rose from my seat, and to cheer them up, I asked about a photo of a cottage on the wall. "Is that where you grew up?"

"Don't we wish!" Olivia drew near it. "That was our grandparents' beach house."

Next to it was a very small painting of a sunflower. Even with the simple black frame it wasn't any bigger than five inches by five inches. "Did one of you draw this?"

Olivia stopped smiling. "We've had it for years. I don't even remember where we got it."

I nodded and thanked them for an enjoyable evening. But I felt that I left on a sour note. What was with that sunflower?

As soon as I got home, I settled on the sofa and drew the sunflower from memory. It wasn't perfect, but it was close enough.

I doodled as I thought about Maisie and Percy. Who'd have thought he would be at the root of Dolly's problems with Maisie? I was sketching his head, but it wasn't coming out quite right. He had a narrower jawline and a prominent chin. Now it looked more like him. On the surface he was sort of pretty, but he was a hollow shell. Maisie had given up a relationship with her mother over a man who hadn't cared enough to stick with her.

I took Peaches to work with me again in the morning. She walked to the store eagerly. Maybe she liked being with people all day long instead of hanging around home alone. I went through my routine of opening the store, poured a cup of coffee for the professor, and walked upstairs with Peaches racing ahead.

But Professor Maxwell wasn't there. It wasn't like him at all.

When I returned to the first floor, Veronica had arrived. The advantage to having a sister who is not only a knockout but immensely popular is that by high school you develop a well-honed ability to recognize the people who want to use you.

So when Percy showed up at Color Me Read wearing a brown short-sleeved shirt covered with the Gucci monogram, I knew something was up. After all, he was the one who had said no one wanted to buy books anymore.

He walked in somewhat tentatively. That should have come as no surprise to me. He found himself in a land where books were prized. They were the big feature. It must have felt foreign to him. When he saw me, he smiled. Chill bumps ran along my arms.

"I'm looking for Florence Fox."

I was tempted to say that no such person worked in the store. Florrie wasn't short for Florence. But that would have been unkind and silly. "I'm Florrie Fox."

"I heard you were cute."

Ugh. He was trying to kiss up to me. "How may I help you?"

"I heard . . ."

At that very moment, Veronica walked by with an armful of books to change out the window display for the upcoming signing.

Percy's gaze followed Veronica all the way to the window.

He turned back to me. "I was told that you authenticated a coloring book called *The Florist?*"

"I wouldn't say I authenticated it. I'm not an expert, but it appeared to me to be an original copy."

He leaned against the checkout counter and gave me a sideways look that I thought was supposed to be flirtatious. "This isn't the best place to talk. I'd like to get to know you better. How about having dinner with me tonight at Porcino? It's impossible to get a table on short notice, but they know me there."

I bit my lip to keep from laughing. He was well-known at a restaurant called *pig?* With enormous relief, I said, "Thank you for your kind invitation, but I'm seeing someone."

He straightened up. "You're kidding."

I should have been insulted, but I laughed at him. He wasn't good at this. I stepped out of my polite bookstore manager shoes for a moment. "I think we both realize that you're not here to date me. And I know you don't buy books. What is it that you want?"

He held up his palms. "Okay. I can see that you are all business. As a man of industry myself, I can appreciate that. He took out a checkbook. "How about a little business transaction between the two of us?"

There were two things in the world that I was certain about at that moment. The first was that I would never take a check from Percy, even if he forgot himself and wanted to buy books. The second was that there wasn't a business transaction of any kind that I would be willing to enter into with him. "This is a bookstore. If you would like to buy books, I would be delighted to sell them to you. We don't take checks."

"Gotcha." He winked and pointed his index finger at me. "I understand what you're saying." He left the desk, sidled up to Veronica, and said something that made her giggle.

Zsazsa and Professor Goldblum hurried into the store.

"We need to speak with you," said Zsazsa.

"Privately," added Goldblum.

"I'm almost finished here. I'll meet you upstairs?" They nodded their agreement and stopped by the coffee to help themselves.

Percy returned with two books from the show window. He handed me a dark dystopian detective book and a mystery by a Swedish author written in the original Swedish.

"You read Swedish?" I inquired.

"Is that what that is?"

Had I been a meaner person, I would have rung them up. Instead, I set them aside. "Why don't you just tell me what you want?"

Percy took a deep breath and for the first time, I thought

the real guy was speaking to me. "Look, I sold *The Florist* at an estate sale by mistake."

"I was there."

"Funny, I don't remember you."

No kidding.

"The woman who bought it has died and no one can find the book. The woman who hired me to arrange the estate sale is going to sue me for the value of the book, which is apparently a small fortune. I don't have that kind of money." He pointed at me with his whole hand. "Since you're the one who identified it as being old"—he flicked his pen on his checkbook—"I thought maybe we could enter into an arrangement that would change your recollection of the book?"

"You're asking me to lie about it?"

"No!" His eyes blinked open wide. "I would never ask that. Perish the thought! I'm just saying that maybe for one hun . . ."

I shook my head.

"One thou . . ."

I shook my head again.

"What's your price?"

I took a deep breath of air and shook my head.

"Oh, come on. I would do this for you."

Now I couldn't help laughing out loud. "No, you wouldn't. You can put your checkbook and pen away. There is no amount of money that would bribe me to lie about this."

His mouth twitched back and forth and for just a second, I thought I saw a flicker of tears coming on. He was very stressed about the lawsuit. Not that I could blame him.

"If I find the book and bring it in to show you, will you authenticate it for me?"

Did he have the book? Or know where it was? That didn't compute. If he had it, he could hand it over to Ms. Dumont and solve his problem with the lawsuit. I didn't think that would be legal, but if he had it, that was the least of his legal problems. "Sure," I lied, hoping he still thought I was an authority even though I wasn't. "If you bring the book in, I will tell you what I think." I omitted mentioning that he would still have to have it properly authenticated. After all, if he brought it in, he would be the number one suspect in Dolly's death.

He started to leave but turned back. "Where do you think it is?"

Was he pretending he didn't know? I didn't want to say something out of turn that could interfere with the police investigation. I told him the truth. "Dolly was holding it the last time *I* saw it."

"And where exactly was that?"

"Here. In the bookstore."

"So it's probably in her apartment . . ."

I had no idea why he drew that conclusion, but I didn't bother correcting him. If he didn't have it or know where it was, maybe he would find it when he put Dolly's possessions up for sale. But that still wouldn't solve his problems, because as far as I knew, it still rightly belonged to the estate of Dolly Cavanaugh.

The second he left, Veronica rushed over to me. "What did he want?"

"He wants me to lie about *The Florist*. Apparently, he was engaged to Maisie at one time."

"No kidding? I don't know why I'm surprised, he's so dreamy!"

"Veronica, he's a worm."

"You're exaggerating. I think he's sweet. How can you resist those deep brown eyes?"

"*Eww.* How is it possible for you to be attracted to someone like him? He has no brain."

"You'd be interested in him if you didn't have cute Sergeant Jonquille hanging around."

As if mere mention of his name made him materialize, Eric walked into the bookstore.

"I can assure you 100 percent that I wouldn't be attracted to Percy if he were the last hope for mankind to survive."

"Let's hope earth doesn't devolve to that point! So these are the famous flowers," said Eric. "Did this Percy person send them?"

"I very seriously doubt it." I leaned across the checkout desk for a kiss.

Eric pecked me on the lips. "Impressive arrangement."

Veronica did not help at all by gushing over them like they were the Hope diamond. "Florrie just won't tell us who her admirer is."

If she hadn't been on the other side of the checkout counter, I would have bumped her in the shin to shut her up. "They're probably from some nice old lady whom I helped in the store and don't even remember."

"Like we'd believe that," Veronica teased.

The two of them gazed at me as though waiting for me to confess. "I don't know who they're from, and it doesn't matter. Someone did something nice for me, and I appreciate it."

"Jack Miller." Eric, who always took everything in stride, said Jack's name glumly.

"Who's that?" asked Veronica.

Eric glanced at me before turning to Veronica. "You don't know him?"

Ohhh. This was getting me into so much trouble. Hastily, I said, "Veronica was busy at the time Jack came in. And he was here very briefly. The fact that I didn't mention him to Veronica should prove to you how insignificant his presence was."

There. That should do it. I smiled at them.

I could see on Eric's face that he wasn't buying it. "A detective from homicide should be by today to question the two of you. Nothing to be worried about. Just tell him what happened the way you told me."

"Should we have an attorney present?" asked Veronica.

"Not unless you were involved in Dolly's death."

Veronica play-punched him.

"He may ask for a list of the members of the coloring club."

Veronica nodded. "I'll get that ready for him. Are they suspects?"

"Probably not. But they might know something. In the meantime, I'd better get back on my beat." He winked at me when he said, "Stay away from that Jack Miller."

But before he made it out the door, Goldblum jogged down the stairs. "Are you coming, Florrie? Hey! I didn't know Sergeant Jonquille was here. Bring him up here with you."

"What's that about?" Veronica gazed up the stairs at Goldblum.

"I have no idea."

My sister grinned at me. "You seem to be pleading that to a lot of things. Like the man who sent the flowers."

"You can stop that now. But stay away from Percy. He's trouble."

"Bad boys can be fun sometimes."

Where did she get such crazy notions?

"We'll be upstairs." Eric and I rushed up to meet with Zsazsa and Professor Goldblum.

When we walked into the room, they simultaneously said, "Close the door."

Chapter 18

Eric closed the door behind us.

"We have news." Zsazsa motioned for me to sit down. "The young man, Edgar, is not a student."

"Edgar? Dolly's tenant?" asked Eric.

Zsazsa explained her concern that he didn't understand German.

"He's not even enrolled." Goldblum lowered his voice and looked at Eric when he said, "I still have some connections."

"Maybe he's planning to enroll in the fall," I suggested.

"Applications for the fall term have closed." Zsazsa shook her head. "He is not in the department of German and European Studies. I knew it!"

"There are other universities in this town," Eric pointed out.

"An excellent observation. None of them have a graduate program in German and European Studies," said Goldblum with great satisfaction.

"We need to see his driver's license or the registration on his car." Goldblum looked at me eagerly. "To find out who he really is. Maybe his name isn't Edgar Delaney."

"Why would he claim to be a student?" I wondered aloud.

"It's an easy cover." Eric pulled out his little notebook and

wrote something. "Most people don't happen to run into retired professors who would ask them questions in German.
Maybe he thought that department would be an easy bluff. I'll
pass this information along to homicide."

Goldblum scowled when Eric left. "That was certainly an-
ticlimactic."

Zsazsa ticked items off on her fingers as she spoke. "He
claims he's from Ohio. He has no apparent good reason to be in
Washington. He lied about being a student. And he lives in
Dolly's house. Isn't that enough to suspect him?"

Goldblum paced the floor. He came to an abrupt halt. "We
should search his apartment."

"Whoa." I held up my palms. "That's definitely illegal. No
breaking and entering. Not even the police can do that. They
would have to get a warrant."

"But Maisie wouldn't. Can't the owner of the building go
into the tenants' apartments?" Zsazsa cocked her head.

"I want to find Dolly's murderer as much as anyone else,
but I don't want to land in jail, nor do I want that to happen to
the two of you. Besides, I don't think you'll find Maisie to be
very cooperative."

I heard Veronica shouting my name. "I'd better get back to
work. Please don't go getting into trouble." I left the room and
scrambled down the stairs expecting to find Veronica with an
irate customer.

The man with her could have been Santa Claus had he
worn red and added a white beard. He was clean-shaven, with
a head of fluffy white hair and a belly that wouldn't need any
stuffing. His sport coat hung open. I suspected that it wouldn't
close over his abdomen.

"This is—" began Veronica.

The man interrupted her. Flashing a badge, he said, "Detective Lieutenant Holberstein. I'd like to speak to each of you
individually."

"You go ahead," I said to Veronica. "The professor is out if you want to use his office."

Veronica led the way upstairs, looking terrified.

In less than fifteen minutes, she came back. "Your turn."

"How did it go?"

She shrugged. "I felt like I was boring him. I gave him the list of Hues, Brews, and Clues members like Eric suggested, and he didn't even look at it. He just folded it and stuck it into his pocket."

A few minutes later, I understood what she meant. I had explained how we found Dolly and told him about the skeleton in her wall and *The Florist*.

"A coloring book," he said in dull disbelief.

"It's a rare book from the 1700s," I explained.

"O-kay," he sang in two tones. "Thank you, Ms. Fox. I'll be in touch if we need anything else."

He stood up and slowly walked down the stairs. I followed him and watched as he ambled out the door.

Veronica was ringing up a sale for a woman.

"Was that Detective Holberstein?" asked the customer. "He looks awful. I suppose it's no wonder."

Veronica must have smelled gossip. "Do you know him?"

"Not very well but I heard what happened. Such a shame. I thought for sure that he would retire. He must be counting the days."

"What happened?" I asked.

"He had major heart surgery. Must have been about a year ago now. I understand it was touch and go for a while. On the day of his operation, his wife and son were on their way to the hospital when a poorly secured load of metal tubes on a truck came loose on the beltway and went straight through their windshield. In a split second, he lost his entire family."

Veronica and I shared a look. No wonder he had been so lethargic and uninterested.

"I understand he sort of gave up on life after that. Who could blame him?" The customer tsked loudly. "You ladies have a great day."

The second the door shut, Veronica said, "If we don't do something, Dolly's murder will go unsolved."

"Maybe he doesn't work alone. I'll ask Eric."

"I feel so sorry for him. But Dolly matters, too. And how do we know that her killer won't poison somebody else if he's not caught?"

I agreed with her entirely. I didn't think that Detective Holberstein had it in him to care anymore.

At 8:41 that night, my phone rang. Zsazsa sounded completely hysterical. She was always in control and self-composed. I had never heard her like this. Words spilled out of her in a crazy mix that made no sense.

"Zsazsa, I need you to calm down. Speak slowly."

"They are here. They think I killed Dolly."

"Who?" I asked. "Where are you?"

She whispered, "I have to go. They're taking me to the police station. Florrie, you must help me. I beg of you!"

The line went dead.

Chapter 19

I wasn't sure whom to call first, Professor Maxwell or Eric. In the end, while I slid on sandals and was grabbing my purse, it was Professor Maxwell whom I phoned. Zsazsa was an old friend of his. Unless I missed my guess, she needed a lawyer, and the professor would be able to roust one on short notice.

Mr. DuBois answered the phone. "This had better be important. *True Tales of Evil* is on TV."

When I told him about Zsazsa's phone call, he changed his tune. "Maxwell isn't home. To be honest, I'm worried about him. He has completely abandoned his normal schedule. He's out and about at odd hours. I shall try to reach him on his cell phone, but don't hold your breath. Most of the time he does not answer."

I hung up, got into my car, and drove to the Second District station. When I parked, I called Eric and explained the situation as I ran into the building.

Of course, they didn't let me see Zsazsa. Only a lawyer would be able to talk with her. I waited impatiently, walking in circles. I had dealt with Professor Maxwell's attorney before. I checked my phone. Strickland, Wheeler, and Erba was still listed under my contacts. Because the professor was an important client, I had the direct number to Ms. Strickland. Zsazsa probably couldn't afford her fee, but in my panic, I phoned her anyway.

Ms. Strickland promised to send someone over. When I hung up, I made one last desperate call to Professor Goldblum. He and Zsazsa were old friends. Maybe he could do something for her.

The wait dragged on. Half an hour passed. Forty-five never-ending slow minutes passed. Business went on as usual at the station house. Only those of us who waited for news were agitated.

A petite woman about my age walked in and asked for Zsazsa at the desk. I flew over to her and introduced myself. She was from the law firm that handled Maxwell's affairs. She disappeared into the back, but I felt a teeny bit calmer. At least Zsazsa had someone on her side back there with her.

Eric strode in with Goldblum. I rushed over to them. Eric promised to find out what was going on and brushed past me.

Before Eric disappeared into the back, Goldblum said, "I'll bail her out. I have the name of a good bondsman."

When it was just the two of us, Goldblum started asking questions. "What happened? Why would they bring Zsazsa in for questioning? What had she done? How could she possibly be a suspect?"

I had no answers. But when Goldblum asked *what had she done,* I began to worry. What if she had tried to search Edgar's apartment? Had she been caught and arrested for breaking and entering?

At long last, Eric returned with the attorney. We gathered outside in a private corner of the parking lot.

"Zsazsa has *not* been arrested," said the attorney. "My appearance put an end to the questioning. She should be out here any minute. They don't really have much on her yet."

"Yet?" I squeaked.

Eric shot me a reassuring look. "The manager of Zsazsa's apartment building happened to be throwing something in the dumpster when he saw a bottle of antifreeze and a big container of orange juice. They were both empty."

"What kind of craziness is that?" yelled Goldblum. "There must be a hundred tenants in that building."

Eric nodded calmly. "They compared the list of tenants with the names of your coloring club members, and Zsazsa was on both."

"They can't arrest a person for that." Goldblum was furious.

"They *didn't* arrest her." The attorney spoke soothingly. "But it doesn't help that she appears to have been the last person to have seen Dolly Cavanaugh alive. They brought Zsazsa in for questioning. It's a standard maneuver. Sometimes people confess under pressure. The police watch their demeanor, see how they respond. You'd be surprised by the things people say and do during an interrogation."

"I'm confused." I tried to keep my voice even. "Zsazsa is a suspect?"

"Oh yeah." Eric didn't even hesitate.

"So that guy Holberstein will take this information and try to build a case against Zsazsa?" I asked.

"Right." Eric let out a long breath.

"Can she leave the country? What if I take her to Belize? She can't be extradited from there." Even in the poor light of the parking lot, I could see Goldblum's agitation.

"*Don't leave the area* is TV baloney," said Eric.

The attorney added, "And Belize entered into an extradition treaty with the US about twenty years ago. It's no longer a haven for people hiding from United States authorities."

"So what can we do?" Goldblum sounded frantic.

The attorney smiled at him. "*You* can't do anything but be her friend and offer moral support. In the meantime, we'll probably hire a private investigator to see if we can find out exactly what happened that night. If we're lucky, someone else might have seen the victim alive after Zsazsa left her, and we have to hope Zsazsa will have an ironclad alibi for the time up to Dolly's death."

"And the police will continue to investigate," said Eric.

I didn't want to argue with him. But having spoken to Holberstein, and having dealt with homicide not too long ago, I had a bad feeling the police would think they had their woman. Holberstein was in no condition to pursue a case that he thought was already sewn up.

Zsazsa emerged from the building.

Goldblum ran to her, nearly falling over his own feet in his haste.

The other three of us walked toward them.

"What a horrible experience," cried Zsazsa. "All I want is a steaming shower and a hot cup of tea."

"I'll take you home," I said.

"No! I cannot go back there. They will come for me in the middle of the night, breaking down my door with guns blazing."

The attorney said soothingly, "That's in movies. You aren't a fugitive or a gun runner."

"I don't care. I don't think I will ever feel safe in my own home again."

"You could come home with me," I offered.

"Maxwell! Yes, I must speak to Maxwell. He has been through this and survived. But they put him in jail. I can't go to jail. I'll perish. I will! I might not be a perfect person, but I pay my taxes, I always go to vote, and I have never murdered anyone!"

"Maxwell was considered a flight risk," I reminded her.

"They'll say the same thing about me. No, I must go somewhere safe."

Goldblum held out his arm like a gentleman walking the

bride down the aisle. "They don't know about me. You will come to my house. While you take a shower, I will make you a cup of tea. I have a couple of guest rooms, so you can have your own room and feel perfectly safe."

Relief flooded Zsazsa's face. "You are very kind. That sounds perfect." She placed a hand on her chest. "I don't mean to inconvenience you, Florrie. But perhaps you could pick up a change of clothes and some toiletries for me tomorrow?"

"I would be happy to do that."

Zsazsa handed me the key to her apartment. "Thank you, darling." She turned and looked back at the police station building. "I never want to come here again."

I drove home on Wisconsin Avenue, the main drag that ran through Georgetown. People were still out and about. I stopped for a light and waited for it to turn. On the corner across the street, Professor Maxwell emerged from a bar with none other than Frederic van den Teuvel and a short man whom I didn't know. He wore his hair slicked back and his eyes roamed like a wild animal scanning the savanna.

No wonder Mr. DuBois was worried about Maxwell. What was the professor doing with scummy van den Teuvel?

I was still pondering that when Jack Miller, the guy who had been bleeding at the back door of Color Me Read, emerged from the bar. He stretched and looked around before casually ambling after the professor and van den Teuvel.

A horn honked behind me. Instead of driving straight ahead as I had planned, I turned right to follow the motley gang. I double-parked briefly, letting the engine idle while I watched Jack follow the other three men. At the end of the block they split up. Van den Teuvel and the wild-eyed guy got into what looked to be a sleek black Jaguar.

Professor Maxwell walked in the direction of his home with Jack on his tail. I followed them slowly, intending to pick up the professor if necessary. When the professor turned up the driveway to his property, Jack stood on the other side of the street and watched briefly before moving on.

That night I set my alarm two hours early. In the morning, I made a mug of tea but skipped breakfast and took a walk over to Zsazsa's apartment.

I had been there many times before. In order to compete with the ease of buying online, Color Me Read delivered books in the Georgetown area. Each time I brought books to Zsazsa, she had tea and a pastry waiting for me. I always enjoyed paying her a visit.

This morning, her apartment looked the same, but it felt lifeless without her vibrant presence. Zsazsa's apartment was filled with books and fascinating art that she brought back from her travels. The walls and curtains were warm golden beige, as though the sun were kissing them. Touches of firecracker red reminded me of her vivid hair color.

The apartment was tasteful and gracious. She didn't have nearly as many knickknacks as Dolly, but I could understand why they had felt comfortable together and become fast friends. They were both independent women with a dramatic flair.

I walked into Zsazsa's closet and looked around. It was more difficult than I expected to select outfits for someone else. I spied a suitcase and matching hanging bag with wheels, and filled them quickly.

In the bathroom, I collected a selection of makeup, her toothbrush, shampoo, and conditioner. It didn't take long to fill a small case with toiletry items.

Just when I thought I had everything, I remembered shoes and grabbed some jewelry, too. As I walked through the bedroom, I looked out the window and saw the dumpster.

Leaving everything in the apartment, I locked the door

and took the elevator downstairs. I located a door to the rear of the building and walked outside.

The dumpster was surrounded by a fence on three sides probably to make it less of an eyesore. The open side faced an alley. I walked over to it and looked up. Everyone in the building who had a view of the alley could see it.

Of course, no one would think twice about a tenant putting trash into the dumpster.

The alley ran through the block and was open on both ends. Anyone could easily have walked or driven through and disposed of the antifreeze in the dumpster without drawing any attention.

I had to discount the importance of the orange juice. Even if Dolly had consumed the antifreeze in a glass of orange juice, it was such a staple in households that half the people living in Zsazsa's building probably had some in their refrigerators at that very moment.

As I gazed around, trying to imagine how a nonresident might have disposed of trash there, it dawned on me that there was no light. I saw one at the back door to the building. But there was no lighting at or even near the dumpster. "For day-time dumping only," I muttered, "unless you're trying to get rid of poison, in which case, it was ideally located for a night-time visit that wouldn't be noticed."

I returned to Zsazsa's apartment, picked up her clothes, and delivered them to Goldblum's house, which was a mere two blocks away.

As far as I knew, Goldblum had never asked us to deliver anything to him. At least I had never been there before.

His house was immaculate outside. The brick walls had been painted soft cream, which provided a nice background for forest-green shutters. A gate beside the house appeared to lead to a garage in the back. I rang the bell.

A rosy-cheeked Goldblum opened the door. He wore an

apron that said *Bacon is my Superpower.* "Florrie! You're just in time for breakfast."

Zsazsa zoomed toward me. "I hope you brought my makeup! I dislike the way I look without it."

She did appear a little washed out without her usual eyeliner, but I was happy to see she had her verve back. "You bet."

"I'll take these upstairs for you," said Goldblum.

"Not the makeup!" Zsazsa grabbed the smallest bag. "Is this the correct valise, Florrie?"

I assured her it was.

Goldblum loaded up the rest and struggled up the stairs with them.

"I'm so glad to see you feeling better." I gave Zsazsa a hug.

"Come to the kitchen and have a cup of coffee. Do you like bacon? That apron he's wearing is no joke. I have known Goldblum for years, but I had no idea he was such a baconista."

I followed her into a modern kitchen with marble countertops and an eight-burner range. "Goldblum likes to cook?"

"Apparently so." She handed me a mug of coffee. "Help yourself, Florrie. He made enough for a football team." She opened the makeup bag, flipped up a mirror, and applied her eyeliner with a practiced hand. She peered down the hallway and whispered, "I think Goldblum likes having company."

"Do you feel safer here?"

"Definitely. I have already phoned the apartment building manager and given my notice. It's a nice building, but I have lived there quite long enough. I'm not going back. I will find a new place. Perhaps Nolan knows of a nice condominium. And I already feel more like myself now that I'm wearing eyeliner." She motioned for me to sit at the counter.

She took both of my hands into hers. "You helped spring Maxwell from jail. You will help me stay out of jail, too. Yes?"

"Zsazsa, I will do anything I can to help you. You know that. But what you really need is the lawyer who came to your rescue last night."

"Hah! Lawyers!" She waved her hands as if dismissing the thought of them. "What I need is you."

Goldblum joined us in the kitchen. "She's right, Florrie. Zsazsa and I have brilliant minds, but you seem to have a knack for this. Zsazsa and I were up late last night discussing her situation and we have come to a conclusion. The person who murdered Dolly does not like Zsazsa."

Chapter 20

"Why do you think that?" I asked.

"The killer is obviously trying to frame me." Zsazsa dug through the makeup bag and found a lipstick the color of a pink grapefruit. She applied it to her lips, smacked them, and smiled.

"That's certainly possible," I said. "But I saw someone running in Dolly's alley that night. If I had just murdered someone and almost gotten caught in the act, I think I would have thrown the murder weapon, as it were, in the first reasonable place I saw to dispose of it. The killer must have realized the police would be on the scene soon and looking for him."

They glanced at each other. "Just a moment," said Goldblum. "The killer wouldn't have brought a bottle of antifreeze to Dolly's house. He would have mixed the drink elsewhere."

"Or he might have made it in Dolly's house, but he had the antifreeze in a flask," suggested Zsazsa.

"You make excellent points," I agreed. "Not to mention that there could be no connection whatsoever between the orange juice and the antifreeze in the dumpster, and Dolly's death. It could very well be that someone in your building happened to throw out a container of orange juice and another tenant happened to throw out antifreeze."

"There's only one small glitch with that scenario." Zsazsa clasped her hands together so tightly that they turned white under her fingers. "The police informed me that both bottles had been wiped clean of fingerprints."

Uh-oh. No wonder they pulled her in for questioning.

"Did you two come up with any ideas about who the real killer might be?" I asked.

"We thought it must be someone who knows Zsazsa. Probably someone in the coloring club." Goldblum picked up a slice of bacon. "Would you care for a fried egg, Florrie? Over easy is my specialty."

"Thanks, but I can't stay long. I have to get over to the store."

"But then it dawned on us," said Zsazsa, "that most of them probably don't know where I live."

"But it would have been easy for any one of them to follow her home and make note of her address." Goldblum refilled my coffee mug.

"So then we need to figure out which one of them would have been desperate enough to kill Dolly for *The Florist.*"

"Exactly." Goldblum held a platter of pancakes out to me. "We're looking for someone in desperate need of money."

"Edgar Delaney, if that's his real name." Zsazsa nearly spat the words. "I'm sorry but why else would he lie to all of us? I don't understand why he targeted me, but it's quite obvious that Edgar is the killer. We just have to prove it."

I was ashamed that I wolfed the pancakes. They were fabulous, and I told Goldblum so. "Please forgive me, but I have got to get going to open the store."

Even though I hurried along the sidewalks, I was two minutes late. I hated being late. Bob hadn't arrived yet, but Olivia waited at the door.

"Good morning. I'm so sorry to make you wait."

"No problem," said Olivia. "I wanted to talk with you."

We walked inside. I asked if she could wait a few minutes while I switched on the lights. The process of opening up, of starting the music and coffee calmed my nerves. When I was done, I spied Bob helping a customer, and found Olivia sitting in the parlor with a fresh cup of coffee.

I perched on the chair beside hers.

She swallowed hard. "Florrie, the homicide detective came by yesterday to ask what Priss and I remembered about the night Dolly died. You know how it is when that happens. Everything just flew right out of my head."

Olivia fidgeted uncomfortably. "I did remember something but now I'm in an awkward position. I thought maybe you could tell your nice Sergeant Jonquille for me."

She appeared to be rambling. "Okay. You're afraid to tell the detective?"

"No, no. It's nothing like that. You see, the night Dolly was killed, I saw Nolan leaving our building. At the time, I didn't think a thing of it. He was clearly interested in Dolly, whether to date her or to sell her house is irrelevant at this point. But I saw him leaving and I feel the detective should know that. Even if he had nothing to do with Dolly's death, maybe he saw her killer on the street or something."

"I agree. The detective should know." I didn't think it would make any difference to him now that he had his sights on Zsazsa, but he should be informed. "So what's the problem? Why can't you tell him?"

"That's why I came to you. Not only do you have a direct tie to the police, but you have a sister so you'll understand my dilemma. Priss has a thing for Nolan. If I report him to the police, she'll never forgive me."

I *did* understand. Sisters could be completely unreasonable. "Did you tell Priss that you saw Nolan?"

Olivia shot me a frustrated look. "What would Veronica do if you tried to tell her you saw her dreamboat at the murder scene?"

"She would be furious. But I would tell her anyway. Shouldn't Priss know? It might change her mind about him. And what if he murders *her?*"

Olivia laughed without humor. "These are the things that keep me up at night. What if my sweet, gullible sister is chasing a killer? It happens, you know. I see it on the news all the time. The sister disappears with some guy and comes back in a body bag."

Olivia was hitting a little bit too close to home for my comfort. Veronica was easily swayed by men. A word of flattery, a cute smile, and she was hooked.

"I understand. I'll be happy to share that with Eric. But I can't guarantee that the detective won't show up at your apartment to ask you about it."

"I guess that's a risk I'll have to take. Thank you, Florrie."

"Now that Nolan's laid up, I suppose he won't be finding you a new place to live."

"There's another thing that keeps me from sleeping. Maisie has given us our notice. We were in a month-to-month lease with Dolly. We had lived there so long. I never gave any thought to what would happen if Dolly died. Anyway, we have to be out in a matter of weeks."

"Zsazsa's apartment is coming available. But it's a one-bedroom."

"Too bad. That's a nice building. To be honest, I think it might be time for Priss and me to leave Washington. It's gotten so expensive here. Our incomes would go a lot further in the suburbs or in some small town."

"I hope you change your mind about that. We'd miss you."

"Nothing is settled yet. Dolly would never have imagined the number of people impacted by her death."

After she left, it was a quiet morning at Color Me Read. I had a thousand things to do, but I couldn't get Dolly and Zsazsa out of my head.

I stood at the checkout counter, doodling a picture of Zsazsa with a slate-blue colored pencil. Her dramatic eye makeup came first. I had known her for years. She and Goldblum were close friends of Professor Maxwell. They spent countless hours in deep and fascinating discussions with him at the store. She was kind, and interesting, and charming. I doodled her hair, which wasn't the same in blue. Her hair was the color of sugar maple leaves in the fall, glowing in the afternoon sun. Funny how different she looked without that burst of color on her head.

This was the first time I had seen her afraid of anything. I would be scared of going to jail, too.

But as I drew her mouth, I couldn't help wondering if she could possibly have murdered her friend. I wasn't under the impression that Zsazsa needed money. Had they argued over *The Florist*? Which one of them actually found the book at the estate sale? Was it possible that Zsazsa felt she was entitled to the book? Money drove people mad and caused them to do unimaginable things.

But the lips I had doodled on Zsazsa smiled at me, and I was convinced that she would never have murdered Dolly.

"That's a pretty good likeness."

Eric's voice jerked me out of my thoughts. "Thanks."

"How's she doing today?"

"Feeling better."

"I stopped by because they have some preliminary information about the skeleton in Dolly's house. It was definitely a man, about five feet, ten inches tall. Most likely he died as a result of a broken neck. It's hard to tell if he broke his neck falling into that wall or if someone stuffed him in there."

The Coloring Crook

57

"I don't have any doubt about that. How could someone
fall into a wall?"

"There's a case in Texas where something similar happened. There was a rotten floorboard and they think it gave
way and she slid down into the wall."

I shot him a look of disbelief. "As improbable as that sounds,
in our case, the man would have had to fall into the wall from a
hole in the roof. I drew a rough sketch of the roof and the wall.
So he was on top of the roof, it gave way, and he happened to
fall *behind* the bookcase, breaking his neck in the process. And
in all the years he was there, no one ever noticed there was a
hole in the roof? Not to mention the smell."

Eric threw his head back and laughed. "I didn't say it was
logical. I just said that it had happened somewhere else."

"I believe the cops need to rethink that theory. In any
event, I don't believe that's what happened here. Do they have
any idea when he died?"

"The house dates back to the 1800s, but the bones are
modern. Oddly enough, it's the remains of the shoes that are
the biggest clues. They were a brand and style that were sold
around twenty years ago. Give or take five years and that's the
time frame."

My hopes sank. "Then he was probably hidden there when
Dolly owned the house."

"I know she was a friend of yours, but I can't help wondering if he wasn't a tenant whom she killed."

"Good heavens! Like *Arsenic and Old Lace*?"

He tilted his head. "In a way, I guess. But this victim wasn't
poisoned as far as we can ascertain at this time."

"Does Maisie know yet?"

"Someone from homicide is going over to talk with her. I
wanted to tell you before wild rumors start."

"I still can't imagine Dolly as a murderer."

"There's the possibility that her husband did it."

"That would be more plausible. Maisie isn't very likeable, but I keep feeling sorry for her. I just can't imagine how horrible it would be for my mom to be murdered and then discover that she had hidden a body behind a wall. My head would spin. I would have to rethink everything I had known to be true."

Eric nodded. "She didn't like her mother to begin with. This takes everything to a whole new level."

"Eric, I heard what happened to Detective Holberstein."

"He went through a very tough time."

"Do you think he's ready to get back to work?"

His eyebrows jumped. "It's very kind of you to be worried about him."

"That would be nice of me, but I'm more concerned about Zsazsa and Dolly. Zsazsa didn't murder anyone. They've got nothing on her. I saw the dumpster. Anyone could have thrown out antifreeze there."

"You went and looked at the dumpster?"

"I happened to be over there getting clothes for Zsazsa. I'm worried that Holberstein will take the easiest route instead of performing a thorough investigation."

"The sad fact is that the easiest route, the one where everything fits together, is often what happened."

"Are you saying you think Zsazsa murdered Dolly?" I was appalled.

"I'm trying to tell you that Holberstein is a professional who will do his best."

"That's so not true," I cried. "You should have been there when he talked with me. I honestly don't think he understands the importance of *The Florist*. He acted like I was talking about some mass-produced children's coloring book."

Eric laid his hand on my arm. "Let's give Holberstein a chance. Okay?" He shot me a funny look. "Your mother called me."

"What?" Oh no! What was she up to now?

"There's a concert in the park on Saturday night. Your mom's bringing a picnic dinner and asked me along." Eric forced a smile, but his eyes narrowed as though he wasn't sure about it. "Thought I'd better walk it by you first."

Why was I the last to know about this? Why hadn't she called and told *me* about the concert? I must have shown my irritation because Eric began to chuckle.

"I gather this is all news to you? It was nice of her to invite me. But if you'd rather I didn't go . . ."

"Of course, I want you to go. I only wish she had told me first."

"Maybe we should keep our mothers apart for a while. There's no telling what they might do if they got together." I reached across the counter and high-fived with him.

A customer approached the counter with a stack of books on World War II.

I waved to Eric as he left. We had only been dating for a month. It was far too soon for my mother to be so involved. While I rang up the sale, I debated whether I should talk to Veronica first to find out what was up.

But no sooner had I finished than Edgar sauntered into the store. He browsed around for a while, but I noticed that he kept looking at me. He finally sidled up to the checkout counter. Tilting his head bashfully, he said, "I understand we're married."

Chapter 21

I hadn't expected that. My breath caught in my throat. "Ohhh, you must have talked to the guy from the flea market. I guess I deserved that." I managed to choke out, "I understand you're not a student."

Edgar's face went as pale as paste. "Could we talk? Somewhere else?"

I tried to think of a very public place. "Sure. How about the café across the street?" I didn't know his financial status, so I quickly added, "My treat."

"At noon?"

"That sounds great."

At exactly five minutes before twelve, I asked Bob and Veronica to mind the store. I crossed the street and found a table in the window as I had hoped. Very public, but not so close to other tables that everyone would hear us. I ordered an iced tea to sip while I waited.

I studied the bookstore from my vantage point. It was amazing to me that the guy who had jumped on the awning hadn't ripped through it. There had been two of them. Did van den Teuvel have a partner? Or had he and Orso broken in to Color Me Read at the same time? That didn't make sense. It had to have been a team of people.

Time ticked by. I checked my watch entirely too often and was beginning to feel like I had been stood up on a date.

By the time twenty minutes had passed, I was sorely irritated. Other people didn't go by the clock as precisely as I did, but I had waited long enough.

I paid my check and walked out quite miffed with Edgar. When I crossed the street, a bicycle delivery guy zoomed past me, nearly hit a woman, and crashed into a car. People ran to help him, but I turned and power-walked down the street. What if something had happened to Edgar?

The day was hot and humid, typical summer weather for Washington, DC, but lousy conditions for rushing. I slowed to a walk. The brownstone appeared tranquil as I approached it. It had been foolish of me to imagine that something might be wrong with Edgar.

I slowed down but continued to Dolly's house anyway. I knocked on the outside door that led to the basement. "Edgar?"

There was no answer.

I huffed. He stood me up, and now I had imagined terrible things when the truth was that he wasn't even home. He probably forgot all about it and went somewhere else. I had turned to leave when I heard something crash inside.

"Edgar?" I shouted. I tried the doorknob. It twisted easily.

I pulled my phone from my purse and held it at the ready in case I needed to call 911. With the other hand, I pushed the door open slowly, worried about what I might see.

At first I couldn't make out much. My eyes had to adjust. The underground apartment had windows, but coming from the bright summer sun, it seemed dark.

It appeared to be a compact apartment. I was looking at a combination living and dining room. I guessed the kitchen and bathroom were toward the rear. I listened quietly. Could the sound have come from upstairs?

I heard another thud. There was no way I was going inside. "Edgar? Are you all right?" I shouted.

Still standing in the doorway, I dialed 911 but felt foolish when I told the dispatcher, "I think something is wrong because the door was unlocked, and I can hear thuds inside."

She was nice about it and promised to send a car by to check on the situation.

I was looking down at my phone when someone wearing a baseball cap plowed into me with his head down like a bull.

I flew airborne for a couple of feet and landed on my back, momentarily stunned. I had heard about people having the wind knocked out of them, but I had never experienced it before that moment. I lay on my back gasping and hoping nothing was broken.

By the time I sat up and looked for the guy who had flattened me, he was long gone.

Feeling creaky and sore, I managed to get to my feet. "Edgar?"

The door was still open. I peered inside. "Edgar?"

Someone whimpered. Edgar sat on the floor with his arms wrapped around his knees. I wished I were hearing the siren on a police car. I was leery about going inside.

My cell phone lay on the ground where it had fallen. The glass on it was cracked in a starburst pattern. I picked it up and pushed the button to call 911 again. Nothing happened. It was dead.

"Edgar," I called, "is anyone else in there with you?"

He sniffled and shook his head.

I debated. The easiest thing to do would be to run upstairs in the hope Priss, Olivia, or Maisie was home. Not that they were strong, but they could call 911 again and they would be good backup if someone else was hiding in Edgar's apartment.

I looked at him again. There was something so pathetic about his appearance that I didn't feel I should leave him alone at that moment. Had he been through some kind of trauma?

I propped the door open with a footstool in case I needed to beat a hasty retreat. Holding my breath, I entered the apartment with great caution. "Where's your phone?"

Edgar still sat on the floor. I kneeled beside him. "Are you hurt?"

"Lock the door," he whispered.

That made me uneasy. Edgar could be Dolly's killer or there could be someone else in the apartment. I wasn't taking any chances. In case anyone could hear us, I said in a loud voice, "The police are on the way. They'll be here any minute."

"He'll come back. Lock the door," he wailed.

"Let's go outside. We'll be safer out there." Edgar's glasses lay on the floor. I picked them up and handed them to him. "Where is your cell phone?"

He looked around the room and shivered. Was he in shock?

"Florrie?"

I was thrilled to hear Eric's voice. Part of me wanted to run to him and moan about being knocked down. But Edgar was in far worse shape than me. "In here, Eric."

Eric stepped inside. "What's going on?"

Edgar didn't say a word. I nudged him a little bit. I was close enough to see tearstains and fear on Edgar's face. "Tell Eric what happened. Who was that?"

Edgar swallowed hard. "I don't know. I've never seen him before. He knocked on my door and when I opened it, he burst inside." In a tiny voice he said, "I thought I was going to die."

"Was he alone?" asked Eric.

"As far as I know. He tried to choke me." Edgar whimpered and tears rolled down his cheeks. "I thought my mother would never know what happened to me. I would disappear and never be heard from again, just like my dad."

There was no doubt in my mind that Edgar had been through a harrowing experience.

Eric walked past us and down a hallway that I suspected led to the kitchen. After checking out the closet and bathroom, he returned. "What did he want?"

I stood up. "Maybe I should let you talk with Edgar alone."

"No!" Edgar fastened his fingers on my arms like talons. "Don't leave me. Please, Florrie. Don't leave me alone!"

"All right. It's okay. Relax, I won't go anywhere."

Behind Edgar's back, I made a bewildered face at Eric.

Eric crouched. "Let's see your neck."

He took a closer look and nodded. "You better get that checked out. What did he say to you?"

"He asked, 'Where is it? Where is it?'" babbled Edgar.

"*The Florist*?" I asked.

Edgar shrugged. "I guess. I don't know. He never mentioned it by name."

"Why would he think you had *The Florist*?" Chills ran down my spine. Had Edgar murdered Dolly? I was glad Eric was present.

"I don't know. I'm confused. I . . . I was so scared that I didn't know what to say." He turned his head to look at me. "Why? Why would he threaten me? I don't have any money."

Eric continued to ask him questions while I untangled myself from Edgar's clutch. I wandered around the room being shamelessly nosy. After all, Zsazsa and Professor Goldblum thought he was lying about being a student. I didn't see any textbooks. Maybe he took notes on his computer? It had been a while since I was in school, but I didn't see many books at all. He had a map of Washington on the dining table, along with a list of antiques stores.

And then my breath caught in my throat. A photo lay on the table. It showed a remarkably handsome man standing on the stoop of Dolly's house. There wasn't a doubt in my mind that it was the same house. The iron gate and fence were in the front and the windows matched, right up to the dormer on the third floor. Something was slightly off, though. I had to study it for a moment before I realized that the vegetation was smaller. The tree in the front wasn't nearly as large as it was now.

I flipped it over, hoping to find a date. Nothing was written on the back. Still, it was odd that Edgar had a photo of the house from years before. Maybe Dolly had given it to him?

Eric was making notes. "You're sure you had never seen him before?"

"Positive. He wore a baseball cap pulled down low over his face. I'll never forget his voice. I used to like English accents, but this was like the devil himself."

"British?" I walked over to them. "Are you certain?"

"Did you see him, Florrie?" asked Eric.

I told Eric about the man ramming into me. "I didn't see his face at all. But there is one person who wants *The Florist* and has a very distinct English accent—Frederic van den Teuvel."

"Could it have been the man who was following Edgar? Jack Miller?" whispered Eric.

I didn't want to think that. A lot of people could do an excellent English accent, but I hoped it wasn't Jack. Still, I understood why he might think that. Then again, Jack *had* been following Edgar. "I didn't see his face, but that's probably a good bet."

"Maybe you should get checked out, too. Let me see your eyes."

I walked behind Edgar so he wouldn't see me.

"Florrie!" Eric was annoyed.

I flashed the photograph at him.

He followed me. "Stop that and look at me. Hmm, pupils look okay. Still, that kind of fall is nothing to mess around with. Do you have a headache?"

The only thing annoying me at that moment was his refusal to pay attention to the photograph in my hand. "I'm fine." I held the picture up to his nose so he couldn't avoid seeing it.

He gazed at it for a minute, flipped it over, and examined the back. "Let's get an EMT crew in here."

Eric radioed in. When he was finished, he asked Edgar if he could stand up.

Aside from the marks on his neck, it seemed to me that most of Edgar's wounds were psychological. It wasn't that he couldn't stand up, he was just too scared to.

Eric helped him to the sofa and asked for his driver's license. "Edgar Delaney," he read aloud. He showed him the photograph. "Want to tell us about this?"

"It's my dad."

Chapter 22

I moved closer to see Edgar's face while he spoke.

"I found the picture in my mom's room when I was seven or eight. She denied that it was him, but she didn't have any other pictures of him, so I always imagined him looking like this, living in this house."

"You never met your dad?" asked Eric.

Edgar shook his head. "Mom was super sensitive about him. I have a twin sister, Lucy, and when we would ask questions about him, Mom would always clam up. Lucy said it was because he left her in the lurch, pregnant with twins, and disappeared. Maybe she could never forgive him for that. You can't imagine how many days I stayed by the window hoping he would walk up to the front door. When that didn't happen, I watched the cars that drove by. I thought maybe he was ashamed to come home, but he'd want to know how we were doing because he still loved us, and he might drive by." Edgar shrugged. "Maybe he did and I never knew about it."

He appeared to be a little bit more relaxed now. "When you're a kid, your parents are superstars, you know? I guess every kid thinks a missing parent will show up one day with a story about rescuing the world."

His hand trembled as he focused on the photo. "I spent my whole life on the lookout for him. Hoping I would see him in a crowd or a store somewhere."

I reached for the photo and glanced at Edgar, comparing him to the man in the picture. They both had dark hair in a similar cut, and a slender build.

He smiled. "Mom always said he was the best-looking man she ever saw."

"Is she still alive?"

"She's in Ohio, living in the house where I grew up. Never did marry anyone. I think he was the only one for her. Even all these years later, I wonder if she's still waiting for him to find her."

"Find her?"

"They lived in Washington at the time they were dating. But she moved home when she was pregnant. They weren't married. I guess she needed family around to help her with two babies. But now Lucy needs a kidney. I'm not a match, and none of the relatives on my mom's side are matches. It seems like a long shot that a man who never bothered to find us would donate a kidney, but I had to try. She's on the kidney transplant waiting list, but the doctor recommended trying to find Dad anyway. If he has other children, one of them might be a match."

"You're just going around town asking if people know him?" Eric looked at him in disbelief.

"Pretty much. We tried Facebook and other social media, but we couldn't find anything. I even submitted a"—he made a fist and circled it in front of his mouth—"swab to be tested for a DNA match. That didn't yield any helpful results, either. It must seem stupid to you. The first thing I did when I got to Washington was look for the house in the picture. Imagine my amazement at finding the exact house. I was so excited. What if he lived in the house? There was a sign out front that said *Basement Studio for Rent*. I sucked up all the courage I had, imagining that he might answer the door when I knocked on it. But it was Dolly who answered."

"That must have been disappointing." I sat down beside him.

"I hoped she might have a husband and when she told me her husbands had all died, I asked if I could see pictures of them. Even though he wasn't one of her husbands, I felt kind of like I had found him. At least, I knew he had been here. He had walked these sidewalks. He had come to this neighborhood and strolled by all these houses." Edgar wiped his nose. "It was kind of magical, you know? I found a place where I knew my dad had been."

"Did Dolly recognize him?"

He sniffled and coughed. "She didn't know him. I had hoped he might have been attending a party here or something. It's silly but I feel like his spirit is here. Even if he was just passing by when he posed for this photo. He was here! My mother's sister had never said a single thing to me about my dad in all the time I was growing up. He was off topic. Not a word. But when I was getting in my car to drive down here, she stopped me out of earshot of my mom." He smiled a little. "She gave me a package of freshly baked chocolate chip cookies for the trip and said, 'Edgar, you need to understand that your dad might not want to be found. If you go asking the wrong people about him, you might scare him off.' "

My heart went out to him. I could see the little boy in him still suffering because Daddy never came back. I couldn't imagine how awful it would be to not know my father. It would be like a part of me was missing.

"He might have another family now," said Edgar. "If he heard I was looking for him, he might hide or leave town. I could be the last person in the world he wants to see."

I gazed up at Eric, wondering if he was thinking the same thing I was. I couldn't say it out loud. Not in front of Edgar. A man who disappeared? Surely the thought must have crossed

Edgar's mind by now that his father might well be the skeleton in Dolly's attic.

Edgar's sad tale made me feel a little bit guilty for having slightly whacky parents who loved their golden retriever, Veronica, and me more than anything. Edgar's anguish would never leave him as long as he didn't know what had happened. Maybe if he found his dad, he could get some resolution and put that part of his life in perspective. Even worse, if he didn't find him, his sister might die. It was a long shot all right, but if it were Veronica, I would do everything I could to help her, no matter how unlikely it seemed.

"What's his name?" asked Eric.

"Thomas Jones. It's so common that it's almost hopeless. Still, I have to try for Lucy."

"What are you doing to find him?" I asked.

"When I told Mom I was coming here to search for him, she said he used to be a trader."

"Stock market?" I asked.

"Flea market," he said. "He traveled around to flea markets where he sold things and acquired new stuff to sell." He tilted his head sheepishly. "I'm checking around town with antiques dealers and junk shops, hoping I'll run into someone who recognizes him."

I had such mixed feelings. Edgar's story about his sick sister, Lucy, made my heart go out to him. But there must have been a reason that his assailant thought he had *The Florist*. Could this sweet and anguished man have murdered Dolly for the book? But wouldn't he have taken off if he had? It would have been easy enough for him to disappear into the night. True, one would hope the cops would have found him. I didn't know what to think about Edgar Delaney.

Eric's presence bolstered my bravery. I looked Edgar straight in the eyes and asked, "Do you have *The Florist*?"

"No. And it would be fine with me if I never heard of it

again." He looked at Eric. "Do you think it's safe for me to stay here? What if he comes back and kills me?"

"I'll ask for a car to swing by here now and then. In the meantime, don't open your door to anyone you don't know."

The EMT crew marched in at that moment. They tended to Edgar first, but one came over and checked me out, too. I insisted that I was fine, but he warned me to rush to the emergency room at the slightest sign of a headache.

I was beginning to feel the strain on my muscles, but other than that, I was okay.

Eric and I left Edgar in the capable hands of the EMTs. He was refusing to go to the hospital, which I took as a sign that he felt better and was getting over the shock of being attacked.

We paused at Eric's car, and I asked, "Do you think the skeleton could be Edgar's dad?"

Eric took a deep breath. "For the sake of Edgar and his sister, I hope not. When he's a little calmer I can ask him about the possibility of doing a DNA match."

"They can get DNA off bones?"

"Sure. Unfortunately, the time frame fits. The picture doesn't mean much, but it does place him here, assuming that it *is* his dad in the picture. It would be interesting to know if the Beauton sisters recognize him."

"By the way, Olivia wanted me to tell you she saw Nolan at the house the night Dolly was murdered. But you're not supposed to let on that it was Olivia who ratted on him."

"Because?"

"Priss has a thing for him."

"Heaven forbid a murder investigation get in the way of a romance," he quipped. "I may have to pay them a visit. As long as I don't tread on homicide's turf."

I waved as he left. I had been away from the store for hours. Bob and Veronica would be wondering what happened to me. I stretched a little bit to see if the gardening lady across the street happened to be outside. Maybe she had gotten a good look at Edgar's intruder.

I crossed the street and walked up to her front door. But when I knocked, there was no answer. On a whim, I peeked into the garden behind the house, but she wasn't anywhere to be seen. When I returned to the sidewalk, I noticed a baseball cap hanging on her climbing roses as though someone had thrown it in haste. Someone who had just threatened Edgar and who had plowed over me.

I jumped up to snatch it but missed. The curse of being short. Dolly's neighbor was too precise about her garden to leave twigs or sticks lying around. I jumped repeatedly until I managed to knock the baseball cap to the ground. Proud that I had managed to retrieve it, but sore from my encounter with the mysterious man, I finally headed back to Color Me Read. The second I walked into the store, Veronica and Bob descended upon me.

"If you're going to take half the day off, you ought to tell a person," growled Bob.

"I have been calling your phone for hours. Where have you been?" Veronica demanded.

Bob looked at my hands. All I held was the baseball cap. "At the least you could have brought us lunch."

I pulled my phone out of my pocket and showed it to them. "I'm sorry that I left you in the lurch, Bob."

When I told them what had happened to Edgar, their tunes changed.

"What's going on around here?" asked Veronica. "I understand needing money, but people are irrational about that book."

I sent Bob out to get lunch for all of us, then hung the baseball cap on a hook near the register. It might contain a hair that could be used to collect DNA. The cap would probably be the last thing the police would check for DNA, if they were willing to do it at all. Still, I planned to hand it over to Eric.

Over barbecued chicken sandwiches, Bob, Veronica, and I tried to make sense of the bizarre things that had happened.

"It all started with the discovery of *The Florist*," said Bob. "Before that everything was normal."

"Then Dolly was murdered, and *The Florist* went missing." I bit into my sandwich.

"You know it's kind of ironic," said Veronica. "The two people who broke into the bookstore committed a crime. Yet it would be to their advantage for us to know who they were because it means they didn't kill Dolly. If they had, they wouldn't have been nosing around here for *The Florist*."

"Have either of you seen anyone else looking around the store as though they were searching for *The Florist*?" I asked.

"There was the guy Helen was freaked out about." Bob popped a potato chip in his mouth.

"I don't recall hearing about that." I looked at Bob, waiting for him to swallow a gulp of soda.

"You know how Helen is. Anyone who isn't wearing the latest fashion is immediately suspect. He was an older guy. Lots of wrinkles. I didn't say anything to you because there wasn't anything wrong with him. He said hello and browsed around like he wasn't in any big hurry." Bob shrugged. "I didn't see the problem. Helen can get a little hysterical over nothing."

It wasn't much of a description. Most older people had wrinkles. "Did he have a British accent? He might be the one who threatened Edgar."

"British accent?" Veronica sighed. "We have loads of customers from the British consulate."

"It's hard to imagine that anyone could be so desperate that he threatened and choked Edgar. It sounds to me like it was Frederic van den Teuvel, so be super careful if he happens to come into the store." I took a sip of water.

"What does he look like?" asked Veronica.

"I'll draw a sketch of him. We can leave it by the cash register."

"What about Percy?" asked Bob. "Everybody is talking about the lawsuit Lucianne Dumont is bringing against him. No one is more desperate than Percy. If she gets a million-dollar judgment against him, he'll be ruined for life."

"We can't let that happen," said Veronica. "Percy is really a very nice guy."

I looked over at her. "Really? You're defending the dufus who put the book in a yard sale in the first place?"

Veronica glared at me.

Oblivious to her ire, Bob said, "Lucianne . . . would she hire someone to find the book?"

I shrugged. "I feel like we ought to put up a sign on the door that says *The Florist is not on the premises.*"

As afternoon shoppers drifted in with questions, we all got back to work. I drew a sketch of Frederic van den Teuvel and taped it near the cash register in a spot where it wouldn't be seen by customers. I had just finished when Olivia came in, poured herself a cup of coffee, and hung out around the checkout desk.

"Where's Priss?" I asked.

Olivia groaned. "You and I have a lot in common, Florrie. The older girls in the family are smarter, but the young ones get the men." She watched Veronica when she spoke.

I was taken aback. Maybe it was true, but she sounded bitter, while I didn't care a whit. "Priss is out with Nolan?" I guessed. "Can he walk yet? Maybe he's showing her apartments."

"Wouldn't that be a nice switch? I'm the one who does all the legwork. Just like you do."

"No luck yet? Did you check out Zsazsa's building?"

"I loved it. It's so modern. Quite a switch from Dolly's house. The two-bedroom unit is way too expensive for us, though. They showed me Zsazsa's apartment, which we could swing if we took on a little more work, but I don't see how we could carve another bedroom out of it. One of us would have to sleep in the living room."

"Like Dolly did when Maisie was growing up."

"Exactly." Olivia gazed at the table of new releases. "I just don't know. Stay here in Georgetown but live in a cramped situation, or move out of town and have some space and privacy. I think I'm getting too old to bunk on a sofa bed permanently."

While we were speaking, Percy waltzed into the store carrying a folder the exact size of *The Florist*.

Chapter 23

With a big grin, Percy plopped the folder on the checkout desk. "There you go."

"What's this?" My pulse quickened. Had he found the book?

"*The Florist*. You said you would authenticate it if I brought it in."

I opened the folder and didn't even have to flip the first page. It was painfully apparent that he had bought brand-new parchment paper designed to look old and had printed the pages off the Internet. I stared at him in shock. For once, I truly didn't know what to say.

Was he really that stupid? Or did he think I was that dumb? If Percy was actually so clueless, then I didn't want to hurt his feelings. On the other hand, part of me was offended that he would even try such a con. I opted for the simple truth and tried to say it without a tinge of irritation in my voice. "This is a copy of the book and it has no value."

At that very moment, Professor Maxwell walked into the store.

"But it's an *authentic* copy," Percy protested.

Huh? I had no idea what he meant by that but played along. "All right. It still has no value."

Percy blinked hard. His face brightened up and he said, "Thank you! Books are worthless. I tell everyone that, but they never want to believe me. Of course it has no value. That's what I need you to testify to. I'll give your name to my lawyer."

Professor Maxwell frowned at Percy. "I'm glad you weren't one of my students. No book is worthless. Between the covers of books lie the answers to the mysteries of life that men have pondered through the ages."

Percy stepped back and pointed at me. "She's the one who said it has no value."

"That doesn't sound like Florrie."

"He downloaded a copy of a rare book and printed it on paper made to look like parchment," I explained.

Percy appeared to be afraid of Professor Maxwell. He grabbed his papers and backed toward the door. Pointing at me again, he said, "You'll hear from my lawyers. Thank you for your help. You have saved my life."

He turned and ran out the door fast. I felt truly sorry for him. He didn't seem to be capable of understanding reality.

"Percy? Is that the fellow who sold Lucianne Dumont's priceless book?" asked the professor.

"The very same." I wandered over to the show window and watched him. Lucianne Dumont stood on the sidewalk speaking to no one. I assumed she was yelling something at the woman in her Bluetooth earpiece. I didn't think she saw me because she focused on Percy.

But then, when I least expected it, her eyes locked on mine like a gunsight on its target. Moving swiftly like a panther, she stalked toward the store and tried to rip off the sign we had hung in front announcing the upcoming release and reading of *From Fame to Infamy: The Dumont Family Curse.*

I muttered, "Lucianne is trying to tear down our sign."

The professor walked up beside me. "What is it attached with?"

"Chain from the hardware store. The sign is a tough vinyl with a backing so it can stand up to the weather."

"And apparently to Lucianne," chuckled the professor.

Lucianne pulled and tugged, but she couldn't rip it off. I thought I might have heard a few swear words. Her face had turned a frightening shade of purple. I had a bad feeling that she expected the hapless Angie on the other end of the phone to magically cause the removal of the sign.

"Lucianne had a few choice words to say about you," said the professor.

Uh-oh. I wanted to shout *I can explain!* But that would sound so lame.

I braced myself, but before I could come up with a defensive response that didn't sound juvenile, Professor Maxwell winked at me. "Keep up the good work, Florrie."

He ambled up the stairs.

Olivia shook her head. "If I hadn't seen that myself, I wouldn't have believed it. What a dolt. Maisie has no idea how lucky she is that she didn't marry Percy. He's a con artist but not smart enough to be a good one."

Veronica marched up to me and handed me her phone. "It's Mom." She walked away but only a few steps. She clearly meant to hear the conversation.

"Hi, Mom."

"Veronica says your phone is broken. Honey, I want you to get another one right away. I don't like not being able to reach you."

"I plan to, Mom. As soon as I get off work."

"Florrie, sweetheart—" I tried not to groan aloud. When she started a sentence that way, it could only be something she thought I would not want to hear. I took a very deep breath.

"—there's a concert in the park under the stars tomorrow night. I thought I would bring a late picnic dinner. I'm making the fried chicken you like so much! Anyway, I called your Sergeant Jonquille to see if he could come and he's available. Would you mind baking something for dessert?"

"Why did you call Eric first? What if I had broken up with him?"

Mom gasped. "You didn't! Oh, you're teasing me, Florrie. He would have said so if that had been the case."

"You do see the problem, don't you?" I asked.

"Is your sister there?"

"Four feet away from me."

"Pretend like I'm telling you a recipe. Two cups of rice. Veronica is bringing someone she likes. Your father and I are so worried about her. She says you don't like this fellow. What's wrong with him? Three cups of water."

"Is she pretending to give you recipe ingredients?" Veronica grabbed the phone from me. "Mom, I know that trick. You'll meet him and like him tomorrow night. And I expect everyone to be on their best behavior. Especially Florrie."

Veronica hung up the phone. "Please be nice to him, Florrie."

"Who is this guy? I didn't know you were seeing anyone."

"You'll meet him tomorrow night. If you love me, you'll be welcoming."

Oh swell. My eyes met Olivia's.

"You two sound just like Priss and me."

"Do I always criticize the guys you date?" I was immediately sorry I had asked.

Veronica's mouth fell open, and she gazed at me with an incredulous look.

"Okay. I get what you're saying. I promise, no matter who you bring, I will do my very best to be accepting. After all, you're the one dating him, not me."

"Thank you, Florrie." She waltzed off, smiling.

Now that I had to bake something for the next evening, I was relieved that Bob and Veronica were scheduled to cover the store that evening. Despite the fact that I had spent hours away during the day, I bailed out as soon as I could, with Peaches on her leash. My first stop was the phone store, where they informed me that they weren't sure they could transfer information from my old phone to a new one. It all depended on how extensive the damage was. I left it with them and hoped for the best.

When I was leaving, I heard someone call my name. Maisie sat at an outdoor table at the restaurant next door. I strolled over with Peaches.

"What a beautiful cat! And look how smart she is walking on a leash." Maisie picked up Peaches and cuddled her. "I miss my kitties so much."

She pointed to the other chair at the table. "Please join me. I hate eating alone. Besides, I owe you an apology."

I sat down while she continued to stroke Peaches.

"I'm sorry for the way I treated you. I've been inexcusably rude. I know I complain a lot about Mom, but if there's one thing she taught me it was manners, and I've been just awful. I hope you understand. First she was dead, then it turns out she was murdered, and then there was a skeleton in the wall. It seemed like every few hours there was another horrible development. It was all overwhelming."

Her phone rang and she glanced at it. "Ugh. I was stressed out even before Mom died. Last month I was driving at night when a deer jumped out of the woods and collided with my car. The deer leaped away as though nothing had happened, but the car was demolished. The trouble was that I still owed money on the lease, and I had to buy a new car. Insurance covered some of it, but not enough. Collection people have been hounding me. Phone calls day and night. They just don't understand that I can't pay the lease if I don't have a car to get to work. It's been a nightmare. And then on top of it all, Mom died. I've been at a breaking point for a while and, well, I'm sorry if I snapped at you. It wasn't anything personal."

"You look tired."

"I am. I can't sleep. I wasn't close to Mom for a long time, so I don't know what mischief she may have been entangled in. The police are convinced that it's that Zsazsa woman who murdered her." Maisie slugged back what appeared to be a daiquiri. "They tell me they found her lipstick in Mom's apartment under the coffee table."

"The cream-colored table?"

"That's the one. I guess that links her to Mom that night."

"They went out together for a late tea. Maybe she dropped it when they got back."

"Maybe that was when she murdered Mom. I'm with Olivia and Priss on this. There are a surprising number of people looking for that coloring book. I bet Zsazsa has it. The police are getting a warrant to search her apartment."

She ran a hand over her face. "Olivia and Priss—I feel so guilty. I had to give them their notice so I can sell the house. I don't know what they're going to do."

She set Peaches on the sidewalk to sniff around. "The remorse is overwhelming. They're really the only family I have left and here I am kicking them out."

"You're related to Olivia and Priss?"

"Not biologically. They were always there when I was a kid. Babysitting me, taking me to the movies with them, making popcorn, and watching the stars at night in the park. They were very good to me. Just like aunts. I remember going to them with my problems instead of to my mom. Sometimes it's easier to talk with someone else."

"I don't mean to abandon you, but I need to get going. I'm having some issues with my own mom."

Maisie was pretty and looked like Dolly when she smiled. "It's universal, isn't it?"

I collected Peaches and hurried along the sidewalk toward the carriage house.

"Florrie! Florrie!"

I paused, still holding Peaches.

Edgar loped toward me. "I never thanked you for coming to my rescue today. There's no telling what might have happened if you hadn't shown up when you did."

"I'm glad I could help you. And I'm terribly sorry about your sister."

"Sergeant Jonquille talked me into supplying some DNA." Edgar bit his upper lip and blinked hard. "He's worried that my dad might be the guy in Dolly's wall."

"Why don't you walk with me?" I suggested. "Let's hope that's not him. At least you'll know for sure."

"So why did you tell the flea market vendor we were married?"

I was on the spot. "Why did you ask him about *The Florist*?"

"I wanted to know what it was worth. Everyone was talking about it. I had shown him the photo of my dad. He's about the same age, so I hoped he might know him. He didn't. No one does."

"Edgar, with all respect for your aunt, maybe you should put that picture on Facebook and ask people to share it. If it wasn't your dad in Dolly's attic, he could be anywhere. He could have moved to California or Alaska."

"But what if he sees it and goes into hiding?"

"If it were me, I think that might be a chance I would take. Isn't it just as likely that he would contact you?"

"Maybe you're right. I'll think about it. I don't know what else to do."

Poor fellow. I gazed up at him. "My family is going to the park tonight for a starlight concert. Would you like to come along?"

"Sure! That sounds really nice. I've been kind of lonely since Dolly died. Should I bring something?"

"Not a thing. We'll have enough food to feed a football team." I gave him the time and told him how to find the carriage house.

I walked home, hoping I hadn't invited a killer to a family event.

Chapter 24

I spent the next few hours baking. The chewy salted double chocolate brownies were first. I watched the mixer beat the eggs with the sugar until they became creamy and thick. There was something about the ordinariness of sprinkling flaked salt on the brownies that I found comforting. No skeletons, no antifreeze, no beloved friends dying. I popped them into the oven to bake, watching the time carefully. I didn't want them to lose the satisfying chewiness.

When they rested on a baking rack on the kitchen counter, I started cupcakes. I had a package of sweetened shredded coconut that had to be used and my family loved coconut cupcakes. I cut back on the sugar in the batter just a little bit because the cream cheese buttercream frosting would be super sweet.

Methodically, I spooned the batter into the cupcake liners, making sure they were three-quarters full. When they were in the oven, Peaches and I ventured out into our garden. It was a lovely summer evening, the kind when the warm air feels like an embrace.

I drew a sketch of Edgar, wondering what his sister looked like. He resembled the man in the picture, but I wouldn't have known they were related if he hadn't said so. Maybe it was the

old-fashioned yet newly popular glasses he wore that made
him look different. Or maybe he looked more like his mom. I
drew the glasses with the dark tops and the clear bottoms.
They were a style that made a person look serious. Favored by
nerdy types, it seemed.

My thoughts turned to Zsazsa. I wondered what other evidence the police might have found in Dolly's apartment. Lipstick could have fallen on the floor any time. Even I could
defend that and I wasn't a lawyer.

Zsazsa and Goldblum had hit on something important. I
doodled a glass as I thought. Whoever had murdered Dolly
had either made a drink in Dolly's apartment, or brought her a
drink. The police were focused on orange juice, so I had to
believe they had found remains of it in her stomach. I switched
to a tangerine coloring pencil and filled the glass. I doodled a
straw and a wedge of lemon as a garnish.

I planned to take a cooling thermos to the starlight concert
the next night. That would be an easy way to transport a
deadly drink. It would be even easier for someone who lived
close by. Edgar, Olivia, Priss, or even Dolly's gardening neighbor might have made drinks and brought them over on a tray.
Of course, one would have to be careful that Dolly got the
toxic drink.

I hoped Zsazsa didn't have a cooling thermos. She probably did. So many people took water everywhere with them
that they were very common. No one would think a thing
about it.

The other point that stuck in my mind was that it must
have been someone Dolly knew well. She had opened the
door to that person. Unfortunately, it didn't eliminate many
people.

The timer went off in the kitchen. I hurried to rescue my
cupcakes. I slid them out of the oven and placed them individually on baking racks. When they cooled, I would frost them.

Satisfied that the bulk of the baking had been done, I returned to the garden where Peaches stalked a mouse.

Poor mousie. It was a good thing Peaches was well-fed. Her instincts forced her to focus on it. I hoped she wouldn't catch it.

For fun, I opted for an electric violet pencil and drew a little mouse peeking out of a hole. I hoped the real mouse had a hiding place to scamper to.

It was the calmest night I'd had in days. Even as the sun set, I stayed outside and drew, but as I checked the pages of my sketchbook, I found I had more faces than I did garden vignettes for the coloring book.

I was very glad I had swapped days with Helen. In the morning, I would go to Dumbarton Oaks for inspiration and try to get back on track.

I rose feeling fresh and eager to get going. I should have waited until the phone store opened to check on my telephone, but I decided it was better to do without it. I would go to Dumbarton Oaks, spend the morning sketching without interruptions from my mother, and then check on the phone.

I spooned Crabby Cat Crabmeat into a bowl for Peaches. She ate with gusto. I assumed it was tastier than mouse.

When she was through, she sat in a sunbeam and carefully washed her whiskers.

I made myself an insulated stainless steel water bottle full of hot tea with just the right amount of sugar, sealed it, grabbed my sketchbook, and said goodbye to Peaches.

She didn't seem to care. It was naptime now that her tummy was full of Crabby Cat.

Dumbarton Oaks was a historic estate, now open to the public. The sprawling gardens were still carefully tended. I opted for the fountain terrace and settled on the grass.

An iron gate hung open as though welcoming visitors.

Stone pillars and fences enclosed the area. Overflowing summer blooms lined the enclosure. And in the middle of a manicured lawn were two pools, each with a small child in the center holding a fish from which water spouted.

There were inspiring views everywhere I looked. I focused on the magnificent fountains and sketched, wondering if the artist of *The Florist* had done something similar in his quest to draw precise images of flowers.

I focused on my work, oblivious to the other visitors who came and went, until someone sat on the grass beside me.

"I hope you don't mind if I join you?"

I looked to my right. "Mike, right?" It was the man who had left a drawing of me in my sketchbook. The truth was that I did mind, but what could I do? If he talked too much, I would make an excuse and find another spot. "That drawing of me was great."

"It's been a long time. I'm quite rusty. This is a magnificent place. Imagine what it must have been like to live here."

"Like royalty," I said. "But think about the cost of upkeep."

"No kidding. I'm sure they didn't mow their own lawns." He smiled at me.

"Are you visiting every park and garden in the city?" I asked.

"I lived here for years without ever knowing about this place. No, I am here to enjoy the beauty and wonder of life."

I looked over at him again.

"Like that hummingbird. I'm told they are a healing symbol. They're supposed to help us endure and see the positive when we are troubled."

"I should incorporate one in my coloring book. We all need that!"

I flipped the page and doodled a hummingbird.

"Are you troubled?" he asked.

"A dear friend was murdered and I think they have the

wrong suspect. But I'm not making much progress in figuring out who really murdered her."

"That would be a woman named Dolly?"

"How did you know?"

"I read the newspapers. The skeleton in her attic ensured a lot of publicity about her death. I, too, am looking for someone."

"A long-lost girlfriend?" I teased.

Fortunately, he smiled. "I'm looking for a man who"—he held up his hand and snapped his fingers—"disappeared into the mist of humanity." His mouth twitched from side to side. "He stole some very valuable items and vanished. But, you see, I intend to find him. While there are many faraway places on this planet and many places to hide, he will not escape me. Not even if it's the final thing I do in my time on this earth."

"You're scaring me a little bit. You don't intend to harm him?"

"Ah, that's where the concept of forgiveness comes in. I could say bygones can never be recaptured and let it go. But he took over twenty years of my life. I am sorry to say, that I don't think I can simply wash that away. It clings to me like a coffee stain on a crisp white shirt."

I was almost afraid to ask exactly what he meant. "How could anyone take years of your life?"

"I went to prison for a crime he committed. For twenty-seven years I was incarcerated and could not live my life. Meanwhile, the real criminal was never arrested. Each day he was able to sit in the sun, to hold the hand of a loved one, to lick an ice cream cone, and hear the melodious laughter of children."

Why hadn't I stayed home and sketched in my tranquil garden with Peaches prowling around the koi pond?

"You needn't look so distressed. The point is that I did *not* commit a crime. But now everyone thinks I did. I paid the price for someone else's crime. And it was a very dear price.

Now I bear the grand title of felon. Most undeservedly. There are no jobs available to me. Who wants to hire a felon? I wouldn't."

"But if you find this man you can prove that you were not the thief."

He cocked his head. "Maybe. Twenty-seven years is a long time. There's no telling what he did with the items he stole. As far as I know, they never turned up again. Either he still has them or he sold them on the black market. If so, the current owner spent many years with the knowledge that I was not the one who stole them, and he allowed me to rot in prison rather than give up his precious acquisitions."

"Does this have anything to do with Orso?"

His eyebrows lifted. "You know Orso?"

I smiled at him and shrugged. "I read the newspapers."

Mike bellowed. His hearty laugh rumbled through the garden. "It's too bad I never had children. I would have enjoyed a daughter like you."

He got to his feet. "I hope we meet again, my dear Florrie."

While his face was fresh in my mind, I tried drawing it. Like Professor Maxwell, his face was a roadmap of wrinkles. I would have to study him to get them right. He had the standard horizontal worry lines across his forehead like Nolan. And the equivalent of a quotation mark between his eyebrows. His lips were so thin that his mouth was little more than a slit. I added a longer tip to his nose. It was prominent but attractive. It suited his face, but there was no pug nose on that man.

By midafternoon, I was pleased with my progress and ready for a bite to eat. I closed my sketchbook and returned to the phone store.

They proudly brought out a new phone with all my old information on it. One item accomplished!

All day long, I had dreaded the starlight concert in the park. Normally, it would be the sort of thing I enjoyed, but the pressure was on to be warm and welcoming to Veronica's new beau. I wasn't my sister's keeper. And I didn't want to be like Olivia and Priss. If this mystery man was the man of Veronica's dreams, the least I could do was welcome him into the family. Right now, I reminded myself, they were only dating. So all I had to do was be civil.

In the early evening, I wrapped up the brownies and coconut cupcakes I had baked. I packed them into a picnic basket along with two large thermoses of fruit spritzer. Eric and Edgar arrived just as I was pulling out an old blanket to sit on.

I opened the door and did my level best to sound cheerful. "Ready to relax under the stars?"

I handed the picnic basket to Eric and the blanket to Edgar. As I was locking the door, I spied Mr. DuBois looking out the window. Excusing myself, I hurried to the back door of the mansion and knocked on it.

Mr. DuBois opened it. He was leaning on his crutches. "We're headed to the park for a starlight concert. Would you care to join us?"

Mr. DuBois gazed at Eric and Edgar. "Thank you for your kind invitation, but I must decline."

I raised my eyebrows. "We can help you walk."

"Miss Florrie, I abhor leaving the premises after dark. Sitting in a field on the ground among hundreds of other sweating people is not my idea of a pleasant experience. Concerts are to be enjoyed in a concert hall with finely constructed acoustics. One dresses for such an event and sits in a chair without the smacking noises of one's neighbor consuming potato chips."

"Aww, come on. I think you would enjoy it."

"I fear you have a wildly misguided notion about what would please me. Have a pleasant evening."

The three of us walked away, but not before we heard the bolt on the door snap shut.

"What's with him?" asked Edgar.

"He's very proper, but I have a suspicion that he's somewhat agoraphobic."

Edgar glanced at me, evidently confused.

"He likes to stay home," explained Eric.

The park wasn't far from the Maxwell mansion. Eric and I spotted Veronica and my mom immediately. They had staked out one of the best spots. It was out in the open where we would be able to see the stars and the orchestra.

And then I spotted Veronica's new boyfriend. The one she had made such a fuss about. The one she wanted Mom and Dad to meet.

Percy McAllister.

Chapter 25

I could feel my cheeks growing pink. Maybe it wasn't fair of me to categorize Percy as a dolt. I knew he was wrong about books. And bringing me a homemade copy of the book everyone was looking for was peculiar at best. I wanted to bang my head against a wall. How could Veronica fall for him? I sucked in a deep breath. All I had to do was say hello and make a point of sitting as far away from him as possible.

I forced a broad smile. "Hi, Percy."

I introduced Edgar to everyone and spread the blanket on the grass. It was the first time Eric had met my dad. I knew Eric was a great guy, but even if my dad wasn't as impressed with him as I was, Percy would make Eric look like Einstein.

The sun was setting, and the orchestra began tuning. Mom set out an array of olives, pickles, dips and chips, and baskets of her famous fried chicken. I passed her my brownies and coconut cupcakes to add to her spread as she liked.

We sat around in a circle, noshing on the goodies.

"So, Percy," said Dad. "I hear you handle estate liquidation. That must be an interesting job."

Percy picked up a chicken leg. "You'd be surprised what I

find going through people's personal stuff. One lady had a buckeye in every drawer in the house!"

"That's so sweet," said Mom. "They're for good luck."

"I threw them away," said Percy. "The dumpster is my best friend. There was a man who filled sketch pads with pictures. Dozens of them. He had a ton of paintings on the walls, too. Nobody wants that junk."

I caught Veronica's desperate look in my direction. Ordinarily, I might have said something, but I didn't need to bother. Percy was doing a fine job digging his own hole.

"What's the most interesting item you ever sold?" asked Edgar.

"That's easy. A restored 1964 roadster Mustang. Coolest car I ever saw. I'd have bought it myself if I could have afforded it."

"Are your parents in the estate sales business?" asked Dad.

"Nope. My mom works at the Department of Labor."

"And your father?" Mom asked sweetly.

"He split before I was born."

"Kind of like my dad," said Edgar. "He didn't split, though. He just disappeared."

"I'm so sorry for both of you," said Mom. "I'm sure they would have been proud of you."

The music started as the first stars became visible. An hour later, most of us were on our backs or leaning on our elbows gazing at the night sky. I could hear Percy telling Veronica how beautiful she was. *Barf.*

Eric lay on his back between Edgar and me. Eric had just turned on his side to look at me when we heard a bang like a firecracker had been set off. In the night sky, I watched a glowing missile soar upward, arc, and drop, heading straight for us.

Everyone scattered. I grabbed Eric and rolled him away into the spot where Edgar had been. For a moment, I thought the firecracker had missed us. But Eric jumped up with a howl and flicked the burning remnant off his bare leg and onto the grass. The grass caught fire immediately. The music screeched to a halt.

I could smell singed hair burning and promptly dumped an entire bottle of ice water onto his leg.

Edgar grabbed the blanket, threw it on the grass, and stamped out the flames.

My dad took a closer look at Eric's leg. "Son, I think we'd better get you to the emergency room."

I could hear my mom calling 911.

A stranger ran over. "I'm a doctor. Everyone okay?"

We all pointed at Eric's leg. I could see that he was in a lot of pain. He was trying hard to be brave about it. But I felt enormously guilty. If I hadn't rolled him in that direction, he might be all right.

The EMTs arrived within minutes. They had Eric on a stretcher in no time. I grabbed his phone and wallet, and promised to meet him at the hospital.

Veronica volunteered to open the store in the morning. Leaving the blanket and picnic basket to my mom and dad to take care of, I rushed out of the park and hurried home. I opened the carriage house only to grab my car keys, and then I was off for the hospital.

By the time I got there, the place was swarming with cops. I asked if I could see Eric, but the nurse merely said, "Get in line, honey."

Eric had a lot of friends. I could hear them talking about it.

"It had to be illegal. None of the legal fireworks could cause that kind of burn."

"It was probably some idiot kid who had no idea what he was doing."

"I was there. It took everyone by surprise."

It seemed like an eternity, but a doctor finally appeared. "I'm looking for a Florrie Fox?"

I could feel the heat rising in my face when I jumped up with everyone watching me.

He led me into the emergency room. Eric lay on his back. I walked over to him and clutched his hand. "I'm so sorry."

He murmured, "They want me to stay."

I could tell he had been given a heavy dose of something.

"Eric will be fine," said the doctor. "All things considered he was lucky. He sustained a third degree burn on his left leg. We're keeping him overnight as a precaution and to mitigate pain, but most likely, assuming all goes well, he'll be released tomorrow. He'll have to stay off that leg for at least a week. We'll give you detailed care instructions tomorrow."

"Okay. Can I stay with him?"

"Sure. But you might want to head home and get some sleep. He'll be out of it most of the night."

"I think I'd feel better if I stayed."

The doctor nodded knowingly and left. An orderly smiled at me. "I'm taking him upstairs now. Don't you worry, we'll take good care of him."

I followed along to his room. In a matter of moments, the nurse came in and checked his IV. While she did that, I peeked through his wallet. Ordinarily, I would have considered it the height of rudeness, but I needed to call his parents. I supposed it was unlikely that he had their phone number, but it was worth checking. I was fairly sure I had a card with my parents' names in my wallet so they could be contacted in an emergency. No such luck in Eric's wallet.

It was the first time I had used my new phone. I hoped there weren't many people named Jonquille in Paris, Virginia.

Unless . . . taking a chance, I rode the elevator back down to the main level and hurried to the emergency waiting room. But the cops were gone.

I stepped outside for a breath of air and spied two uniformed officers chatting in the parking lot. I hurried toward them. "Excuse me. You wouldn't happen to have come here because of Sergeant Jonquille?"

"Yeah," said the one with a mustache. "How's he doing?"

"He'll be okay. But I need to call his parents to let them know he's here, and I don't have their phone number."

Both of them pulled out their cell phones. Between searching the net and calling the station, it was only minutes before one of them dialed the number and handed his phone to me.

"Hello?"

It was a man's voice. "Mr. Jonquille?"

"Yes."

"This is Florrie Fox. I've been dating your son, Eric? I'm so sorry to tell you this, but he was in an accident tonight." I hurried to say, "He'll be fine but he's in the hospital. They want to keep him overnight."

I could hear a woman in the background asking him questions.

I gave him the name of the hospital. He promised they would be there as soon as possible.

After thanking the cops, I returned to Eric's room. He was sleeping peacefully. An hour later, the nurse came in to let me know that Eric's parents had arrived. "Only one at a time in the room with him," she warned.

I had hoped to meet them under better circumstances. It was two-thirty in the morning, and I was beginning to look like something the dog dragged in. Taking a deep breath, I marched out to the waiting room to meet them.

"Florrie?" Eric's mom flew at me. "Is he okay?"

As calmly as I could, I said, "They tell me he will be fine. In fact, the doctor said he was lucky."

"What happened?" asked his dad. "I thought he wasn't working tonight."

I told them about the concert in the park and the fire-cracker that had come out of nowhere.

"That should be illegal," his mom exclaimed.

"It is." His dad reminded me of Eric.

I worried that his mom might hyperventilate. In spite of her panic about her son, she was sweet. Someone I thought I would like. "The nurse said you can go back to see him but only one at a time."

His father was clearly the stronger one of the two, or maybe he was simply trying to keep a stiff upper lip for his wife's sake. "Go ahead, sweetheart."

Eric's mom wasted no time leaving to check on him.

A willowy woman about my age with long blond beach waves appeared to be with them. She blinked at me. "I always thought there was a height requirement for nurses. And aren't you supposed to wear a uniform?"

Uh-oh. I had met her type before. I held out my hand to her and forced a smile. "Florrie Fox. You must be one of Eric's sisters."

She pulled her hand toward her chest as if shaking my hand would be repulsive. "I'm the fiancée."

Chapter 26

What? What did that mean? Who called herself *the fiancée?* I didn't have to fight back the temptation to demand clarity. I wasn't the type to engage in a catfight. And I certainly didn't want to have this discussion in front of Eric's father.

"Do you know there's blood on your clothes? Don't they make you change if that happens?" she asked.

I looked down. She was right. But I could barely speak. Was she Eric's fiancée? "Everything happened so fast that I didn't realize it."

Eric's father had drifted to a window. He stared out at the night, his hands in his pockets.

"You're not a nurse?" she asked.

"No." I desperately wanted to get away from this woman. The conversation was surely going to take a nasty turn soon. But I couldn't return to Eric's room. Nor could I wake him and ask what the deal was with *the fiancée.* "Excuse me," I muttered as politely as possible.

I did my level best not to run down the hallway. I found a ladies' room but there weren't any paper towels, only an electric hand dryer. Great. Just great. I dabbed some water on my shirt but only succeeded in making a mess. I might as well have smeared it with mud. I immediately regretted looking in the mirror.

There wasn't much I could do. On so many levels this had been the worst possible way to meet his parents. But then, if the willowy mean girl was Eric's fiancée, it really didn't matter anyway.

I inhaled a deep breath of air and returned to the waiting room. Eric's dad had disappeared, but his mom had returned.

"Florrie, thank you for calling us. I feel much better now that I've seen him. If you don't mind, I'd like to stay with him the rest of the night. Eric's dad will drive Rebecca home and come back for me in the morning."

It was only right for her to be the one staying with Eric. If it were me in that hospital bed, my mom would want to be with me. I smiled at her. "I'm sure Eric will appreciate that. It will be reassuring for him to see you when he wakes. It was nice meeting you, even under these terrible circumstances. Good night."

"Good night, Florrie. And thank you."

I walked out with my head held high. What else could I do? But in the parlance of Ricky Ricardo, when Eric was better, he was going to have "some 'splainin' to do."

My phone woke me at eleven minutes past eight in the morning.

When I answered, Eric whispered, "Please rescue me. I have to talk fast because Mom will be back any second. Please, please, please let me sleep on your sofa for a couple of days. She's trying to spoon-feed me Cream of Wheat. Gruel, Florrie! Gruel!"

"Sure." The word slipped out of my mouth before I remembered Rebecca. Why did tall, leggy women always have romantic names like Veronica and Rebecca? And why wasn't he going to Rebecca's place if she was his fiancée? That discussion was one better had in person, I decided. "What time should I pick you up?"

"Come as soon as you can. The doctor has to swing by to check on me before they can discharge me, but I need to get out of here. Thanks, Florrie. I owe you."

I heard his mom's voice and the phone went dead.

Peaches jumped up on me and purred right in my face. Cat talk for "I'll have my breakfast now, thank you."

I crawled out of bed, flung on a bathrobe, and stumbled down the stairs.

I was feeding Peaches when someone knocked on my door.

"Miss Florrie? Miss Florrie?"

I recognized Mr. DuBois's voice and opened the door.

"A police officer was injured last night at the concert. That wouldn't have anything to do with your middle of the night arrival at the carriage house, would it?"

"Tea?" I asked.

"I knew it! You see what happens when people wander about in the nighttime?"

I made tea for both of us, loaded it on a tray with coconut cupcakes that I hadn't packed the night before, opened the French doors to the garden, and invited Mr. DuBois to the table. "It was an accident."

"Nonsense. It's all over the news that they're seeking a boy who was seen by several people."

"It was still an accident. It could have happened to anyone."

"Miss Florrie, you will please take note that it did *not* happen to me because I had the good sense to stay home. How is Sergeant Jonquille?"

"He has a fiancée."

"Oh my! Actually, I meant his injury, but that is rather disturbing."

"Yet he wants to stay with me while he recuperates."

"Oh, Miss Florrie! You didn't agree?"

"I did."

"Well, I'm not serving him. Are these coconut cupcakes?"

"Yes."

"Is this what you think is an appropriate breakfast food?"

I tried not to smile, but I did bait him. "Yes. Are you intimating that one does not eat cupcakes for breakfast?"

"There is no need to be a smarty. They're rather tasty. Eggs, butter, flour. All reasonable breakfast ingredients commonly consumed in pancakes. You have simply rearranged them into a delicious little package. One always learns new things. Back to Sergeant Jonquille. He carries a gun and if I am not mistaken, he will be expected to have it here with him, so I have no objection to his presence on the premises. Particularly since there was another garage break-in and Maxwell has been keeping irregular hours."

"I just don't understand what someone would want in a garage unless he was after the car. Did he steal the car?"

"He did not. But what he stole is irrelevant. It was only two houses away!"

"Mr. DuBois, you have that fancy security system we had installed earlier in the summer. Whoever is breaking into garages would be a fool to come here."

Mr. DuBois appeared pleased and sipped his tea. "Especially now that we will have our own armed guard on the premises. What time did you say you were picking him up?"

When Mr. DuBois went home, I stood under a hot shower for longer than I should have. I was hoping it would wash away the tiredness I felt, but it didn't work out that way.

In case Eric's parents were there when I went to collect him, I made a point of wearing my favorite lavender dress that I thought brought out the green in my eyes. Not that they would care, but it made me feel like I was putting my best foot forward, and it didn't have any blood stains on it. Besides, the reading of the Dumont book was that evening and who knew if I would have a chance to change clothes before then?

I drove over to the hospital, hoping the doctor had okayed Eric's release. I dreaded the whole thing. All I wanted to do was curl up at home with a book and Peaches. That wasn't possible because I had to work. Still, in a perfect world, that's what I would have done. Clearly, my world wasn't perfect. Why had I put myself in this position? This was the time to walk away from Eric. To leave him to his fiancée. We hadn't been dating long. It didn't matter how much I liked him or how lovely he had been to me. For all I knew, maybe he was like that to everyone.

But I parked my car in the hospital garage, braced my shoulders, and took the elevator up to Eric's floor. A small crowd had gathered outside his room and a nurse was trying her best to shoo them all into the waiting room.

As I drew closer, I recognized his weary mom and dad, the dreaded Rebecca, and the two cops from the parking lot the night before. "Good morning. It looks like Eric is having a party."

The nurse turned to me. "Rules are rules. I'm sorry but we cannot have all of you here."

Eric's mother and one of the cops said, "Hi, Florrie."

The nurse's eyes brightened. "You're Florrie? You may go in. Everyone else to the waiting room."

Eric was sitting up in bed. "Thank goodness you're here. I love my mother, but she's been smothering me with love since I woke up. Can you get me out of this joint?"

"Has the doctor signed your release?"

"He's supposed to be doing that right now." Eric ripped the tape off his arm and slid the IV needle out.

"I don't think you're supposed to do that."

"Hand me my clothes?"

I really couldn't blame him. As upset as I was about Rebecca—*and why exactly was she here again this morning?*—I could relate to his desire to escape the hospital. I hoped we could at least remain friends. Handing him fresh clothes that someone, probably his mom, had neatly hung up, I asked, "Are you sure you want to come with me?"

Eric had swung his legs over the side of the bed. One was wrapped in bandages. He stopped and looked at me. "I would be a pest at your place. You think my mom should take care of me?"

I was horrified that my initial reaction to his question was to think that if he went home with his mom, Rebecca would be with him constantly. Was I turning into one of those terrible women who played games? I chose my words carefully. "Not at all. I only want you to be comfortable."

He blew a huge breath of air out of his mouth. "Thanks, Florrie. I'd much rather be here with you."

I was basking in the glow of his words when the nurse returned. "What are you doing?"

"I'm going home."

"You didn't know that you're not supposed to disconnect yourself from your IV?"

"You should be glad. Now you don't have to do it."

Under her breath, the nurse said to me, "It's probably a sign that he's feeling well. But I pity you, honey. Try to keep him off that leg." She handed me a stack of papers with instructions on them and, in a regular tone so he could hear, she rattled off what he was supposed to do. "Mainly, I want you to bring him to a doctor if it looks worse. And make sure he takes those antibiotics. He tried to weasel out of them this morning."

The nurse tried to coax him into a wheelchair. I wasn't getting in the middle of that argument. "I'll go get the car."

I scurried by the waiting room and fetched the car from the garage. When I pulled up at the front door to collect Eric, he was standing on one crutch surrounded by his parents, his cop friends, and Rebecca.

His dad helped him into the passenger seat while his mom whispered to me.

"Please call me a couple of times a day to let me know how he's doing. I know he'll try to make it sound like he's back to normal no matter what is really happening." She reached out and hugged me. "I'm so glad he has you to help him."

Rebecca wasn't as warm. She glided toward me like an iceberg and whispered, "You may have won this round, but the war has just begun."

Lovely. I slid into the driver's seat and closed my door to get away from her.

The cops were joking with Eric, but made a point of saying they would retrieve clothes and necessities from his apartment and bring them to the carriage house. That would delight Mr. DuBois. Three police officers hanging out behind the mansion would be like a dream come true to him.

I was relieved to see Veronica's car parked at the carriage house. She hadn't forgotten that she had to open the store for me. Happily, Eric had no trouble limping inside with one crutch.

"I don't need this thing." He stashed it in a corner before settling on the sofa.

Peaches wasted no time making him welcome. I brought him a mug of coffee and some snacks. After making sure he had his phone and a throw in case he grew chilly and wanted it for a nap, I was off to Color Me Read.

So much had happened that it was hard to focus. I tried to force myself to think about the event that evening instead of

Eric. The doctor had said he would be fine. As for Rebecca, that conversation would simply have to wait.

Veronica and Helen asked about Eric immediately. I assured them he would be okay.

"Thanks for being nice to Percy last night," said Veronica, giving me a hug.

"Sure." I glanced at my watch. "Is it really twenty past one? We need to get going."

The rest of the afternoon was consumed by preparations for the reading that night. We brought chairs up from the basement and arranged them in rows in the parlor where Don Moosbacher would read from his book. Veronica placed stacks of the book on the checkout counter and new-release table so people could find them easily to purchase them. I was planning to send Helen out for pastries, but I thought it would do me good to get out, so I went instead.

While I was looking at the selection of pastries in the bakery, I heard rapping on the window.

Edgar waved at me. He barged inside. "How is Eric?"

"He ripped out his IV this morning and escaped from the hospital. I think the nurses may have been glad to see him go."

Edgar smiled. "He must be okay if you're joking about him."

"How's your sister?"

"Spending a lot of time in dialysis. No matches have come up for her yet."

Edgar volunteered to help me carry pastries. The two of us were like children at the bakery, selecting all the yummy items we wanted to try. In the end, I bought petit fours, mini-cream puffs, orange chocolate tarts, spinach and Gruyère filled buns, lemon tarts, Snickerdoodles, and an assortment of cupcakes. I suspected we had bought far too many until we returned to the store. It was so crowded that I worried the fire marshal might show up and tell us we had exceeded our capacity.

Don Moosbacher shook hands and walked through the crowd like a celebrity. I overheard one elderly gentleman saying how glad he was that someone was finally brave enough to reveal the truth about the Dumonts.

Veronica and I arranged the goodies on tables that she had set up in the children's book room. Veronica kept the coffeepot filled, and I stationed myself at the front desk to direct people.

As they drifted into the parlor and took a seat, Professor Maxwell trotted down the stairs. He looked as tired as I felt.

"I assume you know that Mr. DuBois is upset about your irregular hours?"

"DuBois is always upset about something. You gave him the best gift imaginable."

"Coconut cupcakes? I hardly think so."

"Your charming Sergeant Jonquille. As we speak, DuBois is preparing Beef Wellington for him and two of his buddies."

"He said he wouldn't serve Eric. He's never done that for me."

"You, my dear Florrie, are not a policewoman."

"And to think I was going to buy a takeout pizza on the way home tonight." I smiled at him. "You look worn out."

"I am. I had hoped Orso would put my little van Gogh painting on the black market. It hasn't been easy finding the current underground dealers."

"That's what you were doing with van den Teuvel. I saw you coming out of a bar with him and some scuzzy-looking guy."

"As much as I loathe van den Teuvel, his roots run deep in the underground art market. It's big business, and he's a player. I've been touching base with people who might know if Orso had a van Gogh for sale. But I haven't had any luck. It may have gone straight to someone like van den Teuvel, who had a buyer waiting."

"I presume he wouldn't tell you if that were the case?"

"I doubt it. Not unless there was a hefty commission in it for him."

"Do you have a photo of it?"

"Of course. I should have realized my little artiste would appreciate it."

He trudged upstairs but returned quickly. Professor Maxwell handed me a picture that nearly made me choke.

Chapter 27

"Do you know if prints of your van Gogh sunflower were ever made?" I asked.

"Not to the best of my knowledge. It was bought by my great-grandfather in the late 1800s. I suppose someone could have arranged for the sale of prints during the ensuing hundred years, but I doubt it. Is it familiar to you? Have you seen it somewhere?"

I nodded reluctantly, my heart pounding. "I saw it or something very similar hanging on the wall in Olivia and Priss's apartment."

The creases between the professor's eyes deepened. "Are you certain? I'm under the impression that they would not have the funds for something like that."

"Maybe they don't realize what it is. People are always finding famous paintings in garages and attics."

"I'd like to see it. How could we arrange that?" he asked.

I was spared having to answer. Everyone grew quiet.

And then someone called, "Yoo-hoo! Florrie? Where are you?"

Veronica, the professor, and I were standing in the doorway to the parlor, watching as Mr. Moosbacher arranged his notes.

I knew that voice. Veronica whispered, "You'd better go shut him up."

I hurried through the hallway. Sure enough, Norman stood at the checkout desk looking around.

I whispered, "Shh. We're having an event. Why don't you sit down?"

From the parlor doorway I watched him take a seat.

Mr. Moosbacher began to speak. "Since we are in Washington, the hometown of the Dumonts, I'm sure many of you have heard stories about them. In my book"—he held up a copy—"I sought to sort fact from fiction. And let me tell you, it wasn't easy. For instance, who has heard about Ambassador Dumont's son, Lawrence, driving through town in a convertible in the buff?"

At that moment, Lucianne Dumont marched into Color Me Read with a man in a suit and a police officer.

She strode into the parlor, turned to the audience, and held up a document. "I have in my hand a restraining order against the publication of Mr. Moosbacher's libelous book about my family. It's nothing but lies," announced Lucianne.

Some of the audience appeared to be in shock, but a few of them snuck out of their seats. I knew where they were going and rushed to the checkout desk just in time to see someone who looked suspiciously like van den Teuvel leaving the bookstore. I had no time to peer out the window, though. People streamed toward the checkout desk. If Lucianne wanted to prevent people from reading the book, she had done the wrong thing. Now everyone would be itching to buy it. No one had shown *me* a restraining order. I was more than happy to ring up sales.

If Mr. Moosbacher was still speaking, I couldn't hear him.

Lucianne wound her way through the crowd and shrieked when she saw me selling the book. The man dressed in a suit, whom I assumed might be an attorney, and the policeman broke through the cluster of people, too. And Norman was right behind them. I heard Professor Maxwell's voice in back of me. "Keep selling, Florrie."

Norman pushed his way to the counter. "Florrie, I have something to tell you."

"Norman, I'm busy right now. Can it wait?"

"I'll stay right here until you're finished."

Ack! He was in the way of everyone waiting to buy the book. "Could you tell me tomorrow?"

As much as he annoyed me, I felt terrible about the disappointed look on his face. And he was still blocking everyone and slowing us down. "Maybe you could wait for me in the parlor?"

He drifted away, sad as a dog on a diet.

I sold books as fast as I could. Veronica slid them into bags and passed them to the customers. As far as I was concerned, Lucianne's restraining order was just too late. The horses were already out of the gate.

I could hear Professor Maxwell discussing the restraining order with the man in the suit and the cop. "We're not *publishing* it," said the professor. "This document makes no mention of a restraint on the *sale* of the book. Hundreds of bookstores around the country have this book in their possession and are currently selling it. We're no different."

Lucianne stared daggers at me. I had a very bad feeling she would make life hard for me if she could.

Mr. Moosbacher's book sold out. We didn't have a single copy left, which made me rather sad because now I was itching to know what was in it that Lucianne had fought so diligently to keep quiet.

When the hubbub died down and Mr. Moosbacher had left, I asked the professor, "What could it contain that would be so outrageous?"

"Every family has its secrets. I know mine does. The sad

thing is that Ambassador Dumont was a highly respected man. His grandfather, however, made a penny every which way he could including a few highly questionable ways, and the ambassador's son, Lucianne's father, spent every cent he could. That's not a secret. The man was a thief who considered himself above the law. My guess is that Moosbacher uncovered something wildly illegal that they did to build the family fortune."

Veronica and Edgar packed up the leftover pastries while the professor and I locked up the store. I turned off the coffee and the music, then walked the basement and the first floor to make sure that no one lingered behind. I returned to the front door and flipped the sign to *Closed*. Only when I turned around did I realize that the baseball cap was gone. Someone had swiped it. I hadn't seen van den Teuvel that night. Admittedly, it had been a zoo. And it was possible that the cap disappeared hours ago, but I hadn't noticed until now. Chills rose on my arms when I was forced to acknowledge that Edgar's assailant had been in the store.

The four of us walked back to the mansion together. While Edgar and Veronica told the professor what had happened to Eric, I was thinking about getting another look at the sunflower painting in Olivia and Priss's apartment. When we reached the carriage house, I entered first to be sure Eric wasn't sleeping.

He sat on the sofa with his leg up, playing poker with his two police friends and Mr. DuBois.

I waved at the professor, Veronica, and Edgar. "You can come in."

We opened the package of pastries, the professor brought over a couple of bottles of wine, and we had an impromptu party.

I was in the kitchen when Eric limped over to me. He whispered, "Is it okay with you if Edgar spends the night?"

I shrugged. "Sure. But I don't have anywhere for him to sleep."

"Mr. DuBois has offered a camping cot that Maxwell takes on his adventures."

"It's okay by me. Is Edgar afraid to go home?"

"He's scared that guy will come back. Homicide ran a background check on him. Everything he told us was spot on, right down to the sister in need of a kidney."

"Did you ever question van den Teuvel about attacking him?" I asked.

"He's slick, Florrie. Except for the accent, we haven't got anything on him."

The cops, Veronica, and Professor Maxwell finally went home. While Edgar accompanied Mr. DuBois to retrieve the cot, I collapsed in a chair, dog-tired. I thought it would be best to get a good night of sleep before I broached the subject of Rebecca.

"Did you change your bandage?" I asked.

Eric grimaced. "It looks awful. Thanks for putting me up. I won't be in your way long, I promise."

Maybe it was because I was exhausted or maybe I just couldn't stand it anymore, I blurted, "So who is Rebecca?"

Eric didn't squirm. He didn't seem one bit uncomfortable about my question. In fact, he grinned. "She's my Norman."

"Norman!" I leaped to my feet. "I forgot all about him. He must have gone home." I explained about him coming to the bookstore during the mad rush to buy a scandalous book.

"He'll get over it," Eric assured me.

"So Rebecca is your Norman." I had not expected that response. I could understand and relate to that. "She's not your fiancée?" I asked just to be perfectly sure.

Eric snorted. "Is that what she told you? Good grief. I hope she's not telling anyone else that. I'd better check to make sure she hasn't convinced my parents we're engaged. Although I can't imagine my mom not mentioning it. Rebecca is a friend of my sister's and hangs out at my parents' house all the time. In fact, she works at my dad's restaurant. We joke about her adopting our family. We've all grown used to her being there."

"So your parents called her when they heard you had been hurt?"

"They didn't have to. Mom said Rebecca was the first to know. She had heard on the news that a police officer had been injured, and she drove over to their house. She was sleeping on the sofa when you called."

I nodded. "That sounds like something Norman might do."

Eric's expression changed to worry. "Oh, Florrie. Did you believe her? I'm so sorry. If I had known, I would have explained sooner." He reached for my hand and squeezed it. "For a couple of people who haven't been going out very long, we've certainly encountered some bumps in the road."

He scooched over, wincing when he moved. "Just to be perfectly clear, I'm not interested in seeing anyone else. I know you think you're boring, but I think you're pretty amazing."

I was about to kiss him when Edgar barged in carrying a camping cot. I spent the next few minutes bringing him blankets and helping him get settled.

It was past midnight when I fell into my own bed with Peaches by my side.

I slept until nine in the morning. I bolted out of bed when I saw the time. I had to open the store at ten. No lingering for me this morning. Maybe Edgar could pick up some breakfast for Eric. I rushed into the shower. When I was dressing in a sleeveless periwinkle shirt and an icy-white skirt, I heard voices downstairs. Peaches was nowhere to be seen. The scent of coffee and bacon wafted up to me.

I slid my feet into white sandals and walked down the curving staircase.

Mr. DuBois was serving breakfast in my garden. Hampered by his crutches, he told Edgar where to place the dishes. Stacks of blueberry pancakes with pats of butter melting on top of them got my immediate attention. "Good morning, Miss Florrie. I have your tea waiting, just the way you like it—a spoon of sugar and a splash of milk."

I sat down at the table between Eric and Professor Maxwell. I sipped my hot tea and pronounced it perfect.

Mr. DuBois beamed.

Eric was already eating pancakes. "Now we know how the other half really lives."

At Mr. DuBois's direction, Edgar passed me bacon and sausages.

Professor Maxwell appeared to be finished with his breakfast.

I checked my watch. "I would love to eat, but I need to open the store."

Professor Maxwell placed his hand over mine. "Bob is taking care of that this morning. You and Veronica have the day off. Fear not. I have made the arrangements. Helen will be there to assist Bob."

I looked at the professor. "What's up?"

"I should like to visit Olivia and Priss's apartment to see the sunflower."

Eric stopped eating. "Is there something special about their sunflower?"

Professor Maxwell told them the story of Orso while I indulged in the fluffy pancakes and salty bacon. My teacup was instantly refilled when I drained it.

It was a gorgeous summer day and still early enough to be comfortable. Peaches roamed through her private jungle and birds twittered in the trees.

"You're sure it's the van Gogh, Florrie?" asked Eric.

I excused myself and fetched my sketch pad. I located my quick rendition of what I had seen.

Professor Maxwell was looking over my shoulder. "That's it! Florrie, that's the painting."

"I don't understand," said Edgar. "Why would Olivia and Priss have a painting that was stolen?"

Chapter 28

It was a good question. There was only one answer I could think of. "Orso gave it to them?"

Eric held out his hand for the sketch pad. "May I?"

I handed it to him.

The professor leaned back in his chair. "Of course. Orso removed the four items from the delivery truck and gave them to someone for safekeeping. I had been working on the presumption that they were hidden but everyone knows it's easier to hide things in plain sight."

"Edgar, where's that photo of your dad?" asked Eric.

Edgar pulled it out of his wallet.

"Show it to the professor."

Edgar passed it to him.

"Is that Orso?" asked Eric.

Professor Maxwell peered at it closely. "No. He looks a lot like Orso, but that's definitely not him."

Edgar exhaled noisily. "I'm glad to hear that!"

The professor drummed his fingertips on the table. "It appears that Olivia and Priss are now key. Shall we pay them a visit, Florrie?"

"You can't just barge in and demand your sketch," said Mr. DuBois. "You need a pretense for visiting them. Otherwise they'll clam up."

"Quite right, DuBois. But if I were interested in buying the building, I would surely be expected to tour the house, including their apartment . . ."

"Florrie," said Eric, "do you think Nolan is up to showing the building this morning?"

"If he thought he was going to sell it, he would do backflips with two broken legs." I looked up his number and called him.

I admit that I felt just a hair guilty for lying to him. He would get his hopes up about selling the house. But just as I had expected, he was raring to go and agreed to meet us there at eleven o'clock.

Eric pushed back his waving hair. "I wish I could be there."

"No way. They would clam up. Not to mention that you're supposed to keep your leg up."

"Indeed," said Mr. DuBois. "I acquainted myself with the instructions for your care, and I'm afraid you haven't been following them."

"I get it. I would ruin the whole plan. I'll stay here and console myself by studying Florrie's sketchbook."

At ten minutes of eleven, Professor Maxwell and I set out for Dolly's house. "They live in the second-floor apartment. When you walk in, you'll see a wall full of paintings and photographs. The sketch is on the left in a black frame about an inch wide all the way around."

"I hope they haven't damaged it."

The professor greeted Nolan warmly, asking all the right questions about the house. "What kind of heat does it have? Does each unit have its own electric meter? Has it been rewired?"

Nolan did his best to limp along. But I noted that stairs were an issue for him. "You don't need to come down to the basement with us," I said.

"I should be with you when you view any occupied units of the house. You can see the third floor on your own." Nolan opened the door to the basement and stopped cold. "Seeing that it's you, maybe I can trust you to look at the basement unit by yourselves?"

I assured him that he could. The professor and I made quick work of the basement. Not that there was much to see. The laundry room, a utility room that appeared to double as a storage area, and Edgar's small apartment, none of which were remarkable or surprising in any way.

We walked back up the interior stairs.

Nolan knocked on the door of Dolly's apartment. We could hear footsteps approaching on the other side. The door swung open and we stood face-to-face with Percy. There was no mistaking what he was doing there. He wore a woman's robe of cream-colored silk embroidered with flowers. Yet he didn't appear to be the least bit self-conscious about his attire or, far, far worse, the fact that *I* had caught him with another woman. Most men would have been ashamed, or at least embarrassed, but Percy asked, "Is it eleven o'clock already?"

Nolan scowled at him.

I was taken aback. "I thought you were dating my sister."

Percy nodded. "Veronica. Nice girl."

Really? That was all he had to say? No shame? No blushing? No rapid chatter to try to defend himself? I had been right about him all along. He was a worm.

"Don't look so astonished, Florrie. See, Maisie and I were engaged once. And when she came back to town because of her mom's death and all, we sort of hooked up again."

"Good try, Percy. You were out with Veronica only a couple of nights ago."

"Yeah, I like Veronica. We have a real good time together. So, you wanna come in?"

Percy stepped aside and yelled, "Hey, Maisie! Nolan's here!"

I gasped when we walked inside. The paintings had been taken off the walls and the furniture had been moved.

Nolan glanced at me. "We're getting ready for the estate sale."

Maisie ambled out of the bedroom dressed in high-fashion jeans and a T-shirt that sparkled with blue and silver sequins in an abstract design. "Hi. Excuse us. We'll be outside." She crooked her finger at Percy and ushered him out the front door.

"Well that was awkward," said Nolan.

While he showed the professor the bedroom, I remained in the kitchen, wishing I had thought to study it before Maisie arrived. Finding orange juice now would be meaningless. If Dolly's killer had made the antifreeze drink in her kitchen, everything would be washed up or thrown away by now.

Finally, it was time for us to see the second-floor apartment. Nolan climbed the stairs slowly. After three steps he said, "Florrie, run up there and see if Olivia or Priss is home. Maybe I don't need to walk up. Here's the key for the third-floor apartment."

"No problem, Nolan."

The professor and I walked up to the door. I knocked on it. The pretty wreath and the pillow on the bench were gone.

Priss opened the door. "Florrie! Nolan told us he was showing the apartment today. Where is he?"

Whispering so I wouldn't embarrass him, I said, "His ankle is killing him, so he's going to wait downstairs."

"Poor Nolan. That fall really banged him up." Priss flitted out to the railing and looked down at him. "Hi, Nolan! How are you feeling?"

She kept talking to him, so the professor and I stepped inside and greeted Olivia. While the professor made small talk, my mouth fell open. There wasn't a single thing left on the wall.

"Your wonderful paintings," I gushed. "They're gone!"

The professor didn't show any sign of dismay. "Pity. Florrie was telling me about a painting of a sunflower. I collect them and thought I might be interested in buying it from you."

Olivia avoided my gaze. "Really? I don't think it's worth much." She eyed some boxes that clearly contained paintings. "We're packing up for our move. I think it might be in this one."

She dug in the box and pulled out a black frame that I recognized. I could hardly breathe.

Chapter 29

Olivia held it out to us. "Is this the one?"

The frame was the same, but the image inside had been drawn with a black pen and colored very well with beautiful mustards and apricots. But it clearly was not a painting.

The professor glanced at me.

I had no idea what to say. Mostly I was angry with myself because I hadn't been prepared for this. "Do you have another one? One that is a painting? An oil, I think it was."

Olivia tilted her head like a confused puppy. "No. This is the only sunflower that we have. It's the one you admired the other day. Would you like to have it, Professor Maxwell?"

At that moment, my opinion of Olivia took a nosedive. How could she keep a straight face? It made me question everything she had ever said to me.

The professor surprised me when he pulled out his wallet. "What are you asking for it?"

Olivia handled the situation smooth as silk. "It's not worth anything." She held it out to him. "You'd do me a favor by taking it. One less thing for us to pack. Unless . . . will you be looking for tenants if you buy the house? Priss and I would love to stay."

"I haven't decided whether to buy the house. But I promise I'll call you if I do."

"Thanks. It's very stressful having to move after all these years. We're pretty comfortable here."

The professor and I took a quick look at the kitchen and bedrooms, all of which were in the process of being packed.

At the door, Professor Maxwell paused and asked Olivia, "By any chance, do you know Orso?"

"I don't believe so. The only orzo I know is the little pasta." Olivia smiled. "Does he have an apartment for rent?"

"Not that I know of. He's an old acquaintance. I thought we might have a mutual friend."

After thanking Olivia and apologizing for having disturbed her, the professor and I trekked up the last flight of stairs. I slid the key into the door and opened it.

"So this is where the skeleton was hidden?" asked Professor Maxwell.

"Right there." I pointed at the spot where it had been.

"Not a bad little efficiency."

"You wouldn't find it creepy to sleep here knowing that someone had been hidden in the wall?"

Professor Maxwell laughed. "My dear Florrie. Better to know it was removed than to sleep here not knowing it was behind the bookcase."

We walked out, and I locked the door. Professor Maxwell stood at the top of the stairs and gazed down the stairwell. "I wouldn't want to fall down these stairs. No wonder Nolan wanted to remain safely at the bottom."

We walked down to Nolan, who was flirting with Priss.

"Ready to make an offer, Professor?" he asked.

"I'd like to think about it. Thank you for allowing us to see it. I hope your ankle is better soon."

"If you need any more information, just give me a call."

We said goodbye and hustled out to the street. We were

two blocks away before I said, "Olivia knows something about your van Gogh."

"Undoubtedly. She probably knows she has stolen property. I did find it amusing that the replacement piece was so childish. Didn't they think an artist would know the difference? It's most peculiar. But I got the feeling that she really didn't know Orso."

"I don't know. She was doing a fabulous job of lying about the van Gogh with a straight face. Besides, if she doesn't know Orso, then how did she get the van Gogh?"

"Therein lies the mystery. How did she get the treasure Orso stole, and what has she done with it?"

When we reached the mansion, Professor Maxwell thanked me for my assistance and went home. I could hear laughter coming from the carriage house before I reached the door.

I opened it to find Eric and Edgar examining my sketch pad with Zsazsa and Goldblum.

"Did she have the van Gogh?" asked Eric.

"She had taken it out of the frame and replaced it with a sunflower that she or Priss must have drawn and colored."

"So they know what they have." Goldblum frowned. "I suppose that makes them the most likely candidates to have murdered Dolly and stolen *The Florist*. They clearly have no compunction about possessing that which belongs to another."

I slumped onto the sofa next to Eric. "They must know because she hid it. What I don't understand is why didn't they sell it? I'm under the impression that they don't make much money. Selling that sketch, even underground on the black market, would have brought in a bundle and made their lives easier. They could have bought a condo!"

"Because they value the arts and treasure it?" suggested Zsazsa.

I supposed it was possible, but I doubted that. "So what are you all doing?"

Zsazsa asked, "I suppose you heard that Maisie discovered one of my lipsticks in Dolly's apartment?"

"She told me about it."

Zsazsa's eyes met mine. "It has to be a plant. I didn't lose a lipstick there. I would remember that. You know how I loathe being without my lipstick."

"I believe you, Zsazsa. Maisie said they found it under the coffee table. Maybe I shouldn't have snooped, but when I was going through Dolly's books and searching for *The Florist,* I looked under all the furniture, including under the skirt of that ottoman. There was nothing there. Nothing. I would have seen it. If it had been there, the police would have found it on their first sweep of the apartment. They were there for hours. I find it hard to believe that they would be so sloppy."

"Your drawings are lovely," said Goldblum. "I don't see any of me."

"They're just doodles, really. It helps me think when I draw the people involved. You haven't been accused of murder yet."

"Neither have you, but there's an excellent drawing of you in the sketchbook," he pointed out.

"Mike did that."

Eric raised his eyebrows. "First Jack Miller and now Mike somebody?"

"He's old enough to be my dad. I keep running into him at parks. On that day, I was helping a lady who fell, and he drew a quick sketch of me in my sketch pad. Wasn't that a sweet thing to do?"

"And this evil-looking guy?" asked Edgar.

"That's Frederic van den Teuvel. He's an antiques trader."

"Like my dad!" said Edgar.

"Good grief, I hope not. He's a scum bucket who deals on the black market. Professor Maxwell warned me about him. He turned up asking about *The Florist* right away. It worried me that he knew about it so soon. He's the one who probably choked you."

Edgar paled and took a long look as though he wanted to burn van den Teuvel's face into his memory.

"And the cute mouse?" asked Goldblum.

"Peaches was chasing a mouse in the garden. It reminded me that there's a mouse in Dolly's house that Priss is afraid of."

They chattered on about the lantern I had sketched. But I was still thinking about the mouse and remembered something Dolly's neighbor had said. I sat up straight. "The year of the goat. When was the year of the goat?"

They all looked at me like I had lost my mind. I looked up *year of the goat* on my phone. There were several options, but the only one that fit the time frame was 1991. "It was 1991 when the man in Dolly's attic died."

Zsazsa very kindly asked if I needed an aspirin or a cup of tea.

"Thank you, Zsazsa. But I don't think I've gone over the edge yet. Dolly's neighbor told me there was a time when they had so many rats in the neighborhood they called it the year of the rat, but it was really the year of the goat. It was a neighborhood joke. Everyone acquired pet cats at the time. I'm sorry to gross you out, but I bet the body in the attic was the reason they had a rat infestation. They're like vultures that don't fly. They eat up dead things. It's nature's way of cleaning up."

"That's the year I was born," said Edgar.

"What else happened in 1991?" Eric asked.

"It was the year that the Soviet Union dissolved," said Goldblum.

"I meant a little closer to home," Eric chuckled. "What was going on at Dolly's house? Who were her tenants?"

"Do you think she kept books about her rentals?" I asked. "She must have. Somewhere in Dolly's papers, Maisie must have that information."

"That was twenty-seven years ago. Wouldn't she have thrown them out by now?" asked Goldblum. "I don't think I have bank statements or anything that goes back that far."

Eric reached for his phone. "Those records seem like the kind of thing homicide would have asked for." He held a brief conversation with someone and then hung up. "They're checking to see if they have them."

I grabbed my sketch pad and wrote with a cobalt-blue coloring pencil, *1991* and *27 years ago*.

"How is that going to help anything?" asked Goldblum.

"It isn't," I responded.

Eric wrapped his arm around my shoulders. "On the contrary. It's a starting point. We're no longer casting about wildly. We have a place to begin. Now we need to figure out who went missing in 1991."

It was sweet of him to say that. In a way, I guessed it was true.

Edgar was busily working with his phone. "I'm looking up what happened in Washington, DC, that year."

"Isn't technology wonderful?" asked Goldblum. "Not that long ago we would have had to go to some damp basement and spend days looking through microfiche for that kind of information. What did you find?"

"Hey, you were right about Russia, Professor Goldblum. Looks like the homicide rates were high, and"—he gazed up at us—"you won't believe this. A van Gogh on loan from the private collection of the Maxwell family was stolen in transit to a local museum."

Chapter 30

"That has to be a coincidence," I said. "There can't be any connection."

"But there *is* a link, Florrie," said Eric. "You're the one who saw the stolen item in Dolly's house. There may not be a tie to Dolly's murder, but there's something going on there that involves a man hidden behind a bookcase and Maxwell's missing van Gogh."

"Do you think Olivia or Priss could have been involved in the theft?" asked Zsazsa. "Perhaps Dolly found out about it and threatened to expose them."

"After twenty-seven years?" said Goldblum. "If that was the case, it seems like it would have happened a long time ago."

"The man in the wall! Maybe he was the one who was going to expose them," I said.

"Now we're getting somewhere." Goldblum smiled. "Anyone hungry? I could use a nosh."

"Me, too," said Zsazsa. She plucked at Edgar's shirt. "Why don't you come with us?"

"I'm kind of grungy. I think I should stop by the house and pick up some fresh clothes."

"Excellent!" crowed Goldblum. "I would love to see the inside of Dolly's house."

Goldblum and Edgar rose to leave.

"I don't think I should go there," said Zsazsa. "My presence could be misconstrued. No, no, no. I should not go into that house. Not under any circumstances. Someone might call the police."

"Why don't you stay here with us?" I suggested. "When Goldblum and Edgar are done, they can meet you at a restaurant."

"Think you could bring back some takeout?" asked Eric. "My wallet is on the bookshelf."

"Better yet, Edgar and I will pick up something for everyone, and we'll bring it back here."

The two of them left and Zsazsa got up to brew tea. I felt like a terrible hostess and rushed to help her.

"How are you doing at Goldblum's?"

"He spoils me. A five-star hotel wouldn't do it any better."

A snore rattled through the room. We glanced over and giggled at Eric, who had dozed off.

I preheated the oven and pulled out my mixer. "How do mini-cheesecakes sound to you?"

"I love cheesecake! I've been eating far too much since Dolly died and this horrible nonsense started. It's soothing to me to eat. Isn't that awful?"

"It's hard on the waistline." I pulled out the mini-cupcake baking sheet and little liners. I handed half of them to Zsazsa to insert in the pan. "We have to get to the bottom of this. Maybe we need to look at motive."

"I have no motive to have killed Dolly. It's preposterous that the police could imagine that I would have stolen *The Florist* from her and then concocted a drink to kill her."

"Did you even enter her apartment that night?"

"We walked home from the tea room. I had paid because

she forgot her purse at Color Me Read. She was still so excited about having found *The Florist*. Other than Maisie's birth, I think it might have been the most exciting thing that ever happened to Dolly. Her house is on the way to my condo. I walked inside with her. She asked if I would like to have a glass of champagne to celebrate. I declined because we had already had champagne at the tea room and I had promised to edit a friend's article that evening. I didn't want to be giddy when I did that."

Zsazsa sat down on a stool. "If I had stayed, Dolly might be alive today."

"Or you would be dead, too. How long do you think you were there?"

"Just a few minutes."

"Did you go back to Dolly's that night?"

"No. I was home editing the article."

"So you couldn't have killed her. Unless you carried antifreeze around with you from the time you came to the coloring club until you arrived at Dolly's house that evening, there's no way you could have poisoned her."

"I think that's abundantly clear but that dreadful Holberstein fellow insists there are ways I could have done it."

I suspected there were. She could have planted the antifreeze somewhere or carried it in her purse like I had described. "What does he think is your motive?"

"*The Florist* naturally. That makes no sense at all. I didn't even know about the book until shortly before we came to the bookstore. Does he think I always carry antifreeze in my purse in case I feel like dispatching someone? It's absurd."

She was right about that. I popped two packages of cream cheese into the mixer and let it rip, wincing at the sound. I glanced over at Eric, who stretched.

I watched the mixer's arm circle around, and it dawned on me that whoever murdered Dolly probably planned ahead.

"No one knew about *The Florist* until Dolly brought it to Color Me Read. I wonder how many people happen to have antifreeze at home. I don't, and I don't think Veronica does. For that matter, I don't think my dad has any, either. Dolly's killer had only a few hours to buy antifreeze and concoct something he thought Dolly would willingly consume."

"And it had to be someone she knew. Everyone would be shocked if a stranger showed up at their home offering them a drink."

"That narrows down the field considerably," I said, while spooning the cheesecake mixture into the little liners.

"It would have been easiest for Olivia and Priss," said Zsazsa, "but they had an incentive to keep Dolly alive. They knew Maisie would sell the house if Dolly died, and they would lose their home."

"Which is exactly the fix they find themselves in now." I slid the mini-cheesecakes into the oven and set the timer. The two of us joined Eric while they baked.

I woke Eric when I slid onto the sofa next to him. "I feel just terrible for rolling you over last night. If I hadn't—"

"Edgar would be sitting here with a burn wound instead of me."

"Nah, he moved away. I should have pulled you in the other direction."

"Florrie, you can't make yourself miserable about this. No one knew where that firecracker would land. It was a fluke. It wasn't aimed at anyone."

I sat up. "What if it was? What if someone intended to have it land on Edgar?"

"A kid shot it off. I seriously doubt that he even knows Edgar," said Eric.

"Nolan," I blurted.

"You think Nolan shot off the firecracker?" asked Zsazsa. "Was he at the concert?"

"That's not what I meant. You were there," I said to Eric. "Remember when he fell down the stairs and said a step was slippery?"

"Right."

"And where was that?"

Eric blinked like he was losing his patience. "In Dolly's basement."

"And who lives there?"

"Edgar! I see what you're getting at. You think someone has been trying to harm Edgar?"

"Who was attacked and choked in his apartment?"

"Again, Edgar."

"Are you implying that the killer meant for Edgar to drink the antifreeze?" asked Zsazsa.

"It sounds kind of silly when you put it that way, but what if Dolly drank something intended for Edgar?"

Chapter 31

Eric smiled at me sweetly. "I think that's a very long shot. Besides, why would anyone want to harm Edgar?"

"For something he has. Didn't he say the person who choked him was asking 'Where is it?' "

Eric shook his head. "Your theory doesn't hang together. If Edgar had consumed the antifreeze and died, then he could never tell anyone where 'it' is."

He had a good point. The timer went off on the oven. I hopped up and headed for the kitchen, disappointed that we weren't making any progress. I pulled the mini-cheesecakes from the oven and set them on a baking rack to cool.

I glanced over at Zsazsa and thought about Mike and his anger toward the person who let him take the rap for a crime. I hoped Zsazsa wouldn't end up being convicted for something she didn't do. I didn't think there was sufficient evidence to build a case against her. But maybe the police had information I didn't know about.

The next morning, Mr. DuBois woke Eric and Edgar. I was up and dressed, ready for work, and tiptoeing around.

The first words out of Mr. DuBois's mouth were, "There was another garage break-in last night. Only one block away."

Eric reached for his phone and made a call. He probably hated being out of the loop.

"What did they steal?" asked Edgar.

"They don't know. That's the trouble with garages. They are packed with items one wouldn't miss until they were needed. Young Edgar, may I impose on you to help me bring breakfast from the mansion?"

"Of course. This beats cereal with cold milk any day!"

I watched Peaches while Edgar rolled in a cart loaded with food. The smell was divine.

Mr. DuBois uncovered various platters to prepare a plate for Eric. I dared to steal a slice of bacon.

"Miss Florrie! Sit down at the table properly, and I shall bring you a plate of waffles with fresh blackberries."

I checked the time. "I have a few things to take care of on my way to the bookstore. You fellows enjoy yourselves."

The morning air reminded me of the day Dolly died. I walked over to Dolly's house, thinking that the crisp morning was a hint that fall would be coming soon. Only on this day, it was the contents of Dolly's house that were spread out on her small lawn and the sidewalk in front of the house. I stood on the other side of the street watching as strangers helped themselves to the possessions that she had held so dear. Now that Percy was involved with Maisie, I assumed he was handling the sale. That meant there would be untold bargains. Some people would probably be like me and unknowingly buy something for two dollars that was worth much more.

Lucianne Dumont watched Percy with an eagle eye and spoke to the air again. Poor Angie on the other end of the phone. Did she have to listen to Lucianne all day?

I wondered why Lucianne would be there. Surely she wasn't

interested in any of Dolly's things. She hadn't even wanted the possessions of her own grandfather.

Not too far away, I spied Frederic van den Teuvel watching the goings on at Dolly's house. All of the hawks had come to feast. But I didn't think they would find what they wanted.

The Florist had made a brief appearance, and I for one was thrilled that I had been able to see it and hold it in my hands. Now it would probably be lost forever, or at least until the person who possessed it died. With any luck, it might turn up again sometime.

With a heavy heart, I walked through Dolly's gate, probably for the last time ever.

I walked over to Percy. "Are you selling Dolly's copy of *Winnie-the-Pooh?*"

"Yeah. I think that box is still inside. I'll get it for you."

"Thank you, Percy."

I doubted that he had even looked at the books because they appeared to be in the same boxes I had placed them in days ago. The only difference was that Percy had added a sign that read

Books
50 cents a piece
or
10 for $5.00

The guy was a genius. I couldn't tell Veronica about him, of course. She would have to see what he was like on her own. Maybe I could talk her into coming over to the sale so she would find out for herself. I didn't see Maisie around, but I suspected she must be nearby.

I pawed through the books in the box until I found *Winnie-the-Pooh*. When I lifted it, I noticed a plastic grocery bag on the bottom of the box. I didn't recall lining a box or putting anything into a grocery bag. Feigning great interest in more of the books, I removed just enough of them to pull out the grocery bag. It was heavier than I had expected.

My breath came fast and I could feel my blood pumping. Surely not. It couldn't be. I peeked inside the bag. *The Florist* had somehow made its way into another estate sale.

Painfully conscious of the presence of Lucianne Dumont and Frederic van den Teuvel, I decided not to remove *The Florist* for the inspection I was itching to do.

I slid *Winnie-the-Pooh* into the bag on one side of *The Florist* and a copy of *Cocky the Lazy Rooster* on the other side.

What had Professor Maxwell said? They used couriers who didn't draw attention to themselves and looked like they were simply going about their day. Trying my best to look casual, I rose to my feet and gazed around as if I were still shopping. The lantern that had been on the table in Dolly's garden was only two dollars. I didn't need it, but it would look lovely in my garden and I would always think of her when I lit the candle inside. It seemed fitting. With my booty in hand, I wandered through the tables to Percy.

"Three books and the lantern."

"Three dollars and fifty cents."

I was thrilled that I had correct change. All I wanted was to get out of there before a war started over the contents of the grocery bag.

I avoided looking at Lucianne or van den Teuvel and walked away at a leisurely pace.

I didn't relax until I was safely inside Color Me Read. I locked the door behind me, set the alarm so I would hear if anyone tried to break in, and ran up two flights of stairs to Professor Maxwell's office.

I was winded on my arrival.

The professor was seated at his desk. "Florrie! Are you all right? Your face is flushed."

Taking a deep breath, I very carefully pulled out the contents of the grocery bag, handling them like delicate eggs.

"Children's books?"

"I have to check the dates. I'm not sure they're worth anything. But look at this." I placed the leather cover on the desk in front of him and opened it.

"*The Florist*? Where did you find it?"

I told him what I had done.

He raised his eyebrows. "That's not like you at all."

"Don't worry, I'm going to hand it over to the rightful owner, Dolly's daughter, Maisie Cavanaugh. She can sell it to whomever she wants." I kneeled on the floor and eyed it.

"What are you doing?"

"Aha! Right there. It's the last page." I gently lifted it and turned it over. The bottom outside edge of the book had been torn off. "I'll bet anything that missing piece is what Dolly had in her hand when she died."

I set it down on his desk again and slumped into a chair. "In all honesty, I never thought I would see this book again."

"How do you suppose it landed in the box?"

"All I can imagine is that Dolly placed it in this grocery bag and Percy didn't realize what it was for the second time. If he had bothered to look into the bag he might have recognized some of the pages he printed out and made the connection. Do you mind if we keep it in the locked drawer in your desk until I can turn it over to Maisie?"

"You do realize that technically it belongs to you now? Even if you didn't do the right thing and tell Percy what it was. He sold it to you fair and square."

I shook my head. "It belongs to Maisie."

With *The Florist* safely stashed away, I returned to the first floor, turned on the music, made a pot of coffee, and looked up the phone number for a reputable auction house we had used before. They agreed to send someone over at noon.

I called Maisie and arranged for her to come to the store as well.

It took every fiber of my being not the spill the news to Bob. But when I had calmed down, I realized that my theory about Dolly having placed it in the bag was completely wrong. If she had done that, she wouldn't have had the corner of a page in her hand when she died. Whoever stole the book and murdered Dolly had slid it into the bag. But why? Why leave it in Dolly's house? Remorse? Guilt?

That question plagued me all morning. At noon, I introduced Maisie to Mr. Arthur Fenton and took them upstairs to the professor's office.

When they were seated, I unlocked the drawer, lifted out the bag, and gingerly removed *The Florist*.

Arthur blinked rapidly as he examined it. "This is in very high demand. Everyone in town is talking about it."

"It belonged to Maisie's mother, Dolly Cavanaugh. Unfortunately, Dolly has died, so it now belongs to Maisie."

"Well, you have quite the find here. Are you interested in selling it?"

Maisie looked at me. "Where did you find it?"

"In your mom's estate sale."

"Does Percy know about this?"

I shook my head from side to side.

Maisie paused for a split second, then said, "My mother would want me to sell it."

She looked straight at me as though she needed confirmation. "I think Dolly would want that, too."

Maisie began to cry. "I'm only sorry she's not here to see this happen. She would be so thrilled."

Chapter 32

Maisie accompanied Arthur back to the auction house, and I heaved a sigh of relief. At least the book would be safe until it was sold.

During a lull in the afternoon, I looked up my copy of *Winnie-the-Pooh*. I was painfully aware that prices fluctuate but it was in great condition and valued around eight thousand dollars. A similar copy of *Cocky the Lazy Rooster* had sold two years before for nearly fifty thousand dollars! Dolly always had a good eye.

Now if we could just figure out who murdered her.

It bothered me that the killer had taken the time to slide the book into a grocery bag. That meant it was someone who was very comfortable in Dolly's house. Someone who wasn't in any hurry to get out. Her killer had ripped the book from her hands while she lay dying and had calmly slid it into a grocery bag unafraid of being caught.

I slumped onto the sofa in the reading parlor. I was a complete dolt. They had used me, and I had fallen for their bait. What an idiot I was! I should have realized that Percy couldn't be as stupid as he seemed.

Sure, Maisie had an alibi back in South Carolina, but Percy

had been right here in Washington all along. He must have paid Dolly a visit that evening. Maybe to plead for the return of *The Florist*. He'd brought the toxic cocktail along with him. While Dolly was dying, he ripped it from her hands, slid it into the bag, and left.

But the problem was that if Percy sold it, he would become the number one suspect in Dolly's death. And Maisie couldn't very well claim to have miraculously found it after the cops combed the place and I had gone through all the books. So they took a chance on me. They hadn't forgotten to put that box of books out. They were waiting for me to do exactly what I did.

It was a no-lose situation for them. If I didn't turn it over to Maisie, all they had to do was claim that I was the one who had stolen it. I was a patsy.

I had no idea whether Lucianne's lawsuit had any merit, but it seemed simple enough to me. Maisie would sell the book and collect the money, while Percy filed for bankruptcy. Then the two of them would ride off into the sunset and live wealthily ever after.

Not if I could help it, they wouldn't.

That night, over leftover sweet potato gnocchi, giant grilled shrimp, and spinach salad with bacon that Mr. DuBois had cooked for them, I told Eric and Edgar what had happened.

Eric became very serious. "So when word got out about *The Florist* and Lucianne told Percy how stupid he'd been to sell it, he called Maisie and cooked up this plot? Ouch, but that's cold. Poor Dolly."

"I just don't know how to prove it," I said. Looking at Edgar, I added, "Unless you saw Percy at Dolly's house that night."

"I didn't know anything until I heard the ambulance pull up."

"Phone records," said Eric. "There have to be phone records between Percy and Maisie. He might have even texted her. People can be pretty dumb about that kind of thing." He picked up his phone and made a call.

"When I was going through Dolly's books, a friend of Maisie's came by and recommended Percy to handle Dolly's estate. Maisie acted like she didn't remember who he was. She played her role quite well."

I slept better that night knowing that it was Maisie and Percy that we had to watch out for. As long as they didn't know we were onto them, we should be safe.

Of course, the issue of Veronica still remained. But once Percy was arrested, that should fall in place by itself. I wouldn't have to be the bossy big sister.

The sun shone in my window the next morning, and I had renewed hope that the recent craziness would soon come to an end. I felt awful for Veronica. I couldn't understand what she saw in guys like Percy.

I showered and dressed for work, but this morning I was in no hurry. Edgar and Eric were just getting up when Mr. DuBois arrived with breakfast.

"When Eric goes home, and the breakfast service ends, I'm going to be very jealous," I said to Mr. DuBois.

He whispered, "Then I suggest you convince him to stay."

I probably should have been put out, but I laughed. Things were looking up. We dined on crab crepes, fruit salad, and the ever-present bacon at the table in the garden. Peaches walked the perimeter of the koi pond, watching the fish and occasionally dipping her paw in the water.

Over breakfast, we told Mr. DuBois what had happened. Eric assured him that homicide had been advised and that it was in their hands now.

I left Peaches with Eric and was off to work in plenty of time to open the store. When Veronica and Bob arrived, I already had everything up and running.

"We should receive that shipment of the Dumont book today," I said, looking at the long list of people who had requested it.

Veronica paid no attention.

"What's wrong with you this morning?" I asked.

"Percy showed up at my apartment in the middle of the night."

Oh noooo. "I hope you hid your good jewelry."

"Why do you say things like that? It's just mean, Florrie. You know what I think? You don't like sharing me with anyone else and that's why you hate everyone I date."

"He's seeing Maisie."

"That's a lie!"

"Veronica, I'm sorry. Really I am. I don't want you to be hurt."

"Then stop hurting me." She marched off in a huff and avoided me all day.

At four in the afternoon, Eric called me. "Have you seen Edgar?"

"Not since I left the house this morning. Did you misplace him?"

"I'm getting worried. He went to his apartment to pick up clean clothes. He should have been back by now. He's not answering his phone."

Normally, I wouldn't have been concerned, but someone *had* tried to choke him. I checked the time. "I'm due to deliver some books. I'll look in on him in half an hour or so."

Bob circled the checkout desk and faced me from the other side. "What did you do to Veronica?"

"I didn't do anything. She just has terrible taste in men. I hope she's not being mean to you."

"Eh. I think she'll be okay once you're gone."

I loaded the packages into a bag and felt like Santa Claus when I left the store. Most of the deliveries were close by, so the load lightened fairly fast.

Dolly's house appeared peaceful. The estate sale items were no longer in the yard or on the sidewalk. I sidestepped the stairs to the main floor and knocked on the basement door.

Edgar didn't answer. I tried the handle, but it was locked.

I knocked again. "Edgar? It's Florrie."

I stood in front of his door and called Eric. "He's not answering his door."

"I'm coming over there."

"You're supposed to stay off your leg. Besides, what are you going to do, bust the door down?"

"All right. I get what you're saying. What time are you coming home?"

"Six o'clock."

"Do you think I could convince DuBois to check on him?"

"I suspect he would do anything for you, but he doesn't like leaving the safety of the Maxwell estate."

"How does he get all this food he's cooking for us?"

"He receives grocery deliveries at the mansion from stores all over town."

"No wonder he likes me so much. I'm a captive audience. He must get lonely in that big house by himself."

"I'll see you at six." I hung up and looked around. Out of an abundance of caution, I walked up the steps to the front door of the house. When I tried the door handle, the door swung open just like it always did.

But the house was eerily silent. I walked up to Olivia and Priss's apartment, and knocked on the door. No one was home.

There was nothing to do but continue with my deliveries and return to the bookstore.

Veronica wasn't speaking to me. I could only hope the police would arrest Percy soon.

When six o'clock finally rolled around, I was relieved to go home.

Until I got there.

Chapter 33

Eric and Mr. Dubois waited for me on the sofa.

"Edgar didn't come back?" I asked.

"And he still isn't answering his telephone," said Eric.

"I don't like this, either, but he's not a child. He's an adult. Maybe he met a girl and they're in a bar. Maybe he went to a movie and turned off his phone."

"Do you really believe that?" asked Eric.

"No."

"Miss Florrie, over two thousand people go missing each day. There's no telling what evil might have befallen Edgar."

"You're the cop, Eric. Should we report him missing?"

"I already have. It would help if we had a picture of him."

"I can draw a larger sketch if that would help."

"Wonderful." Mr. DuBois smiled at me. "And I shall make tea."

Fervently hoping that Edgar would return before I finished the sketch, I sat next to Eric and drew Edgar from memory. Even though the type of glasses he wore were popular, they would give him away immediately.

Eric looked over my shoulder. "That's very good. I would

recognize him from that if I saw him on the street. He took a photo of it with his phone and emailed it to the station. "I hate waiting."

"I can call Zsazsa and Goldblum. We could canvass Wisconsin Avenue, look in bars and antiques stores."

"Tea is served. I hope you don't mind that I took the liberty of serving it with your delicious little cheesecakes."

"Thank you, Mr. DuBois."

He sat down with us and sipped his tea.

"I think you'd better call Zsazsa and Goldblum. DuBois, do you drive?" asked Eric.

I held my breath.

"Yes. I have a driver's license. But shouldn't someone remain here in case he returns?"

Eric's eyes met mine. "Good idea. I'll phone Zsazsa and Goldblum."

In the end, Zsazsa, Goldblum, and I split up, each taking a section of Georgetown. Eric drove my car, which I thought a bad idea given the location of his wound, but there was simply no stopping him.

At nine o'clock in the evening, we reconvened at the carriage house. Mr. DuBois had duck confit, roasted potatoes, and celery root puree waiting for us.

At that point, we were too worried to be hungry, but it didn't stop us from gathering around the table in the garden. I made a point of lighting the candle in Dolly's lantern.

"There's just no sign of him at all," said Goldblum. "I stopped by Dolly's house to talk with Priss and Olivia, but they hadn't seen him all day."

"We ought to call his mother," I said. "But who would have her phone number?"

"Anyone know her first name?" asked Eric.

"His sister is Lucy."

Eric excused himself for using the phone during dinner. He called the station and asked for a phone number for Edgar's mom. While he was on the phone, his face brightened. "Where?"

Eric hung up. "Eat up everyone, they found Edgar in Rock Creek Park. Sounds like he's a little drunk. They're taking him to the hospital."

In much better spirits, we devoured Mr. DuBois's fabulous dinner. "Now go get our young man. When you return, coffee, brandy, and chocolate mousse."

Eric grinned. "You don't have to bribe us to come home."

"Maybe you should stay here and put your leg up," I suggested.

"Not a chance."

The waiting room at the hospital was all too familiar to me.

Goldblum paced back and forth. Zsazsa was the most patient among us, sitting primly and waiting.

"What's taking so long?" asked Eric. "Did you have to wait like this for me?"

"I did. Except that night, this room was full of cops."

"Really? You never told me that." He smiled, clearly pleased that his buddies came to his rescue.

At long last, the nurse opened the door and called, "Sergeant Eric Jonquille?"

Eric, who had refused to bring his crutch, hobbled back to see Edgar. He returned twenty minutes later and sat down. In a low voice he said, "I want to tell you this before Edgar is with us. He tested positive for Rohypnol."

"The date-rape drug?" asked Goldblum.

"That's the one. He's very groggy and doesn't remember anything, which is typical. So don't be surprised when you see him. He'll be okay after it wears off. Other than some bruises, he's not injured."

Poor Edgar was able to walk, but I could see why the cops thought he was drunk. He wasn't stable on his feet. We managed to get him into the car and home to the carriage house. He nearly fell into the cot and drifted off right away. I placed a blanket over him and joined the others out in the garden.

Everyone passed on coffee. Mr. DuBois served brandy and the most heavenly chocolate mousse topped with whipped cream. It was the perfect ending to a very strange day.

"Do you think he took the Rohypnol intentionally?" asked Goldblum.

I didn't know much about the drug other than what I had read in newspapers.

But Eric shook his head. "Unlikely. I would wager that someone slipped it into a drink. But I can't imagine why."

"Clearly to knock him out," said Zsazsa. "Look at him. You could steal his wallet or his car keys and he would never know."

Edgar slept through the dinner and the night. When I rose in the morning, he was sitting in the garden watching Peaches chase butterflies.

I sat down with him. "How do you feel today?"

"Groggy. Did I black out or something? I don't remember last night."

"Someone slipped you Rohypnol."

"Why? Why would anyone do that?"

"I don't know. To steal your cash or credit cards?"

He rose too quickly and had to steady himself by grabbing the table. But he walked into the house and returned with his wallet. "Cash is here. Credit cards are here."

"I don't know, Edgar. I'll make some tea. That might help you feel better."

I was in the kitchen pouring water into teacups when he lurched over to the counter and grabbed it. "It's gone. The only thing they took was the picture of my father."

Chapter 34

"Are you sure?" I asked. "Look through the pockets of the clothes you wore yesterday. Maybe you took it out to show someone and shoved it into a pocket."

I could see him across the room, digging through his clothes. He looked up at me with despair. "It was the only picture I had of my dad."

That woke Eric, who slid his wire-rimmed glasses on. He was so adorable in his glasses with his hair mussed from sleeping that I couldn't help smiling at him.

"Morning. Did I miss something?"

"They took the picture of my father!" Edgar was beyond distressed.

Whoever doped him couldn't have taken anything he treasured more.

I poured another cup of tea and carried the tray out to the garden. Eric was yawning when he joined me.

Edgar brought his clothes outside. "Would you go through the pockets?"

"Sure." I checked the pockets of his jeans. They were

empty. His shirt didn't contain pockets. "Would you mind if I looked through your wallet?"

Edgar took his clothes inside and brought out his wallet. He sat down and passed it to me.

I flipped it open. His driver's license picture was better than most. I took each item out and placed it on the table. Credit cards, cash, and a few receipts. "I'm sorry, Edgar. I know how much that photograph meant to you."

After a big slug of tea, I inserted everything back into the wallet and laid it on the table.

"What would someone want with that picture?" asked Eric. "Is there anything you haven't told us about your dad?"

Edgar shrugged. "Thomas Jones. Flea market trader. Lived in Washington twenty-seven years ago. I know so little about him."

"And your aunt said he might not want to be found." Eric took off his glasses and rubbed his eyes. "I hate to suggest this, but what if he was in hiding because he did something illegal?"

Of course a cop would think of that. I watched Edgar's reaction, expecting him to protest.

"Anything is possible, I guess. That would explain a lot."

The knock on the door that we were expecting finally came. "Ahh, breakfast has arrived!" said Eric.

I rose to open the door for Mr. DuBois. The professor was with him and rolled in the cart loaded with food. Mr. DuBois insisted on serving us, but made a plate of hash brown pancakes topped with smoked salmon and hollandaise sauce for himself as well.

"I have to hand it to you, DuBois," said Eric. "My dad is a fantastic chef and I grew up eating some fancy food, but this is unbelievable. I should introduce you to him. I bet he would put this on the brunch menu at his restaurant."

We ate ravenously, all except for Edgar.

"Are you okay?" I asked him.

"I wish I could remember what happened."

"They found you in Rock Creek Park," said Eric. "Does that spark anything for you?"

"No. This entire trip has been a big bust. I don't even have a photo to show people anymore. What am I going to tell my sister?"

Professor Maxwell studied him. "I'm not so sure that it's a bust. Someone knows your father and for some reason, that person doesn't want you to find him. Think about it. He went to a lot of trouble to dope you just to obtain the photograph of your dad. You have ruffled someone's feathers, Edgar. It must mean you're very close to finding him."

Edgar's face lit like a child given a chocolate. "I was ready to give up. You're right. It must mean he's here. Do you think *he* drugged me to get the picture away from me?"

Good heavens. I hoped not! What kind of father would do that?

While they were talking, I retrieved my sketch pad. The picture had shown Edgar's dad in the distance, so the face had been quite small. I tried to recreate it from memory only larger.

While I was drawing, Eric glanced at my sketch. "You're drawing Percy."

I blinked and held it at arm's length. "I am. Rats!"

Edgar stood up and circled the table to stand behind me. "Wow. But it looks like my dad, too. Do you think Percy could be my half brother?"

Oh swell. Poor Edgar came to town looking for his father and now he might have found his half brother who was a murderer? It didn't get any worse than that. On the other hand, if

Percy's kidney was a match for Edgar's sister, he would probably be willing to sell it.

"Maybe Percy's dad was in the same business as yours,"
Eric mused aloud.

I winced when I asked, "Has Percy been arrested yet?"

Eric made some phone calls while the rest of us cleared the
dishes and took them back to the mansion. Mr. DuBois refused all offers to wash the dishes and shooed us out of his
kitchen.

When Edgar and I returned to the carriage house, Eric
said, "Good news. They brought him in for questioning but
released him."

"Like they did Zsazsa?" I asked.

"Exactly like that. They're checking the phone records to
see if he was in contact with Maisie. If they find some concrete
evidence, they'll arrest both of them. Right now they've got
nothing on them."

"Then we should pay Percy a visit, don't you think?"

Edgar and Eric were all for it. I brought Peaches inside and
fed her Tuna Delight which, from the way she gobbled it,
must have lived up to its name.

We were on the verge of leaving when I remembered that
Eric was supposed to stay off his leg. "Maybe you should wait
here."

"Not a chance!"

"At least take the crutch."

Eric planted a big smooch on me. "I'll be fine. If I can't
walk back, one of you can come pick me up."

I reminded myself that sometimes you have to pick your
battles. That was one I wasn't going to win. However, if he was
limping by the time we reached the sidewalk, I was sending
him back to the carriage house.

I locked the door behind us and watched Eric as we

walked along the driveway of the mansion. I thought he was doing amazingly well when he said, "Well! If it's not Mr. Flower Bouquet."

I looked around. Sure enough, Jack Miller was casually hanging out on the sidewalk. "He didn't send me flowers, Eric!"

"No? Then what's he doing here?"

Eric headed straight for him.

Chapter 35

I grabbed Eric's arm. "Please don't do this. Leave Jack alone."

"It's my job to get rid of creeps who follow women. You wait here."

"Eric! Please don't bother him."

Edgar and I waited a few yards away while Eric played cop. He and Jack were all smiles in two minutes.

Eric waved to us to come over.

"It's not you he's following," said Eric. "Meet Jack Miller, of the FBI Fine Art Crime team."

Jack grinned at me. "An art thief was released from prison recently, and we were hoping he'd lead us to the place where he hid the things he stole. I've been tailing him. Then word got around that Professor Maxwell was looking for a van Gogh sunflower painting on the black market, so I was keeping an eye on him."

"That's why you were following him when he left a bar with van den Teuvel."

Jack laughed. "And what were you doing tailing me?"

"You knew?"

"You followed me for blocks. It would have been difficult not to notice you."

"I was making sure the professor made it home okay," I explained.

"Sorry that I scared you the night van den Teuvel broke in to Color Me Read."

"It was you who jumped off the awning?"

"And it *was* Jack who sent the flowers as an apology," said Eric.

"Those got me in a lot of hot water with Eric."

"Sorry about that."

"Then why were you following Edgar?" I asked.

"You were following *me?*" Edgar appeared shocked.

"You were meeting up with a lot of antiques dealers and some black market dealers, asking questions about a Thomas Jones. We know Orso had to stash the goods somewhere and you landed on my radar."

I wasn't smiling anymore. "Orso is also known as Thomas Jones?"

"Not many people call him that, but it's his real name."

I gazed at Edgar. "No wonder weird things have been happening to you. Orso is your dad! Do people think Edgar has the items Orso stole?"

Jack shrugged. "They think he might lead them to their whereabouts. And we all noted that he showed up shortly before Orso was released from prison."

"That's why van den Teuvel attacked you," said Eric.

Jack shook his head. "What a nut job. Did he use the British accent?"

"He's not British?" I asked.

"He's actually Gary Robertson from Pomona, California. A thorn in my side. When he shows up, there's always trouble."

I did note that Eric slyly wrapped an arm around me while we spoke with Jack. It wasn't necessary, but it was sort of cute.

We finally left Jack and made our way along the block in the direction of Dolly's house. Eric was limping a little bit more, but he didn't complain.

As we walked through Dolly's gate, we could hear people yelling inside the house.

The front door opened and Percy stumbled out backward. Maisie and Veronica appeared on the stoop. Both of them were angry and shouting. Percy took one step too many backward and tumbled down the concrete stairs.

Edgar and I rushed to him.

"Are you okay?" I asked.

Percy tried to sit up. "I think I may have broken something." He moaned in pain.

Priss and Olivia showed up behind Maisie and Veronica, who appeared horrified.

"An ambulance is on the way," called Eric.

With Percy and Edgar side by side, I compared their faces. Percy's was narrower, especially around the jaw. Their eyes were brown, but slightly different shapes. And Percy's eyebrows were thinner than Edgar's.

I left them to talk and trotted up the stairs. "What happened?"

Maisie and Veronica gazed at each other.

It was Maisie who said, "He was two-timing us."

Veronica asked, "Will he be okay? We didn't mean to hurt him."

"We wanted to," said Maisie. "And he would have deserved it."

Veronica sat down on the top step. "I didn't want to believe you, Florrie. I hate it when you're right."

"I fell for him twice!" Maisie complained. "How could I be so stupid after he broke off our engagement and dated someone else?"

"He deserves what he got," said Priss.

Olivia appeared pained. "Maybe we should go in."

"No!" Priss was adamant. "You're always bossing me around, just like Florrie bosses Veronica. Birth order does not give you the right to tell us what to do."

Oy. I wanted to walk away. Instead I looked at Veronica. "I'm sorry. I just found out about it first. It's hard not to tell your sister she's being two-timed. But I don't like to see you being taken advantage of and I certainly don't want you to get hurt."

"Well put, Florrie," said Olivia.

"My mom tried to warn me about Percy." Maisie spoke softly. "She hated his guts. Maybe I should have listened."

The ambulance rolled to a halt on the sidewalk and a little crowd gathered.

Just beyond them, across the street, Mike looked on.

Chapter 36

"Mike!" I waved and ran toward him. "What are you doing here?"

"I was planning to ask you the same question. Do you know the owners of this house?"

"Yes. Is something wrong? You seem put out."

"While I rotted in jail and lost the best years of my life, the real thief lived the high life right here."

"Do you mean Dolly?"

"Dolly lived here?"

"She was the owner of the house, but she was murdered a few days ago."

"Was she married?"

"Four times! But her last husband died a long time ago."

"He got what he deserved."

"Someone shot him."

"Ordinarily I do not take pleasure in the deaths of others, but on this occasion, I believe I am entitled to some small degree of satisfaction that he was not rewarded for his poor behavior by a long and wonderful life."

I felt so stupid. How could I have not seen this? "You're Orso."

His eyebrows shot up. "How do you know that?"

"You lied to me. You gave me a fake name."

"I apologize. I no longer wish to be known as Orso. That name carries with it a great burden. I am trying to start fresh. I thought if I gave myself a new name it would be a new beginning for me. Orso Moschello and Tom Jones are gone just as though they died in the prison where I wasted my life."

"Tom Jones?"

"Yes, I know. I've heard jokes about the singer my whole life. I loathed that name."

"Which one is your real name, Orso or Tom Jones?"

"They both are. Orso means bear in Italian. My grandfather called me Piccolo Orso, 'little bear,' when I was a child. My friends picked it up and when I was in the antiques business, everyone knew me as Orso. My middle name was my mother's maiden name, Moschello. I thought it had a more interesting ring to it. I was a young man then and thought it sounded macho, so I was known as Orso Moschello. But my birth certificate says Thomas Moschello Jones."

"When exactly did you go to prison?"

"The worst year of my life, 1991."

My pulse quickened. It couldn't be. Could it? "Do you know a woman with the last name Delaney?"

He studied me in alarm. "Who *are* you?"

"I know someone who would like to meet you."

"Me? Are you sure? Do you know Betty Delaney?"

"I don't. But there's someone else who has been looking for you."

His expression hardened. "Is this some kind of trick? I haven't violated my probation or done anything wrong."

"It's nothing like that. Don't worry."

"Who would want to meet me? My parents passed away while I was in prison. Except for distant cousins, I don't have anyone left on this earth who cares about me."

"Your son does."

"This time you are wrong, dear Florrie. I don't have a son."

"Tom Jones, you are about to embark on the new life you longed for."

I took his hand and was prepared to march him across the street when a moving truck pulled up. Olivia and Priss walked out to talk to the driver.

I tugged a reluctant Orso, or Mike, across the street and through Dolly's gate. We watched as the EMTs loaded Percy into the ambulance. At least the cops would know where to find him.

I motioned to Edgar to join us.

"Mr. Thomas Jones, I would like you to meet your son, Edgar Delaney. He's been looking for you."

I walked away to give them some privacy. Eric held his hand out to me. I grasped it. "How is your leg?"

"Achy. But I wouldn't have missed that for the world."

We watched as movers passed us carrying furniture and boxes. It was the end of an era. Dolly was gone, and now, after twenty-five years in this house, Priss and Olivia would be gone, too. And in one of those boxes was Maxwell's van Gogh sunflower, probably worth millions. It was going away and would be lost again. "There must be a way to stop them," I whispered. "I know I saw the van Gogh."

"Maisie, how old are you?" I asked.

"Thirty. Why?"

"So in 1991, you were three years old."

Eric whispered, "Where are you going with this?"

"Priss and Olivia said they had lived here twenty-five years, but they took care of Maisie when she was three, so they were here in 1991."

"They just rounded the number," said Eric. "I wouldn't put much stock in that."

Priss walked out wearing a gardening hat with a wide brim.

Blood-red roses and dotted midnight-black tulle pinned the brim up in front so her face was visible. She carried a long-handled spade.

"What a cute hat!" said Maisie. "May I see it? Where did you get it? My shop should carry these."

Priss's free hand touched the brim. "I made it myself. I'd rather not take it off, though. You understand—hat head. My hair's a mess."

"That's mine!"

The gardening neighbor from across the street marched toward us. That is my spade, Priss Beauton. You have some nerve."

Priss smiled at her. "Please. It's just a shovel. They all look alike."

The neighbor's eyes narrowed. "That's where you are wrong, missy. That spade has a nick on the back, just above the spot where the handle joins the metal. And over the nick is a smudge of green paint."

Eric said, "Turn the shovel, Priss."

Priss took two steps toward the truck, but the neighbor was surprisingly fast. She tugged at the spade, but Priss wasn't letting go.

A breeze came up, catching Priss's hat. Priss let go of the shovel to reach for her hat, but the wind carried it toward Veronica.

The neighbor flipped the spade so we could see. Sure enough, there was the nick and the green smudge, just as described. The irate neighbor glared at her. "Just so you know, I reported the break-in of my garage to the police. You may have gotten away with stealing from other people's garages in this neighborhood, but not from mine."

She turned on her heel and went home with her spade.

"Are you going to report her?" I asked Eric.

"I guess I have to."

Veronica started to hand the hat back to Priss, but Maisie grabbed it. The hat twisted and a piece of paper fell out of it.

Oblivious, Maisie checked the label inside the hat. "I knew you didn't make this."

I bent over to pick up the paper. It was the photo of Edgar's father.

Chapter 37

"Oh, Ms. Beauton," moaned Eric. "What have you done now?"

To me Eric said, "Hold on to that hat."

Maisie handed it to me, while Eric walked over to the moving men and showed them his badge.

He made a phone call, and then said to Priss, "Let's go inside and have a little talk."

I peered in the hat to see if she was hiding anything else in it. She'd done a good job, but I dared to wedge a fingernail under the fabric. And there it was. It hadn't been in a box after all. My fingers trembled. I was holding an original van Gogh sunflower in my hands.

"Maisie," said Eric. "I'd like you to come, too."

Maisie's face paled until it was almost a toasted gray. She went along, though, and the rest of us fell in line.

Orso caught up to me. "Is that the van Gogh? How did she get hold of it?"

I handed Edgar the photo of his dad, which he promptly showed to Orso.

"*This* is your father? Well, I must say that's a disappointment. I rather liked the idea of a daughter and son. I enjoyed it if only for fifteen minutes."

"It's not you?" Edgar asked.

"No. This is Randy Johnson, the man who ruined my life. The one who ran off with four priceless items we were transferring to a museum."

Edgar frowned. "Then how did my mom get this picture?"

Orso rubbed his face. "I was with her the day she took the photograph. It was before Randy scammed me. She dreamed of living in a house like this. We had a lovely day together," he said wistfully.

We gathered in Dolly's apartment. It wasn't the same without Dolly's furniture and clutter. The hardwood floors were fabulous and would help sell the house, but the room was eerie now that it was empty.

Eric turned to me. "Would you go get Olivia? I think she should be here."

I raced up the stairs and asked Olivia to come down. She shut her eyes for a few seconds. "We had a good long run. I guess in the back of my mind, I knew it would all come out one day."

She walked down the stairs in front of me like she was bravely going to her doom.

When we walked in, Orso was speaking. "I hired Randy, the man in Edgar's photo, to help me transfer priceless items to a museum. Unfortunately, on arrival at the museum, it was discovered that four items were missing, one of which was the small van Gogh sunflower. I knew I didn't have them. I've never stolen a thing in my life, but Randy disappeared and was nowhere to be found. The prosecutor insisted I made him up to take the blame. I wasted a lot of years in prison because of this guy. If anyone knows where I can find him, I'd be most appreciative."

I had a very bad feeling that we all knew where Randy

was. What we didn't know was how he ended up behind the bookcase, or why someone put him there.

A look passed between Priss and Olivia. Priss said, "Dolly killed him. She was like a sister to us, so we helped her drag him up the stairs and hide his body."

"Didn't he smell?" asked Edgar.

"Thankfully it was a bitterly cold fall and winter that year, which helped more than you would think."

"That would have been 1991?" I asked. "The year of the rat, which was really the year of the goat?"

Olivia looked pained.

Maisie shook her head. "I knew it. I knew Mom was responsible."

"Dolly?" I asked. "I find that so hard to believe. Why did she murder him?"

Olivia looked down at her hands. "He was three-timing her." Her chest heaved. "He had proposed to Dolly, and to Priss, and to me. He was seeing all three of us, right under our noses. Right here in this house! The man was horrible."

"How did he break his neck?" asked Eric.

Olivia began to cry. "It wasn't Dolly!"

Priss's eyes widened. "Yes, it was. Remember?"

"Oh, Priss. It wasn't any of us. Dolly and I went up to his studio apartment on the third floor and found him with Priss in flagrante delicto. Priss said she was his fiancée, then I said *I* was his fiancée, then Dolly chimed in, and she thought *she* was his fiancée! The fuss moved out into the hallway with everyone shouting, and yelling, and arguing, and smacking him. How could he do that to us? He was moving toward the stairs, undoubtedly to escape us, and the three of us, we didn't mean to, but we all three pushed him. I remember it like it was yesterday." Olivia closed her eyes. "I swear he tumbled down those steep stairs in slow motion. All three of us reached our hands out as if we could catch him or stop him from tumbling.

And then he finally came to a stop. I knew it was bad from the angle of his head. No one can turn their head like that and survive. He was gone. He was there kissing up to all three of us one minute and the next minute, he was just gone."

Her shoulders heaved and fell. She wiped her face with her left hand. "We dragged him up the stairs." She snorted. "I remember old Mrs. Collins dropping by. We were in such a panic. I thought she would never leave. We couldn't bury him. A neighbor would notice that for sure. And he was too heavy for the three of us to put in a car and take someplace. We could barely get him up the stairs. So we propped him up and built that bookcase."

"Why didn't you call the police?" asked Eric. "You could have said it was an accident."

"Are you kidding? We didn't want to go to jail. And none of us had any money for expensive lawyers. And you know the funny thing? For twenty-seven years no one came looking for him. Not a soul. No neighbors asked how he was doing. No friends dropped by to see him. His employer didn't call. Nobody reported him missing, either, as far as I know. He was a man who disappeared and nobody ever came looking for him until the day Edgar showed up with that picture of his dad."

"You're confirming that the man in the photograph is the skeleton behind the bookcase?" asked Eric.

"I thought you had figured that out." She sounded a wee bit sarcastic for someone who was about to go to jail.

"The police did a DNA test to see if the bones were a match to Edgar. That man wasn't his dad," said Eric.

Olivia froze. "We went through all of that for nothing?" She buried her head in her hands and sobbed. It wasn't until she looked up that I realized she was laughing. "Priss tried to kill that boy Edgar seven ways to Sunday. He's destined to live for sure."

"Olivia!" screamed Priss.

"Honey, it's over."

"She's the reason Nolan fell down the stairs?" I asked.

"Yup. She unscrewed the lightbulb and placed a magazine on one of the steps. He flew right on down. Was just the wrong guy is all. It was supposed to be Edgar."

"And the firecracker at the concert in the park?"

"All the news reports said she was a boy. They never would have said that about me, that's for sure. And she clobbered some poor guy who was hanging around. She thought he was Edgar."

Eric looked at me and raised his palms. "Who was that?"

"I think it was probably Jack Miller. Was Priss the one who threatened Edgar by choking him? She could have killed him then."

"Can you believe it? Somebody else almost did the job for her."

"She could have killed him last night when she drugged him," I said.

"I thought I left him belly down in a stream bed. I whacked him over the head pretty good, too, with the neighbor's shovel." Priss sighed. "All I really wanted was that picture of Randy. Without it, he had nothing on us."

"So you were the garage thief?" I asked. I couldn't have been more surprised.

Priss seemed proud of herself. "Where did you think I got the fireworks and the shovel?"

A group of police officers walked in. Priss and Olivia were going to jail.

"Wait!" I cried. "How did you get the van Gogh?"

"It was a gift to Priss from Randy."

"What happened to the other three items?" asked Orso.

"I have no idea," said Olivia. "I imagine Dolly sold them. We had to get rid of everything in the room he was renting, so they might have gone in the trash."

Chapter 38

Now that Maisie, Olivia, and Priss were in jail, Edgar could have stayed in his apartment. But the empty house was creepy. He stayed at my place with Eric and me.

Edgar and Orso had gone for a DNA test that very afternoon. I had no doubt that they were father and son, but I could understand that they wanted confirmation. They were making plans to go visit Lucy. Orso said if his kidney was a match, he would willingly donate it.

Professor Maxwell had already contacted his lawyer, Ms. Strickland, to see if Orso's criminal record could be expunged. Of course, three of the remaining items were still missing and might never be found. But that wasn't Orso's fault.

In the evening, Jack Miller dropped by the carriage house. I served after-dinner drinks and the mini-cheesecakes out on the patio. I lighted Dolly's lantern and wished she could be there with us.

"Thanks for all the work you did to find the van Gogh. Especially you, Edgar. If you hadn't come to town and kicked up some dust, we might never have found it."

Edgar flushed at his praise.

"The reason I came by is we may have solved an old mur-

der as well. Lucianne Dumont hired Frederic van den Teuvel
to locate *The Florist* and procure it for her. Mr. van den Teuvel
isn't known for his delicate manner. He's now been arrested
for attacking you, Edgar, and for breaking in to Color Me
Read."

I knew Edgar felt better with van den Teuvel locked up.

"As part of the investigation of Orso, we looked into the
Dumont's extensive collection of art. Unfortunately, a substan-
tial number of them are pieces that have been missing for years.
In going through some papers, we discovered handwritten
statements of authenticity from Dolly's husband. The metropolitan police are reopening the case of his death. Depending
on what was collected at the scene of the crime back then, we
hope to be able to link Mr. Dumont to the death of Dolly's
husband."

At that moment, the candle in Dolly's lantern toppled over.
I hurried to right it before anything caught fire. But when I set
the candle on its base, it fell again. I finally blew it out and
turned it over to see why it wouldn't stand straight. On the
bottom was a key to a safe-deposit box.

The next morning Mr. DuBois delivered breakfast to the
carriage house again. I had become very spoiled and hated to
think this luxury would end when Eric went home.

As Edgar rolled the cart into my garden, someone knocked
on the door. I opened it to find Norman standing there.

"Hi, Florrie. I've been trying to catch up with you."

"I'm sorry I didn't have time to talk at the bookstore the
other night."

"That's okay. I just want you to know that I have applied to
the police academy."

A chill ran through me head to toe. "Oh, Norman." Surely
he wouldn't be accepted. He would shoot himself in the foot.

His chest puffed up. "Yup. I'm going to be a cop."

"Does your mother know about this?" Even though Norman was an adult, his mother was still trying to be a helicopter mom. I couldn't imagine that she would allow him to do anything so dangerous.

He scuffed the toe of his shoe against the pavement. "Not yet. I wanted you to be the first to know."

I invited him to breakfast but he had to get to work. Apparently there were fairy rings in the grass at a golf course in Maryland.

"It's a grass emergency," he explained.

I thanked him for stopping by, but was planning to call my mom, who would surely phone Norman's mother, who would put a prompt stop to this police academy nonsense.

Professor Maxwell greeted Norman as he left. He stepped inside. "Wait until Jacquie sees the van Gogh. I can't believe that it's back home. I thought I would never see it again."

"When is she coming back?"

"Tomorrow. I'm glad she was away. It's wrenching every time someone thinks they might have a lead on what happened to Caroline."

"They didn't find anything?" I asked.

He shook his head. "Not a thing. Bonnie's father says that's meaningless. Morrissey could have buried the girls in the woods somewhere." His lips bunched together as though he was trying to stay tough. "It never ends."

There was nothing I could do but give him a big hug and steer him to the garden for breakfast.

It took some wrangling to determine who was entitled to open the safe-deposit box. Maisie, Dolly's heir, was in jail awaiting trial for her role in murdering Dolly. The FBI was hoping it might contain the missing items Randy had stolen.

In the end, a court order was issued allowing me to open the safe-deposit box, in the presence of Jack Miller and Sergeant Eric Jonquille.

The bank knew all about the legal wrangling and was waiting for us when we arrived.

They took us into a small room, handed me the box, and closed the door. I slid the key into the lock and turned it.

A letter was attached to the top of a small, flattish bag.

> *Dear Maisie,*
>
> *If you are opening this box and looking at the contents, it will mean that I am gone from this world. It's a long story, honey, but all you need to know is that these items were stolen by one of my tenants. I had nothing to do with the theft. For reasons I can't go in to, I can't turn them over while I'm alive. I'm not sure to whom they belong, but if you'll take them to a museum and tell them you discovered them in your old mom's estate, I'm sure they'll be able to sort it all out. They are extremely valuable treasures and should be preserved. I know you don't think much of my "scavenging" but please do not turn these over to some dealer. Especially not Percy McAllister. They need to be returned to their rightful owners, the people from whom they were stolen. I'm only sorry that I couldn't turn them in myself.*
>
> *Love,*
> *Mom*

I opened the bag and a pair of diamond earrings tumbled out. About three-fourths of an inch in diameter, the outer edges of the earrings were lined with diamonds. More diamonds filled the centers. There was no question in my mind that the diamonds were real, and there were plenty of them.

Jack was elated. "Those are the earrings of Mary Todd Lincoln. I thought for sure they had been melted down and the diamonds were sold individually. They're amazing."

The bag also contained a five-thousand-dollar bill. "I didn't know such a thing existed," I said. "How much money does a person have to have to carry around one bill worth that much money? There aren't many people who could give you change for it."

"They're quite rare," Jack assured me. "And the value is much higher than the face value."

The last item was a brief letter from Martha Washington to her husband. It was sweet and affectionate. She missed him and was waiting for him to return to Mount Vernon.

"I'm glad Dolly saved these. If she hadn't put them in the safe-deposit box, they probably would have disappeared forever." I handed them over to Jack.

"Thanks, Florrie. They're taking DNA samples from prisoners these days. I thought you might want to know about Percy's sample. It surprised a lot of us. In a weird irony, it turns out that Randy, the skeleton in the wall, was Percy's dad."

Eric blinked and shook his head. "So Dolly and friends killed Randy, and Randy's son, Percy, murdered Dolly . . ."

On the day Edgar and Orso were heading home to see Lucy and Edgar's mom, Orso picked up Edgar at the carriage house. I was sorry to see them go.

Orso planted a big kiss on my cheek.

"Any news on the DNA match?"

Orso smiled like the happiest man in the world. "The official DNA results aren't back yet, but it looks like I'm a match for Lucy's kidney. They'll have to do a few more tests when I get to Ohio, but I'm pretty sure her daddy will be her donor."

Orso handed me a little package wrapped in soft tissue and tied with a pink string.

"You didn't have to do this."

"Yes, I did."

I pulled the end of the string and unwrapped a small painting of a hummingbird. It was signed *Tom Jones*. "It's beautiful!"

"To guide you and give you hope when there doesn't seem to be any way forward. You gave me a new life, and I will always be appreciative of that."

"No, I didn't. It was always there, you just didn't know where to find it."

RECIPES

Salted Chocolate Brownies

(makes 20 brownies)

1 8-by-8-inch baking pan
½ cup (1 stick) unsalted butter, plus extra for greasing pan
¼ cup semisweet chocolate chips
2 eggs
1 cup sugar
½ cup flour, plus extra for greasing pan
¼ teaspoon fine sea salt
¼ teaspoon baking powder
1½ teaspoon vanilla
Flaked sea salt like Maldon

Preheat oven to 350 degrees Fahrenheit. Grease and flour the baking pan.

Melt the butter. (Krista does this in a glass Pyrex measuring cup in the microwave.) When melted, add the chocolate chips and stir until they melt. Set aside.

Beat the eggs with the sugar until thick and cream-colored. Beat at least 2 to 3 minutes.

While they are beating, mix together in a separate bowl the flour, the ¼ teaspoon fine sea salt, and the baking powder. Set aside.

Alternate adding the flour mixture and the butter mixture to the eggs. (Hint: After adding flour, beat at a low speed.) When they are incorporated, add the vanilla. Beat well.

Pour into the prepared pan. Sprinkle with two pinches of flaked sea salt. Holding a knife tilted at an angle, gently swirl the salt into the batter. Bake 25 minutes. The edges should look firm. The middle should be firm enough not to quiver when gently shaken. Place on baking rack to cool. (Hint: It's easier to cut them while they are still slightly warm.)

Serve warm or cold. These freeze well. Those with midnight cravings might even find them quite delicious frozen.

Coconut Cupcakes

(makes 15 cupcakes)

Cupcakes

1½ cups flour
1½ teaspoons baking powder
¼ teaspoon sea salt
½ cup (1 stick) butter, softened
¾ cup sugar
2 eggs, room temperature
½ cup coconut milk
1 teaspoon vanilla
⅓ cup shredded sweetened coconut

Preheat oven to 350 degrees Fahrenheit. Place cupcake liners into wells of a cupcake baking tray.

In a bowl, mix together the flour, baking powder, and sea salt. Set aside. Cream the butter with the sugar well. Beat in the eggs. Beat for at least 2 minutes. Add the flour mixture ½ cup at a time. Beat on low after adding, then increase speed. Add the coconut milk, the vanilla, and the shredded coconut. Beat 4 to 5 minutes.

Spoon into cupcake liners about ¾ full. Bake 20 minutes or until they are barely golden and a cake tester comes out clean. Cool on a baking rack.

Frosting

6 ounces butter, softened
4 ounces cream cheese, softened
2–3 tablespoons coconut milk
1 teaspoon vanilla
1½–1⅓ cups powdered sugar
Shredded sweetened coconut

Beat butter, cream cheese, coconut milk, and vanilla until thoroughly mixed. Beat in the powdered sugar ⅓ cup at a time, beating on low speed after each addition. When all of the powdered sugar has been added, beat on high for 4 to 5 minutes.

Spread on cooled cupcakes with a knife. (Don't worry too much about how they look because the shredded coconut will hide flaws.) Place a kitchen towel or parchment paper under the cupcakes. Sprinkle the coconut on them, patting very lightly. Refrigerate. Take out of refrigerator one hour before serving to bring to room temperature.

Blueberry Cake with Pecan Streusel

Cake
2 cups flour
2 teaspoons baking powder
½ teaspoon salt
½ teaspoon vinegar
¾ cup 2% milk
5 tablespoons butter
¾ cup sugar
1 egg
1 teaspoon vanilla
2 cups fresh blueberries

Preheat oven to 350 degrees Fahrenheit. Grease a 9-by-9-inch baking pan.

Place flour, baking powder, and salt in a bowl and stir with a fork to combine. Set aside. Pour the vinegar into the milk and set aside.

Cream the butter with the sugar. Beat in the egg. Alternate adding flour mixture with the milk mixture until completely combined. Add vanilla and beat. Stir in the blueberries.

Pour the batter into the prepared pan and spread to corners.

Pecan Streusel
½ cup pecans
¼ cup flour
¼ cup white sugar
¼ cup dark brown sugar
½ teaspoon cinnamon
¼ cup cold butter

Place pecans and flour in a food processor. Pulse until the pecans are tiny. Add the sugars and cinnamon and pulse to combine. Cut the butter into eight small pieces, add to food processor, and pulse until combined.

Sprinkle over top of batter. Bake 50 minutes or until a cake tester comes out clean.

Allow to rest on a baking rack about 5 to 10 minutes. When cool, top with drizzle.

Drizzle
¼ cup powdered sugar
1–2 teaspoons fresh lemon juice

Whisk ingredients together. Drizzle over cooled cake. If too thin, add powdered sugar. If too thick, add a drop of lemon juice.

Mini-Cheesecakes

(makes 40 mini-cheesecakes)

24 vanilla wafers
2 8-ounce packages of cream cheese, softened
½ cup sugar
1 teaspoon vanilla
3 tablespoons sour cream
2 tablespoons heavy cream
2 eggs
½ cup Smucker's All Natural Cherry Spread (or any jam you like)

Preheat oven to 300 degrees Fahrenheit. Line the wells of a mini-cupcake pan with cupcake liners. Place ½ teaspoon of wafer crumbs in each mini-cupcake liner.

Place the cream cheese, sugar, vanilla, sour cream, and heavy cream in a mixing bowl. Beat until just mixed. Add one egg at a time, beating after each addition.

Spoon the cream cheese mixture on top of the vanilla wafer crumbs, filling the liners full.

Bake 18 to 20 minutes. They will puff up while baking and deflate while cooling, leaving a small dent for the jam. Remove from oven and cool on a rack. When completely cool, warm the cherry spread over medium heat, stirring frequently. Spoon about ¼ teaspoon in the center of each mini-cheesecake.

Killer Cocktail

4 ounces cold orange juice
1 ounce peach schnapps
1 ounce rum
4 ounces cold sparkling wine

Mix together in a tall glass. Garnish with an orange slice.

Turn the page for a preview
of Krista Davis's next
Domestic Diva Mystery . . .

The Diva Sweetens the Pie

Coming May 2019
From Kensington Publishing

Dear Sophie,

My new mother-in-law wins the local pie contest every year. The recipe for her piecrust is top secret, and his family makes a huge fuss about it. She and her husband are coming to visit my hubby and me for the first time. Hubby says a pie is obligatory. Each of her other daughters-in-law bakes a pie for her visit. I'm terrified! What do I do?

Newlywed in Coward, South Carolina

Dear Newlywed,

Bake a cake. There's no point in competing with her, and a cake will last longer than a pie anyway. If someone comments on the missing pie, tell your mother-in-law that you're eager to learn how she bakes her wonderful pies that everyone raves about.

Sophie

Daisy, my hound mix, stopped walking abruptly. I thought she had picked up the scent of a squirrel in the night air, but then I heard rustling in the bushes. In a split second, I was face-to-face with Patsy Lee Presley, and both of us screamed like we were under attack. Daisy barked, which added to the drama.

Wide-eyed, as though she were horrified, Patsy Lee took off running like a woman in her fifties who didn't get much exercise.

My heart still pounding, I sucked in a deep breath. It wasn't long ago that someone had meant to harm me. I guessed I was still wary and a little jittery. The truth was that the streets of Old Town, Alexandria, Virginia, were safe at night. I often walked Daisy after dark, enjoying the lights glowing in the windows of the historical homes that lined the streets.

Now that the momentary shock was over, I wasn't certain it had been Patsy Lee. I had never met her before but I had seen her on TV many times. Patsy Lee Presley was the current darling of the TV cooking world with the number one show. Sweet as the pies she baked, she was slightly chubby, and watching her show was like a visit from a favorite doting aunt. Patsy Lee was due to be in Old Town on Saturday for the Pie Festival, so it could have been her. But what was she doing hiding in bushes and running around like she was afraid?

I looked back in the direction she had gone, but she had disappeared. Whoever that woman was, I hoped she had the good sense to call the police if she was in trouble.

The next morning, I told Nina Reid Norwood and Officer Wong about it while we rolled out dough in Bobby Earl's class on pie baking. Nina, my best friend and across-the-street neighbor, unwisely added drops of water to her dough. I watched as it became sticky and unmanageable, but decided it wasn't my place to say anything. After all, Bobby was teaching the class.

Nina frowned at me. "Why isn't your dough sticking to your hands like mine?"

Wong glanced at her. "Mercy, Nina! Dip your hands in the flour, honey."

Wong focused on her own dough, which looked perfect to me.

"I'll check the log to see if anyone called in last night. It was probably some married woman sneaking home after a rendezvous with a boyfriend. Not to put Patsy Lee down, but a lot of women still wear their hair real big like she does. It could have been someone else."

Bobby Earl approached our group. "Bless your sorry little heart, Nina." Bobby gazed at the sticky lump in front of Nina and patted her on the back. "Why don't you go to the mixer and try again? I don't think that's salvageable."

Bobby nodded approvingly at my pie dough. "Did I hear you talking about Patsy Lee?"

"I thought I saw her in Old Town last night. Do you know her?" I asked.

He snorted. "I taught her everything she knows."

"You did not," Wong scolded him. "On the show Patsy Lee is always talking about her grandmother, from whom she learned how to cook and bake. She was just a tiny thing when she started cooking. So young that she had to stand on a chair to reach the countertop to work next to her Meemaw."

Bobby laughed aloud. "Is that the story she spins? Have you ever seen this Meemaw on her show?"

"Good grief, Bobby," said Wong. "Patsy Lee is in her forties, her Meemaw would probably be in her eighties."

Bobby lowered his voice and said, "Patsy Lee is so far into her forties that she has rolled over into her fifties. And her *MeeMaw* doesn't come on the show because she has a receding hairline, a five o'clock shadow, and her legs are too fat to wear a skirt."

Bobby had done a fairly good job of describing himself. I couldn't help grinning.

Wong's eyes narrowed. "Are you saying there is no Meemaw?"

"I guess she had a couple of grannies, most people do." He shrugged. "But when *I* met Patsy Lee, she couldn't crack an egg without breaking the yolk."

Bobby moved on, pausing to talk to Nina about the dough she was carrying back to our workstation. She sidled in next to me and plunked her dough on the table.

"The secret to a perfect piecrust"—Bobby paused to build up suspense—"is vodka. I find drinking it helps *me*, but a splash in your dough will prevent too much gluten formation.

There are other important factors, like keeping the ingredients as cold as possible, but the vodka is helpful because it makes the crust flaky."

Nina licked the spoon she had been dipping into the lemon filling for her lemon meringue pie.

"You won't have any filling left for your pie," I whispered.

"That's okay. You didn't think I was actually going to bake anything, did you?" she whispered back to me.

Officer Wong shot us a dirty look, "Shh!"

Nina had made fun of me for participating in the class. I had baked plenty of pies in my life, but pie crusts could be tricky. Bobby was a pro, and I figured I would pick up some tips. He baked pies for a living and sold them at Sweet as Pie on King Street in Old Town, Alexandria. Rumor had it that people drove an hour across greater metropolitan Washington, DC, just to buy Bobby's pies. At Thanksgiving and Christmas, they had to be preordered because he couldn't fill all the requests.

He roamed the room as he spoke. The buttons on his short-sleeved white chef's jacket strained a bit against the pressure of his stomach. I could relate. I had my own difficulties maintaining the weight I would like to be.

Wong giggled when he stopped to praise her dough. "I'm so thrilled to be in your class. My grandmother was an expert pie baker. I wish I had paid attention to her techniques."

Was she flirting with him?

Just as he had described, his hair had begun to recede but he was taking it in stride and wore it brushed back off his face. He smiled at her and the little crinkles at the outer edges of his brown eyes deepened.

African American Wong, who attributed her name to the wrong husband by a long shot, wasn't in her police uniform today. Her hair waved to just below her ears in a cut that was shorter in the back and longer in the front. One sassy curl dropped on her forehead.

I looked a little closer. She had taken a lot of care with her makeup. The buttons on her shirt strained a bit, not unlike those on Bobby's jacket. The two of them could be cute together. Nina nudged me, and I suspected she was thinking the same thing.

While the pies baked, Bobby drifted through the room engaging all his students. When he reached Nina he asked, "Is it true that you're judging the pie baking contest?"

Nina turned as red as the cherry filling I had cooked for my pie. "That's why I'm here. I thought I should have a feel for all the work that goes into baking a pie."

Bobby stared at her and appeared confused.

"She has an amazing palate," I offered.

Wong looked over at us. "What's that supposed to mean? I like food, too, but nobody asked me to judge anything."

"I mean that Nina has the ability to taste flavors that the rest of us miss entirely or barely notice. If someone in this class sliced their fruit on a cutting board that was used to mince garlic last night and was thoroughly washed, Nina would still taste the garlic when she ate the fruit."

"I've seen contests like that. They blindfold people to see who can recognize the flavors or textures," said Bobby. "Well, Ms. Nina Reid Norwood, I apologize for doubting you. I guess there's more than one way to judge a pie."

"I hope you entered in the professional category," I said.

"You bet. I can't talk about it in front of a judge, though." Bobby winked at us.

"You're so cute. But it's not a problem," Nina assured him. "The pies won't have any names on them. It will be a blind tasting."

Bobby smiled. "Good to hear. I wouldn't want to be disqualified." He moved on to the next group.

An hour later, everyone except Nina went home with a pie. The class was a small part of the Old Town Pie Festival, which was scheduled to commence in earnest the following day.

Nina offered to carry the pie as we neared my house. She took deep breaths. "Do you think there are calories in what a person sniffs?"

"I'm almost positive there are. I know I weigh more every time I leave a bakery."

As we approached my house, we saw a man peering in the window of my kitchen door. He cupped his hands around his eyes and leaned against the glass to see better. I could hear Daisy barking inside the house.

Connect with Us

Visit us online at
KensingtonBooks.com
to read more from your favorite authors, see books
by series, view reading group guides, and more.

Join us on social media

for sneak peeks, chances to win books and prize packs,
and to share your thoughts with other readers.

facebook.com/kensingtonpublishing
twitter.com/kensingtonbooks

Tell us what you think!

To share your thoughts, submit a review,
or sign up for our eNewsletters, please visit:
KensingtonBooks.com/TellUs.